Captured in Belize

DEBBIE ZESSIN

CAPTURED IN BELIZE

Cover design by Debbie Zessin
Photography and/or graphics credit in part to: Yuri Arcurs; Smallredgirl; and Graham Snook Photography
Author photo by T. Denise Hatch

ISBN: 979-8-99-00573-0-2 (paperback)
ISBN: 979-8-9900573-1-9 (eBook)

Library of Congress Control Number 2024902749

Printed in the United States of America

10 9 8 7 6 5 4 3 2 1

For Jessica

Acknowledgment

First and foremost, I want to express my deepest gratitude to my husband, Eric. His unwavering support, countless hours of patient listening, and willingness to dig through the car console for a pen when inspiration struck have been invaluable. Not only was he my sounding board for plot twists and chapter development but also my biggest critic and my truest fan. His love and support carried me throughout the entire process and encouraged me continually. I graciously thank him for always believing in me.

Next, I extend heartfelt thanks to my sister, Denise. She played an instrumental role in transforming this story from mere digital files on my computer to a tangible book and in the hands of readers. Her unwavering encouragement and shared journey into the world of authorship made this process all the more rewarding.

My children, Jessica and Michael, deserve special recognition. I am truly blessed to have loving children, who inspire me every day. A special thanks goes to Jessica, whose talent for editing and storytelling made the entire editing process more enjoyable and enlightening.

Lastly, I want to acknowledge the Eatonville Writer's Group—a remarkable community of individuals who champion local writers. Their encouragement, positive influence, and wealth of knowledge were a guiding light throughout this creative endeavor.

To all of you, thank you for being a part of this adventure. Your love, support, and belief in my work carried me through every step, and I am forever grateful.

Captured

in

Belize

Chapter One

Unraveled

TESS MARTIN SAT POISED. SHE fought back the explosion of nerves firing through her body, trying to conceal her excitement and anticipation for the evening agenda. Her heart pounded sending deep, pulsating echoes into her eardrums. Roger sat across from her, calm and cool—the complete opposite of her own wear-them-on-your-sleeve-type emotions. She admired his stoic demeanor. From the moment she laid eyes on him, his noble-like characteristics charmed her. She watched him as he pushed back a blonde tussle of hair that fell across his brow. With his nonchalant style, he continued reading over the menu. Tess couldn't help but notice how dashing he looked in his blue Mazari slim-cut suit, casually seductive and true to his character. Delicious, she thought.

Polished silverware, ornate enough for royalty, caught the soft glow of the crystal candle holder—centered perfectly on the white linen tablecloth.

Excited, her thoughts swirled as she gazed around the room. Securing a same day reservation at La Maison was usually unheard of. However, today was different. A cancellation had opened up, and with perfect timing, Roger managed to secure the posh table for two.

Tess rarely frequented the restaurant, especially for personal dates as their menu was beyond her budget. Unaffordable prices aside, it was her favorite place where the elite often dined. Her employer, an upscale design firm located in the heart of New York City, would on occasion meet with clients to impress and secure their business. But for Tess, it was more than just a place for business deals. It was the picture-perfect setting, the ideal romantic ambiance where lovers met, and futures began. Tonight, would be her forever special moment—a memory to last a lifetime and she wanted to enjoy the grandeur.

Gold leaf picture frames decorated the walls, accentuating the expensive art that hung throughout the room. Her gaze shifted to the deep, rich burgundy swags elegantly draped high over the arched windows, contributing to the graceful ambiance. Off to the side, a small covey hosted the evening quartet, the music's vibratos floated across the dining area softening the murmur of polite conversations. High overhead, the grand chandelier gave the room its finishing touch with the magnificent light, featuring rope-like strands of opaque crystals delicately draped across the luminous faux candles. The light danced throughout the dining hall. The tiny black sequins on Tess's dress glistened under its incandescent shimmer and the ambient luster kissed the highlights of her auburn hair.

Given the importance of tonight's date, Tess wanted to look especially elegant. She always kept what she referred to as her 'emergency evening wear,' for those impromptu dinner meetings with high-expectation clients. Tess had gratefully changed into the black minidress and extra pair of heels that she kept at the office. Completing her look she wore her hair swept-up and off to the side. The ambiance, the décor and the music surrounded her, her senses brimmed to their peak. Savoring it all, like a fine French wine, Tess breathed in deeply. Slowly she exhaled, gently closing her eyes, and envisioned the climax to their dinner, the reason they were there. Everything aligned—a perfect setting for a perfect proposal, or so she thought.

Tonight, Roger would propose completing the fairytale of her dreams. *Yes, I will*, she mused, or maybe it would sound better to say, *I do*. Goosebumps danced down her arm. She opened her eyes and looked across the table at Roger giving their order to the maître d'. Her vision dimmed on everything but him, this was her moment and she wanted to delight in it and its perfection.

Tess stared modestly at Roger's smooth bronzed skin that glistened under the light. He spoke with a slight European accent. She loved the way his facial muscles flexed and the deep dimples that formed along his cheeks, especially when he talked about serious matters like tonight. Shivers fluttered down her arms.

Her gaze drifted two tables away. A young man held his date's hand up to his lips. Tess watched the stranger kiss the slender girl's fingers seductively. She drank in their passion, both lovers focused on the other, oblivious to their surroundings. Tess anticipated a similar romantic scenario of her own. She glanced at Roger, then shifted her gaze back to the loving couple. She envisioned the two lovers embracing—their bodies entwined. Raw, passionate love, soaring. Like a chapter from a romance novel, she imagined the scene—the virgin's breasts would heave as the hero's voice, deep and low, seduced her. The lover's hands, strong but kind, would caress the temptress's body held close to him; his warm breath whispering his desire, confessing his love to her.

"Ahem...," a voice interrupted.

Her cheeks blushed as she looked up. A well-groomed waiter stood alongside their table. He wore black fitted pants, a crisp white buttoned-down shirt, void of any wrinkles, and topped it off with a black satin vest, which molded neatly to his slender frame. The man held a platter balanced with one hand. Enchanted by the couple across the room she hadn't noticed the waiter approaching their table. She could still feel the tingling in her rosy cheeks. She froze, hoping he couldn't read her mind. The silver-haired attendant placed the tray on the table. Tess relaxed slightly, thankful for his indifferent demeanor. He took the tall green bottle with its neck topped in golden foil and set it before them. The man pulled a small blade from his waistcoat and with ease the waiter cut through the wrap. Then with swift expertise he removed the cork and poured a small sample into Roger's glass and waited. Tess watched in anticipation, excited by the journey that had led her here, to this moment—her childhood dreams, all unfolding before her.

Roger took the glass by the stem and held it to his nose. Swirling the drink, he then sniffed the aromas before taking a sip. Afterwards, Roger nodded his approval and the maître d' filled their glasses. Tess could smell the fragrant Bordeaux as the wine's bouquet drifted past her nose. The sweet yet bold flavor made her mouth water. Gently, she swirled the goblet, raising it to her lips and took a drink. The fresh oak-like taste warmed her mouth. Everything aligned perfectly.

Tess closed her eyes, savoring her idealistic moment. Roger's familiar voice, a smooth cadence, sounded in the background—a gentle murmur adding to the ambiance. Her thoughts drifted back to earlier that day. Roger's urgent call interrupted Tess's afternoon, insisting they meet for dinner. He said it was important, that he wanted to talk about their future—their relationship. Tess opened her eyes and sighed as if in a dream she never wanted to awaken from.

Again, she glanced around the room, sizing its romantic flare and basking in its exquisite taste. Roger needed to use her credit card for their reservation, she shrugged, but that was all right, she didn't mind. And, while it would have been more romantic to arrive together, she really didn't mind taking a taxi from work. She had become accustomed to his sophisticated and high maintenance appetite along with his busy acting schedule over these past six months. She enjoyed the pretense and sophistication, as well. Tess smiled glancing up at Roger. Tonight's dinner, a fairytale moment and precursor to a marriage proposal from the man of her dreams, made it worth every penny. Roger's finances, or rather lack of, she concluded, were the furthest thing from her mind, at least for tonight. It was merely a minor detail to such an important evening. Besides, she glanced down at the silver embossed envelope neatly tucked into the folds of her purse, life would be taking on a new direction very soon.

A drink became unsettled at the adjacent table and the high-pitched clanking of dishes jolted her back to reality. Again, she heard Roger's voice, but this time, like a tornado upheaving the ground around her, Roger's words tore through her fairytale snow globe.

"I'm seeing someone else," he said.

Tess gasped. His words hung in the air like a crushing, dense fog. Had the fermented spirits played a trick on her? Fearful she might spew the Bordeaux, Tess gulped the remaining wine she had been savoring in her mouth. This time the sweet liquor burned her throat, and she shook her head. *Did he say what she thought he said?*

Tess squeezed her eyes shut, as if that would somehow change the conversation. Her mind reeled. She glanced up, eyes wide. "You...you're what?" Tess stammered. She searched his face in hopes the wine might have gone to her head and distorted his actual words. But there was no mistake. Her fairytale moment had turned into her worst nightmare.

"I'm seeing someone else," Roger repeated.

She stared at his thin deceptive lips and clearly heard Roger's nonchalant betrayal. The restaurant ambiance sank like a fireball burning into the depths of her gut. For a split second, her mouth gaped. Anger and disenchantment spiraled up through her arms and rose into her chest. Her face hardened and her eyes narrowed. Tess's thoughts soared like an out-of-control kite. With her mouth still agape, she stared, watching his jaw, searching for any hint of laughter—something to indicate that this was all just a bad joke. But his accent became more prominent, and while only thirty-seconds ago she had considered it charismatic and attractive, nausea now churned in her stomach. Roger's words betrayed her perfect evening. She felt the blood drain from her face. With her pale complexion, she continued to stare at him. His eyes, she scowled, were cold and unemotional. He leaned closer. Roger tilted his head, as if he had rehearsed this moment many times. Tess's mind flared.

"Tess," Roger continued, "it's just that you're never there, and...," he stared down at his napkin. His hands toyed with the edges, "you've always got your work with you," he said, pointing to her cellphone and tablet-sized client book that she kept by her side. "Seriously, you even brought it to dinner with you, to La Maison of all places!" Roger slid back into his chair.

Her eyes narrowed and her lips quivered. "What are you saying, Roger?" she demanded.

"Look around, Tess. This place inspires passion and yet you bring your office along! That's what I'm saying," Roger smirked. He leaned slightly over the table keeping his tone matter-of-fact like. "Really, Tess, you have no sense of excitement. I need someone spontaneous, someone willing to take risks. I'm afraid that's just not you, Tess, darling. You're more..., well, uptight," he paused, "and somewhat boring."

Before she had a chance to reply, his wandering eyes drifted to the server one table away. Roger ogled the woman, her low-cut dress stretching taut around her voluptuous figure. The dark-haired beauty batted her flirtatious lashes and paraded to their table. Her ruby red lips smiled seductively, and the experienced coquette lifted her eyes to meet his.

"More wine, monsieur?"

Tess fumed as she watched Roger's dimples edge into his skin. He nodded to the hip swaying brunette. Like a third wheel at a drive-in, Tess's nostrils flared.

"No, thank you," Tess scoffed.

The waitress gave her an unimpressed glance then turned her overly coated pouting lips back towards Roger. With another flirtatious smile and brushing the edge of the table with her full-figured curves, the harlot sauntered away. Tess composed herself. Roger's accusations still burned. Who was he kidding?

"Yes, Roger," she kept her voice low but direct, "my clients are important to me. And, yes, I work hard, and it pays for suits like that," she gestured at his newly acquired blue Mazari suit, "and places like this! I'm sorry that working seems boring or that it doesn't appeal to you. But who doesn't work?" she paused. "Oh, I know, Roger," she glared, "you! That's who. You don't work!"

Roger scooted his chair closer. She could see his shoulders starting to hunch. Good, she smirked. She'd landed a blow to his oversized ego. Roger cleared his throat, pulling at his collar. He then looked around before lowering his voice.

"Now, Tess," he said, "you know I'm just between jobs. I'm an actor and actors have down time. I told you that it's only temporary, and besides," he squirmed, adjusting the sleeve of his designer suit, "you said you liked this color on me."

Roger slouched back into his chair. His lips contorted with conceited arrogance. Rage welled up inside her as he reached for the crystal stemware, containing the overpriced drink she was paying for. As if a curtain were drawn back, revealing the truth, Tess saw through his rehearsed act. She wasn't about to let him sit there with his smug grin and dump her.

"Well, Roger, it's been down time these past six months, the entire time we've been together!" she shook her head. Her voice elevated. "Six months,

Roger! That's not temporary, that's pathetic. And, you know what else is pathetic?" she narrowed her eyes, glaring at him—enraged by his calm, arrogant demeanor.

"What, Tess?" he taunted.

"You, Roger, you're pathetic!"

Adrenaline pumped through her veins. Tess stood abruptly snagging the tablecloth. Her wine glass teetered. For a moment the idea of him drenched in the red liqueur flashed through her mind, but that would be a waste of good Bordeaux, she rationalized. Instead, Tess picked up her half-filled glass, threw back her head and gulped the fermented spirits. She set the crystal stemware hard onto the table. The couple next to them stared. She glared at Roger, undeterred. "I may be uptight and boring, darling, but at least I can afford it!" she said.

Tess swiped Roger's glass from the table. The liquid sloshed over the brim. No sense wasting it on him, she sneered. She tossed her head back, nose to the air, and with defiant satisfaction drank it down. The larger-than-typical sip of French wine burned going down her throat. She stifled the urge to cough. Regaining her composure, she gathered her phone, purse, and leather-bound clientele book, and with her head held high and eyebrows arched, Tess stormed out of the room.

***

IN AN instant her ideal relationship had been squashed. Her picture-perfect hero dripped with deceit. Tess slammed the door of the waiting taxi. The stench of vinyl and stale cigarettes permeated beyond the leaf shaped air freshener that dangled below the meter. She ignored the odor and gave the driver an insincere smile followed with her apartment address. She leaned back into the uncomfortable seat as the cab accelerated. *I'm leaving you; I've found someone new,* she mocked. His words played over in her mind. With her arms folded, she looked out the window, her would-be romantic evening a complete and utter failure.

The taxi swerved in and out of traffic. The glare of the streetlights rolled across the windshield and the taste of expensive wine still lingered on her breath. Tess tucked a rogue strand of hair behind her ear and continued staring out the window. Street shop signs and pedestrians blurred past. Despite the warm summer evening, a chill swept over her as she shifted deeper into the taxi seat. Tess pressed her lips tight and mulled over the evening events. Her thoughts were heavy, but the Bordeaux softened her soul. Holding her hand up to her brow, Tess shook her head as tears formed in the corner of her eyes. She fought them back. *How stupid can I be?* Images flooded through her mind, moments she had dismissed until now. She recalled that day, the day when she had run into them, the day she remembered seeing Roger with that woman. It all came pouring back, clearly now.

Her firm had landed a new client, a millionaire heiress and her Australian oil rich husband. She had hand delivered their plans, eager to impress the new account and take the lead on the design team. The little New York bistro, with its delicately scalloped awnings, had been on route to the client's office. Stopping would only take a few moments. She couldn't resist the temptation for her all-time favorite, French vanilla café with a twist of mint and, of course, fresh baked cinnamon croissants. A horn blared and Tess jolted back from the memory. Startled, she glared at the cabbie who gestured to the other motorist. He glanced back at her in the mirror.

"Crazy people, no?" the driver said.

Tess raised her brow slightly and looked back out the window. Her mind drifted back to that day, the day at the café. At first, she hadn't noticed Roger and the blonde sitting together at the back of the small establishment. Instead, she had waited in line enjoying the familiar mid-morning sounds of the coffee bar. Engrossed with the clanking of espresso cups and conversations that buzzed throughout the shop, Tess had closed her eyes and inhaled the aroma. Then she heard the laughter coming from the back of the room. It sounded familiar. Thinking back, she realized Roger always knew the best kept secrets in town. Tess scoffed. The coffee shop had been *their* retreat, *their* covert lover's getaway.

When her job moved her across town, the impromptu stops to the little store had become less frequent. Images of Roger's broad jawline and deep dimples cast across her mind. Tess reflected on their whirlwind relationship, six months of romance. She thought of his touch, their holding hands together and how they had gazed at one another. For her, it had been love at first sight. Life seemed complete with Roger, a sophisticated hero, she had told herself—tall, chiseled, and handsome. The missing link to the image of a perfect life. He was unemployed, but she was willing to overlook that one little flaw. After all, he said he could get work and she believed him. The cab accelerated and Tess watched as neon signs passed by. Her mind swarmed with memories. How cliché of that scoundrel, she sneered, to bring another woman to the same place, the same cafe he had taken her to in the beginning of their relationship. She folded her arms in disgust.

"Man, Tess, you really were stupid!" she murmured.

The pine smell of the car freshener wafted past her nose as the cab driver turned on the air conditioning. Images of the little shop with its sweet fragrance of chocolate and mint, the familiar scent of the bistro, again crept into her mind. She remembered standing there, her client's papers clutched under her arm. She had heard the soft acquainted laughter, and she looked over to the back of the shop. Her smile had faded. There, at a table, Roger and some bottle enhanced blonde sat wrapped in each other's arms. Tess could see it all over again. The full-figured woman's chin rested on petite hands, adorned in diamonds. The two of them, with their faces almost touching, had leaned in closer. They hadn't been aware of Tess's presence. The woman, younger than her but old enough to be a threat, giggled. Tess remembered seeing Roger's pale face after he finally looked up and saw her, like a wolf caught with his sheep.

Tess remembered the echo of her steps, penetrating the thick, awkward silence as she crossed the checkered floor to their booth. It wasn't until she stood beside them that she recognized the young woman, the daughter of her firm's wealthiest client, Mr. Randall Becker. Roger's acting skills kicked in as he tried to play off their chance meeting. Tess fumed at the memory. The taxi sped along. Tess rested her head on the back of the seat, letting out a deep sigh. College friend, my ass. *Well, Tess, you didn't see that one coming did you.* She silently scolded herself. *Roger-Roger-Roger...what a jerk.*

The driver fiddled with the radio knob and flipped through the stations. He settled on soft jazz. It wasn't her favorite music, but the sound of the saxophone relaxed her. The relationship warning signs she had ignored over the past months flashed through her mind. With all the lingering looks and sideways stares, she had tried not to be jealous. "Why can't I see those lies?" she hadn't meant to say it out loud.

The taxi rounded the corner. The driver slowed and stopped at the white marble pillars in front of her apartment building. The high-rise had been one of those items she checked off her perfect-life list. It had taken two paychecks and her company bonus to secure it. An attendant dressed in a red, double-breasted jacket accented with gold buttons hurried to open the taxi door. She gathered up her things. The silver envelope slipped from her purse and spilled out onto the seat. A sense of emptiness engulfed her as she stuffed the papers back into her bag. Tess stepped from the taxi. Her head spun and she tripped over the curb. The attentive doorman caught her arm.

"Guess I may have had a glass too many," she sniffed.

The jolly man offered Tess his hand. "Good evening, Miss Martin."

"Oh, Maurice, it's good to see you," she said, holding on as he steadied her. The ground began to spin slightly, she mused. "You're so good to me, Maurice. I think I love you."

"Ah, Miss, you're a beautiful lass but I suspect my wife wouldn't appreciate me if I flirted with you this evening." They exchanged laughs. He took the money she held for the taxi, leaned into the cabbie, and gave him a wink. "She'll be just fine. Thank you for bringing her home."

The driver nodded and drove away.

"It seems, Maurice, I really know how to pick 'em," she patted him on the chest, "losers, that is!"

"Ah, Miss Tess," his brow wrinkled, "a bad day?"

Her lips puckered. She snickered holding back a full-on laugh. "You could say that."

They walked to the elevators. He pressed the button and held her arm, and the door opened.

"Would you like me to escort you up, Miss?" the attendant asked.

"Oh, you are sweet, Maurice, but I think I can take it from here." Once inside, Tess leaned against the wall. The ride up the lift seemed to take forever. She watched and counted the numbers as each floor passed. The bell chimed. "Finally!" she huffed.

The doors slid open, and she stepped into the hall. A slim polished table sat against the wall. Placed in the middle, an arrangement of fresh flowers billowed over the edge of a porcelain vase. The sweet fragrance of fresh cut daylilies and roses filled the corridor. She continued down the hall, her staggered steps muffled by the carpet.

"Tess let's have dinner tonight at La Maison, there's something I want to discuss," she mocked. "Who takes a person to La Maison and breaks up with them? Who does that?" Her lips pressed tight. "That was his big plan? What a jerk," she murmured.

She stepped around the corner and continued down the hallway. The effects of the wine increased, and her steps staggered. She reached out to the wall and steadied herself. The least he could have done was to let her finish her meal before he ruined the evening, she huffed. Ahead, another bouquet of white scented flowers sat atop a second slender table at the end of the corridor. She stood at her door and looked down at the delicate pedals. The flowers reminded her of the restaurant. Her eyes watered and she bit her lip.

"I am not going to cry over him," she whispered.

Her purse strap slipped partially from her shoulder. Without adjusting it, she reached into the bag and pulled out her keys. The keychain entangled with the silver lined envelope stuffed in the side of her bag. It caught in the clasp as she tried to jerk it free. Tess gave it another tug and the entire contents of her purse flew across the hallway. Her lips quivered. She dropped to her knees and gathered her things. Tears formed and slowly slid down her cheek. "No! I am not going to cry!" she shouted, clenching her fists.

A scuffle sounded behind her. Tess turned to see the neighbor, Mrs. Crabtree, making a grab for her little white fluffed pooch, whisking the animal from Tess's reach.

"Oh," Tess forced a smile, "sorry, I didn't mean to scare you."

"Really!" The indignant woman huffed, tucking the compact-sized canine under her arm. Seeking refuge, the gray-haired woman retreated back inside her apartment, slamming the door.

"Great! Now I'll be known as the wacky single girl next door!" she sniffed.

Forgetting about the old woman and the debutante dog, Tess continued wrestling with her purse. Salty tears trickled down her face and slid onto her lips. Finally, she pulled the tangled set of keys free, aimed for the brass tumblers, and unlocked the door.

Inside, silence surrounded her. A gnawing pit formed in her stomach as her eyes followed the empty, lonely shadows outlining the room. Tess slumped against the door. The truth stared back at her. Roger may have lived with her these past few months, but nothing in the apartment belonged to him and besides his absence, nothing had changed. Emptiness surrounded her.

"Just the same 'ol stuff," she said, looking down at her client book in her hand. "Roger was right. My life is pathetic, and...," she wiped back the tears, "I am boring."

Tess crossed the room, tossing the leather-bound book onto the designer sofa. Stepping over to the window, she pulled back the curtains. The cozy apartment looked over the busy street below and the evening sky illuminated with thousands of twinkling lights. She thought about Roger's phone call earlier that afternoon.

'Ms. Martin,' her assistant paused and fluttered her eyes, *'I have lover boy on the line. He says it's...urrrrgent.'* Tess laughed as the r's rolled across the woman's tongue.

Molly was more than just her secretary. Over the past year they had become good friends. Their personalities were complete opposites with Molly's tangy flare and Tess's analytical tendencies. Molly always looked out for her, especially when it came to men–Molly's forte and choice of sport. Tess had to admit dating was not her strong side and her past had a longer than desired history of losers. But Roger had seemed different, and when he called her office, his voice had been tender. *'Tess, we need to meet tonight to discuss our future,'* he had said. She thought he had gotten the part he auditioned for last week. The role had meant a lot to him, and he did say, *'our future.'*

That was the goal, wasn't it? she asked herself. All the nights he came home late from rehearsal, sometimes not until the next morning, she hadn't complained. He had told her how grueling and demanding the director was, relentless for perfection. Tess had wanted to go and support him, but Roger convinced her she would only distract him. His acting career had been slow despite her not intruding. She hoped things had changed. During his phone call he insisted she finalize their booking with the travel agency, their upcoming getaway vacation. Five days of sand and lust. Tess snorted and peevishly looked across the cityscape. *Get it together, Tess,* she scolded. *All along Roger's been a self-centered, unemployed jerk!* She nodded, now in full silent conversation with herself. *All of this is his fault, and that...platinum tease!* She took a deep breath, exhaling deliberately. *It's been right there in front of my nose. I just didn't want to see it.* She turned from the window, kicked off her heels and laid her purse on the glass table.

"I am so done with men," she blurted, then cringed, not wanting to jinx her future. "At least womanizing-egotistical men," she quickly added. "The next man in my life will be kind, faithful, and most of all, he'll have a job!"

The purse slipped off the stand and landed onto the plush carpet. Light from the window cast a shimmer that caught her eye. She looked down at the satin finished envelope protruding from her handbag. Retrieving the small travel packet, she reluctantly pushed back the torn fold where the clasp had caught. Pausing, Tess leaned her forehead against the window and held back her tears. The cool glass felt good on her skin. She looked down at the silvery envelope and tapped the edge into her palm. Her tipsiness from earlier had now faded and with the card in hand she pushed the veranda doors open.

The mid-summer breeze pressed the thin layers of her dress against her, and the tiny black sequins shimmered in the moonlight. She breathed in the warm night air and stared out over the city. There was something about the quietness from her high-rise at night that softened the bad days, and this, she groaned, was definitely a bad day. Soothed by the flickering lights and distant sounds of the traffic, Tess took a deep breath. A new confidence flowed through her veins as she glanced down at the note still clasped in her hands. Her slender fingers brushed over the words, *Vacation Express, all inclusive.* "Our romantic getaway," she whispered.

She slid her finger under the seal and pulled out the two tickets to Belize. Lost in her emotions, tears formed and slowly slid down her cheek. With the back of her hand, she wiped them away. Taking another deep breath, she exhaled firmly. Tess lifted her chin and squared her shoulders.

"What a farce," she said, her eyes still watering. "Romance doesn't exist."

And with that, Tess wadded up the tickets and tossed them into the wastebasket.

Chapter Two

Rebound

Tess spent the last forty-eight hours sorting through papers and photos and tossing out any reminder of Roger. She found the receipt for their Belize vacation and tried to get a refund, but the travel company wouldn't budge.

***

"I am sorry, but if you had booked through our Executive Membership," the woman's voice heightened over the word "Executive," *keep calm, Tess, just keep calm,* she told herself. The operator's feverous keyboard tapping sounded through the line. "Yes, if you had used the Executive Membership," the voice continued over the phone, "we could have postponed your travel dates. Unfortunately, however, you booked your travel through our Thrift Saver Membership."

"But I just finalized the reservations on Friday."

The uncaring woman continued. "Mm-hmm, it looks like it was made using Mr. Van de Camp's membership," the woman paused, "a Mr. Roger Van de Camp."

"Yes! I told you, the reservations are under his name, but I paid for it with my credit card."

"I see," the voice continued, "and you did receive the best price. However, that membership, I am afraid, does not allow for any changes."

Tess tightened her lips. Of course, it doesn't! I'm sure that was his plan all along. He'd use his membership and pay with my credit card! Her cheeks burned at the idea.

"Is there anything else I can help you with?" the woman asked.

"Yeah, you could erase the last six months of my life," Tess mumbled.

"Ok, thank you for calling. Please let me know if I can assist you with anything else. Enjoy your vacation."

Tess pressed the 'End' button and threw her phone on the sofa. "Well, you got me again, Roger, you cheap bastard!"

***

MONDAY COULD not have arrived soon enough. Tess flung open the glass doors to the design firm, Marcus and White. She headed down the hall beelining to her office. Her patent leather heels echoed as she strode past the reception counter. Spending the weekend stewing over Roger made Tess eager to fill her mind with more important things, like work.

"Hi, Tess!" Molly's perky voice called from behind her desk. "Hey, wait a minute, aren't you and dreamy eyes going on vacation today." Molly looked down at her computer. "Mm-hmm, says Miss Martin out. What gives?"

Tess looked back over her shoulder. "I'd rather not talk about it."

"Whoa, whoa, whoa, what happened at La Maison?" Molly jumped up and leaned over her computer. "Didn't he pop the question?" she whispered.

"No," Tess mouthed back, followed by a fake half smile.

"Well, that man's a damn fool," Molly put her hands on her hips. "I mean why else would he ask you there, to La Maison? Everybody knows that's the place to go if you're going to propose."

Tess reached for the doorknob to her corner office and turned to face her friend. With her head cocked to the side and lips pressed tight, she addressed the question. "That's what I've been trying to work through myself, Molly. Why would he?" she took a deep breath. "Oh, I know. Maybe it's because he's the biggest dramatic rat in the world and has no problem spending other people's money," she paused, "like mine!"

Tess gave her assistant a cheesy grin then took a step back through the doorway into her office and closed the door. A few moments later Molly entered carrying Tess's favorite coffee, French vanilla. Tess was sure the coffee came from the new machine installed in the lounge but appreciated the gesture anyway.

"Hey sweetie," Molly urged, "we've known each other for a while now. You can talk to me, you know that."

Tess took the hot drink and sat back in her chair. "Thanks, Molly. I know I can talk to you, I just," Tess paused, "it's just that I always seem to be in this predicament. I can transform rundown, out-of-style buildings," she pointed to the photos on her wall, "but my love life is in rubble, and not exotic rubble either."

Molly sat on the edge of the desk. "C'mon, Tess, it's not that bad."

Tess contorted her lips and arched her brow. "Seriously?"

"Okay, maybe it's not that good either. So, you don't always pick the best boys on the block," Molly said.

"Exactly!" Tess chimed.

"Oh, come on. You just have to put yourself out there and look beyond tall, dark, and handsome. You know, there is more to life than a picture-perfect photo," Molly gestured to the photos on the wall. "I mean, some of these buildings really didn't need million-dollar makeovers, right? Look at this one," she said, pointing to a Long Island mansion.

Tess looked at the photo. "The Wilhelm account? What about it? It was my first major account and broke the bank at $3.6 million."

"Precisely!" Molly paused, "I mean, really, just because Lady Wilhelm walked in on her husband and their personal chef cooking up more than dinner on the kitchen floor," Molly shrugged her shoulders, "the crazy woman wants to remodel the whole damn house and turn it into a palace for her Shih Tzu," Molly grinned. "Now that's literally going to the dogs," she said and turned to Tess. "I guess she couldn't fathom having another meal cooked there."

Tess laughed. It had been one of her first projects to makeover. It already was a beautiful estate. It featured two wings, twelve bedrooms and fifteen bathrooms, not to mention the separate guest house boasting a mere 3,000 square feet. Prior to the remodel, the Wilhelm's hosted several upscale events. She thought about the luxurious estate. Molly was right. The changes made to the mansion hadn't made it any more glamorous than what it looked like prior to her remodel.

Molly whirled around, legs crossed and swinging her stiletto heels. "My point is, not everything needs a makeover. Maybe you're trying too hard to fix something that's not broken. Sometimes the best things are those left just like they were meant to be. You'll find that guy that's right for you. You've just gotta be yourself."

"I suppose," Tess paused. "You're probably right." She toyed with her pen, lining it up even with her stapler.

"What you need, girl, is to find out who you really are. Then you'll find your perfect guy," Molly said.

"I know what I want; it just never seems to work out," she frowned, "okay, maybe I don't know what I want, or even who I am. Maybe that *is* the problem."

Molly sat upright and her face brightened. "I've got it!"

Tess cocked her head and arched her brow. "What? What are you thinking Ms. Molly McDuff?"

Molly slid off the desk corner. "I am thinking you need a vacation, Miss Martin! Why don't you go to Belize anyway? Forget *what's-his-name*. Go explore, have fun, and let your hair down! A week in the Caribbean air, maybe a little fling with the cabana boy...," Molly rolled her hips and winked, "and you'll come back a whole new woman, you'll see!"

Tess shook her head. "No, that is not what I need!"

"C'mon, you've got nothing to lose. I've already moved your appointments and you've already got the time set aside."

Tess straightened another row of paper clips next to the neatly aligned pen. She tapped her fingers on the cover of her client book. An image of Roger smirking at her for bringing work to the restaurant popped into her head. She looked up, her eyes brightened. "The idea does sound rather appealing."

"That's my girl!" Molly burst.

"Molly, you're right. I may not be able to cancel the trip, but I can sure as hell go on it! I don't need anyone telling me what to do, I'll just...," her smile faded.

"What?" Molly tilted her head.

"I threw the tickets away. I didn't think I'd..."

Molly sprang for the door and bolted to her cubicle. "Don't worry about a thing, Tess. You didn't hire me as your assistant for my looks," she turned and winked. "I keep a file of all your travel itineraries, and I kept the resort number."

"But my flight, it leaves in less than two hours, and I'm not even packed, or anything!" Tess sunk into the chair.

Molly rushed back into the room and shuffled through some papers. "Here," she handed Tess a paper, here's the number. All you have to do is call and confirm your room. You can do that from your cellphone on the way. And like you said, the flight is already booked."

"I still don't have anything packed," Tess said.

"You've got a credit card, don't you? And I know you've been carrying around that passport of yours," Molly grinned.

"Yes," Tess agreed.

"See, there's no problem. You'll just buy what you need when you get there. And when did you ever turn down a chance to go shopping? Look on the bright side," Molly gestured, "you won't have any luggage to check. If you leave now, you'll be able to make it to the airport." She pulled Tess from her chair and pressed her hand firmly onto her friend's back. "Your plane ticket is already in their system. Remember? You couldn't cancel."

"You're right, Molly, as usual," Tess said.

"See, problem solved," Molly grinned.

***

"YES, I'D like to confirm my reservation," Tess stated. She gripped the vehicles grab handles as the cab sped around the corner. "What do you mean they've already been confirmed?" Tess braced herself as the taxi stopped abruptly for the light. "He what?" Tess leaned hard against the seat and placed her hand to her forehead. "Oh—that snipe! Well, he was not supposed to confirm anything! I am the one using our vacation, not him!" she fumed. "Yes, I'll hold."

She could see the cab driver raise his brow as if intrigued by her phone conversation. Their eyes met in the rearview mirror, and she darted him a less than pleasing look. He returned his attention back to the road. Samba music played over her cellphone while she was on hold. Tess looked out the window. A couple sat at an outdoor café. Roger and his harlot seeped into her mind. She sneered at the image. Roger's audacity, how dare he turn their breakup into a love fest for him and his new tramp, and on her dime! Her fingers twisted the end of her hair, a habit she'd had since childhood. Her patience thinned. She waited for the operator to return to the line.

"Señora?" a thick accent burst through the line.

"Yes."

"I am sorry, but your reservations have already been confirmed and because the name on record is under a Mr. Van de Camp, we cannot change them," the man said.

"But...*urrr*," Tess gritted her teeth. Of course, now it made more sense why Roger insisted she use his membership and, because he wanted to feel chivalrous, he asked her to use his name. Argh! When would she learn? She shook her head. They passed a freeway sign, *JFK Airport Next Exit*. "Look, I am the one who paid for the trip. I should be the one to go."

"Yes, señora, I see your name as the credit card holder. I understand the situation and it is unfortunate, but I cannot reserve another room at this hotel, we are fully booked this time of year."

"Yes, yes," her voice quivered, "please, you don't understand, I need this vacation. I'll pay more, anything, please!"

The coarse voice now sounded empathetic. "I could possibly see about a reservation at another location, but I cannot guarantee you the same experience and, of course, there will be an extra charge."

"I'll take it!" Tess cut him off, "wherever it is, yes, I'll take it."

"Very well," the man said. "I will transfer you to the other line. Please hold."

***

TESS PAID the cabbie as he pulled to the curb. With her reservations in Belize now taken care of, she grabbed her purse and hurried to the airport counter. Tess thrust her identification to the woman behind the barrier. "I just need to get my ticket."

"I'm sorry ma'am but you did not confirm your flight, which is mandatory for first class seating."

"Yes, I know, but it couldn't be helped," Tess said. She debated whether or not to go into detail about her philandering boyfriend, or rather, ex-boyfriend.

"Well," the ticket agent continued, "there is a seat that opened in coach, I could..."

"Yes!" Tess blurted. "Coach, yes, that would be fine. Thank you."

The woman pushed a few more buttons and handed Tess a boarding pass.

"Have a nice flight," she said.

Chapter Three

Belize

THE SUN BEAMED DOWN FROM the bluest sky she had ever seen. A warm and subtle breeze brushed across her face as she stood just outside the airport. With the humidity thick, her blouse clung to her skin. She loved the heat but looked forward to some air conditioning. A handful of other would-be tourists stood at the small, yellow sign next to the curb, *Thrift Saver Shuttle*.

"Isn't this exciting?" a jolly faced woman said.

Tess looked over to the woman next to her, not certain who the conversation had been directed towards.

"Oh, I was talking to you, hon," the middle-aged woman nodded. The roundness of her cheeks pushed up the white frames of her sunglasses. She leaned in closer; the brightness of the sun reflected off her vibrant yellow dress. "I just noticed that you were traveling by yourself, too."

"Uh...y-yes," Tess stuttered, "yes, I am."

"Well, hon, sometimes they make the best vacations. Believe me, I've been on some doozies." The woman rocked back and forth from her heels to her toes and back again. Her hand clutched an oversized vinyl, orange purse. "And...the ones that are the best are where you can let your hair down. If you know what I mean." The eccentric tourist slid the bargain store glasses down her nose and winked.

"Really? I'll keep that in mind," Tess said, stepping back from the curb, turning to look the other way. She didn't want to be rude, but she didn't want to dwell on her recent relationship status either, which she realized from the woman's comment, was all too obvious.

***

THE PASSENGER van weaved through the busy streets. Finally, the shuttle rounded the corner and screeched to a halt. Relieved, Tess released her grip on the seat. The driver jumped out and ran to open the side door. He nodded to each passenger as they stepped out.

The second-rate resort lacked the flamboyant appearance compared to the booking she had previously made for her and Roger. There were no grand pillars or valet parking attendants to greet the guests as they arrived. Outside the building, an uneven brick drive that arched in a half circle led to the glass double doors of the flat stucco building. Tess noticed a broken valet cart cast off to one side, leaning against the corner of the building.

"Well, when the booking agent said he couldn't guarantee the same experience, now I see what he meant," she said.

The remainder of guests unloaded from the shuttle. The small group headed for the entrance, each rolling their luggage with a distinct *clunk-clunk, clunk-clunk*, as they crossed the bumpy landing. Tess sensed staring eyes roving over her, questioning her lack of luggage. The brightly dressed woman with her white brimmed sunglasses, the same person who recently pointed out Tess's single status to the world, led the way. Tess followed the group hoping for indoor air conditioning, it would be a welcome relief to the constant, thick temperature that drenched over her. Inside, however, the only breeze emanated from the low-hanging ceiling fans, shaped like palm leaves, woven from bamboo. There were four in total, suspended high over the foyer. To the left of the check-in counter a wide sweeping staircase ascended to the second and third story guest rooms. From the details on the banister and the worn, red floral carpet secured with mushroom shaped brass tacks along the steps, Tess guessed it had been, at one time, a popular destination. The bellhop jumped to his feet taking the guest's luggage into his hand. Tess noticed one man give the attendant cash. Another bellhop, slightly younger than the first, perhaps brothers, ran up to her and held out his hand.

"Oh, no thank you," she smiled.

He persistently followed her, beaming a trustworthy grin. "Your bags, miss?" he gestured.

"Thank you, but I don't have any," she smiled.

Tess snorted at how silly that must have seemed, a tourist without luggage. To be in another country without any belongings was a bit odd, she agreed. However, under the circumstances and like Molly said, '*You'll just buy what you need when you get there!*' Tess lacked Molly's carefree confidence but was excited to step out of her comfort zone and shake up her rigid boundaries. Tess chuckled, amused by her own over-exuberance for paperwork that had proved to be useful. She had been so ecstatic about taking the vacation with Roger that for the past week she had carried her passport in her purse. Without it she wouldn't have been able to get on the plane.

One by one, the guests waited to check in. A neat but indifferent looking man greeted her from behind the tall counter. "Yes, Ma'am, you have reservations?"

"Yes. Tess Martin. I called this morning."

"Ah yes, Miss Martin, we have a room waiting for you. Miguel will take your bags," he said. The middle-aged man snapped his fingers.

The same youth dutifully came over. This time he trudged across the lobby floor slower and hung his head. The poor kid, she mused, he probably wished he could help someone else, someone who actually had luggage. Tess could see his disappointment.

"Oh, no...no thank you," she smiled, embarrassed. "Really, I'm fine. Look...," she held her arms out, "no luggage!"

The man at the counter raised an eyebrow. "Ah, you are here to meet someone perhaps?"

"Y...yes!" she stuttered.

The man narrowed his eyes then looked back at his paperwork. "I see." He placed the room key on the counter and gave her a swift smile.

She cringed, puzzled by his expression. Did he think she was a hooker, in Belize? "I mean no, I'm...I'm not *meeting* anyone in particular...," she frowned. "Well, I'm sure I'll meet someone..."

The man lifted his eyes.

"Never mind, it sounds awful no matter how I put it," Tess sighed. She picked up her key and headed for the stairs. The disappointed boy stood against the wall and shuffled his feet. Tess stopped and called over to him. "Could you show me to my room please?"

The boy straightened up and happily trotted over. He looked at her with his wide smile, then took her by the hand and led her up the stairway. She gave him the key and the young man opened the door then held out his palm.

"Thank you, Miguel," Tess smiled. She found some change in her purse and tipped the eager boy and closed the door.

The smell of dust accompanied by a hint of coconut oil rushed past her nose. She looked up and saw a large ceiling fan, oversized for the small room. The woven blades twirled in rhythm.

"Hmm, air conditioning, I suppose," she said, contorting her lips.

Other than the steady hum of its motor, the room was quiet. She threw her purse onto the bed. In the same moment she kicked off her shoes and flopped across the mattress. The soft down of the comforter engulfed her. The ride in the cramped van had taken over an hour from the airport. She welcomed the opportunity to relax and closed her eyes. The muffled sound of footsteps and totes wheeling down the hall vibrated through the wall as other guests made their way to their rooms. Tess opened her eyes and momentarily stared at the ceiling before rolling onto her side. A clock sat on the nightstand. The rolodex-like numbers were faintly illuminated by a dim light. She stared at it. The tiny motor hummed louder from the outdated clock and the minute number flipped over.

"Okay, Tess, time to do something," she said, breaking the dullness.

She sat up and looked around the room. The survey didn't take long. A single oil painting, portraying an ocean with palm trees dotted along the beach, hung crooked on the cream-colored stucco wall. Within an arm's reach of the bed, two small rattan chairs, both boasting faded green cushions, butted up against a tiny rattan table. Next to it was the sliding glass door.

"Maybe there's a view," she muttered.

Tess walked over and pulled back the linen curtains. She tugged open the slider. The sun had slipped behind the adjacent building. Stepping out onto the veranda, the stagnant hot air took her breath away leaving a hint of salty seawater taste in her mouth. She leaned over the railing. It was futile. A tall palm stood just off the balcony—its fronds brushed against the hotel wall obscuring any view. The hope of seeing white sandy beaches dispersed and she stepped back inside. Her eyes swept over her shabby room, her home for the next five nights. Exhaling, she took another glance across the disenchanting abode. The queen-sized bed took up most of the space. And the beige bedding ensemble had little to zero appeal, which, she grimaced, fit in with the rest of the decor.

"I suppose most people don't come here by themselves, and they probably have other things on their minds," she muttered under her breath. Tess remembered Molly's suggestion and envisioned a brief fling with a well-tanned cabana boy. "Well, if that were the case," she mused, "the room would be perfect."

Squaring her shoulders, Tess took a deep breath. "C'mon, Tess, you can do this. Let's get this adventure started," she whispered. And with that, she slipped her shoes back on, tucked her room key into her mini handbag, and headed out the door.

***

THE EVENING temperatures cooled slightly, and a light breeze ruffled over her as she walked down the path leading to the bar. The older bellhop had directed her, the young man had been eager to tell her of the place. "Yes, miss. Just out the back. You'll see the lights at the end of the path. My brother works there. He will take care of you," the boy smiled. Tess headed down the hallway and out the door.

Vibrant colors formed across the sky, like a vivid painting—orange and pink swept across the cloudless view and the bold harvest-yellow burst from the sun. As she navigated the narrow path, Tess could hear the roar of the ocean growing closer. She inhaled the fresh air, and for a moment, an unfamiliar and welcomed satisfaction swept over her. Tess mused that only hours ago she had sat in her high-rise office debating whether or not she should come to this place. And now, while she had envisioned getting there under different circumstances, she embraced the surreal warmth of Belize.

The trail from the hotel widened, merging with the beach. She found the loose sand made it impossible to walk in, even with her low heels. They were ideal for the office, she noted, but not so much for the white beach granules, which tickled as it sifted between her toes. Tomorrow, she would go shopping and buy sandals.

As the view of the beach expanded in front of her, Tess noticed a young couple about her age walking along the shore. Intrigued, she watched from a distance. The woman playfully kicked water onto the man and then ran away, only to be caught by him moments later. The man wrapped his arms around the slender woman's waist. He leaned in and kissed her. Tess found herself smiling as she took in their flirtatious moment. Her mind shifted to her own relationship, or rather the lack of one, but quickly she dismissed the flinch of sadness and drew on the strength of her friend. Perhaps she would follow Molly's advice, or at least modify it somewhat. Rather than the cabana boy, she thought with a playful grin, she would see what other options were available and put Roger what's-his-name completely out of her mind. Maybe she would let her hair down and enjoy her vacation, she smiled. After all, isn't that what the jolly woman from the bus said she should do?

Ahead, a cantina was just off to the left of the path. It looked more like a movie prop rather than a functioning bar. There were tiki torches lit at each corner where a makeshift half-wall stood. It was about three feet high and made from thick raffia strands. She decided the shortened walls looked more like a suggested perimeter rather than strict confines keeping patrons in the lounge. More dried woven grass lopped over the top of the roof giving it an unpolished, castaway-like appearance, rather than a mainstream hangout. She looked towards the back of the open space where bottles of spirits in familiar liquid colors sat on mirrored shelves.

"That must be the bar. I could definitely use a drink," she muttered.

She made her way past the empty rattan chairs tucked under the lopsided tables. The bar structure looked primitively intriguing. It had a sturdy set of bamboo posts with a set of string lights stretched across the middle. The counter resembled an oversized wooden surfboard, which had been inlayed and polished with thick resin. Crude, but nevertheless, she was impressed that someone had taken the time to coat it with such a thick layer of polyurethane.

Tess ran her hands over the smooth surface. Although there were blemishes where the salt air had dulled it a little around the edges, for the most part, it boasted a good shine that reflected the mirror and drinking glasses beyond. Various stemware of different shapes and sizes were stacked behind the bar. A conch-like carafe caught her eye. It was about the size of a cantaloupe.

"Hmm, wonder what comes in that," she murmured.

Tess settled onto a barstool, her skirt sliding upward, revealing her thighs. Two weathered patrons, their faces etched by time, glanced her way. The bar stool rocked forward with one leg slightly shorter than the other three. Tess rested her elbows on the crude bar which helped steady the crooked chair. Both men lingered at her exposed flesh. The old-timer closest to her arched his brow and smiled broadly. Her cheeks blushed. She gave the men a brief smile and quickly turned her attention to the rest of the room.

Lights flickered from the strands of lanterns tacked along the walls, she figured they were some sort of special bulb that gave the appearance of an open flame but without the obvious fire hazard, as this place would surely be. It certainly lacked the sophistication and social stature of La Maison. She immediately regretted making the comparison as an image of Roger flashed through her mind. Tess didn't want to think about that right now, and especially she didn't want to think about Roger. Just the mere memory caused her shoulders to tense, and a knot rapidly formed in her throat. She took a deep breath and looked around at her options.

"Okay, Tess. Let's see what this place has to offer," she mumbled.

Worn bamboo chairs laced with yellowing palm leaves lined sporadically at the bar. By their looks, she surmised, her uneven chair was not the only dilapidated furniture in the place. Even with the walls open and the night air swirling, the room was bland, and the only illumination seemed to come from the crude lanterns. She squinted, taking in the odd shape at the back of the open room. It was a wooden dance floor, she realized, but mostly just an empty corner. Stage lights hung disheveled overhead with thick coats of dust and gnarly spider webs, no doubt woven by creatures she dreaded. The unkempt space gave her the impression that neither the lighting nor the dance floor had seen any use for quite some time. Perhaps years ago this place had been livelier, but not now.

There was no lack of seating. The one thing that stood out most, she noticed, was that all of the seats were without customers except for the two older men, locals she guessed by their simple linen clothing and worn raffia-like hats.

"Well, there goes the cabana boy idea," she said.

"What can I make for you, Señorita?" a voice asked.

Tess quickly turned; a friendly-faced man stood in front of her. The bartender threw a towel over his shoulder and with his palms on the counter, he leaned towards her. His bronzed skin glistened in the modest light and his smile was warm and friendly. Tess's gaze shifted over his curly dark hair that blended with his surfer-like muscular build.

"Uh...I...I'll have a...uh...," she stammered. A lump formed in her throat. Bar hopping wasn't her typical thing and definitely she did not know what type of drink would be best for her first day of vacation. Molly's words, to let her hair down, gave her just enough push to step out of her comfort shell. She smiled and swallowed hard. After a brief moment she shrugged. "Surprise me."

The man arched his brow and nodded. His white teeth beamed against his suntanned skin. "Alright, you got it!" he said.

The bartender turned around and systematically picked up one bottle from the back shelf and quickly followed it by another. Fascinated, Tess watched his impressive skill. Each bottle had a red pour tip and with expert execution the bartender mixed the liquors. It looked more like a form of art, she thought, as he swiftly and methodically replaced each bottle to its original spot. He briskly grabbed another one, this time blue in color. Playfully, he spun around, wiggling his eyebrows and displaying his broad smile. Next, the bartender picked up a metal cup, filled it with ice and poured the contents into the container. Holding the lid firmly, he shook the concoction over one shoulder and then held it over the other, continuing to gyrate the cocktail shaker.

The faint sound of reggae music echoed from across the beach. Gazing over the nearby surroundings she didn't see anything that resembled a band anywhere. Tess turned back around as the bartender set a tall conch shaped glass in front of her. A tiny pink umbrella swirled on the rim, along with slices of peach and mango fruit, then topped off with a slice of lime. The garnishment looked good enough to eat, she thought, as the delicious aroma of peach and coconut filled the air. Eagerly she took a sip.

"Yum! That is delicious, what is it?" she said, licking her lips.

"One of our finest Belizean specials, this one is called, Bahama Be Your Mama," he grinned.

"Never heard of it, but I'll have to keep it in mind for my next cocktail party!"

"The locals say it will bring out your true spirit. Enjoy!" he said.

The alcohol warmed her throat and went down easily. She could still hear the faint beats of music as it echoed from the beach. In the distance, between the palm trees along the shore, Tess squinted towards the shadow of a distant hotel. She could just make out the small flickers of torches. Turning back to the bartender, Tess motioned with her hand as she continued drinking the fruity beverage.

"What is that over there?" she asked, pointing.

"That is the Grand Simone. Many tourists go there."

"The Grand Simone?" she groaned.

"Yes," he arched his eyebrows, "you know of it?"

The Simone's music echoed from the distance with the occasional faint sound of announcements over a microphone. With the sun setting, the lights from the Grand hotel now reflected through the trees. She hadn't realized how close her hotel was to the immaculate resort, the same resort where she and Roger had made their reservations. The thought of running into the untrustworthy rat made her cringe. Tess looked out towards the nearby beach. Gentle white caps rolled onto the shore. Glancing down at the blue drink in front of her, she twirled the straw and the ice clinked against the glass. For a moment she methodically churned her straw with precise twists. An awkward silence settled over her as she realized the bartender awaited her reply. Tess sighed, almost involuntarily, then squared her shoulders and offered a warm smile in return.

"Actually, I do know of the Grand Simone. I even booked a vacation there. I just didn't know it was so close...to here, I mean. That's all."

"Hmm...," he squinted. "You have a lot on your mind, right?"

"I suppose," she agreed. Tess didn't want to admit she'd flown on a whim to a tropical paradise and now only wanted to mope in a speak-easy-type hideaway frequented only by her and two other uninteresting locals.

"Let me guess, you're here because your boyfriend dumped you, right?" the bartender said.

Tess almost choked on the smooth drink. "Geeze...is it that noticeable?"

"I figured," he grinned. "Our customers are either locals sneaking in for a drink before heading home, or lost souls recuperating from a breakup."

Nodding, she sipped her drink. "Got any advice for me? I mean since you seem experienced in this sort of thing."

He gestured towards the Simone and again threw the bar towel over his shoulder. Leaning over the bar towards her, his brow softened. "A woman, as beautiful as you, should not waste any of her time in this place or give the man who left you any further thought."

"No?" she asked, feeling her cheeks starting to blush.

Tess stopped twirling the straw, wanting to believe him. Her gazed shifted to the Simone, then back to the bartender who again leaned in close. His arms rested across the bar. The faint fragrance of tropical musk filled her nose, and she wondered if it was his cologne or if all the good-looking locals smelled the same.

"Belize is a place where romance lives! That loser didn't know what he had," he paused and dipped his gaze, roving over her. "Now...," his voice softened, "it's your turn to take control of your destiny."

She looked up at him, his eyes shone sincerely.

"Go to the Simone," he said. "Take in all that Belize has to offer and enjoy yourself!"

"Believe me, I would, but there aren't any rooms available. I already checked."

He laughed and pulled the towel from his shoulder rubbing spots off a glass then gently set it on the shelf. "You don't need to stay at the Grand Simone to party there," he said, amused.

"I just thought...," she shrugged.

"No. Many tourists stay here and enjoy the atmosphere at the Simone. I assure you, it's very common and," he paused, glancing towards the men at the end of the bar. "It beats the local activity here," he gestured. "Am I right, Giuseppe?" the bartender hollered towards the men.

Tess laughed and looked down the bar where the two older men eavesdropped on their conversation. The grey-haired patrons nodded in agreement lifting their beers and mumbled something inaudible to her ears. Tess turned back towards the bartender.

"It could be fun, I suppose. I mean the music and all," she said. Tess glanced back at the flickering lights from down the beach. The chances of Roger being there would be slim, she hoped. But then she thought about it more and narrowed her brow. *Even if he is there, maybe I'll tell him how I really feel. Maybe I'll make him stay at this low budget motel while I bask in the pampering at the Simone!* She looked up at the bartender. "I will go!"

"That's the spirit!" he paused and raised the blue bottle of rum, "the Belizean spirit!"

Holding up her glass, Tess toasted to her newfound courage. The co-conspirator locals raised their glasses as well. With the tiny straw she sucked up the last of the alcohol from the bottom of the conch shaped mug. It tickled her throat as she quickly sucked it down and her eyes watered. "I've got to stop doing that," she said, stifling back a cough.

The bartender chuckled. "Enjoy your stay! Belize has enriched the lives of many, and I have a feeling that your journey is just across the way."

She set down her glass and wiped her lips with the back of her hand. With the new energy surging through her, she grabbed her purse, gave a quick smile to the bartender, and set out for the Grand Simone.

"No spontaneity?" she said. "I'll show you, Mr. Roger jerk-face!"

Chapter Four

Stepping Out

TESS MADE HER WAY DOWN the beach towards the Grand Simone. The sun had dipped below the horizon and in its place the moonlight beamed across the water. Silhouettes of chartered boats cruised along the coastline. The dark images twinkled in the distance as their deck lights shone across the sea. Tess gazed out towards the ocean waves. The water rolled up onto the shore with a continuous smooth and methodical cadence. Tempted by the warm, clear seawater, Tess slipped off her shoes. With the straps secured around her fingers she tiptoed into the dark blue moonlit sea. The rush of warm water encircled her ankles and the tiny beads of sand slipped from under her toes as the current retreated. Playfully, she splashed under the Belizean moonlight and continued up the shoreline.

Looking farther up the beach, she could see the outline of the Grand Simone's day bungalows. Thin, linen curtains waved gently in the breeze as tiny lanterns glittered beyond the cabanas. Reluctantly, Tess stepped from the warm water and made her way down the stone path, lit by a continuous line of tiki torches placed along the edges. The Grand Simone was just ahead. Strategically placed lighting illuminated the multitude of the stately pillars giving it an impressive image against the dark blue sky. It was the most beautiful place she had ever seen. But the sting of Roger taking over their suite nagged at her like a toothache.

She took a moment and glanced back out at the sea. An evening breeze rustled the nearby palm trees, and the faint lights of the chartered boats were now far off in the distance. Her mind drifted taking in the peaceful tempo of the Belizean atmosphere. It was a welcome contrast to her hectic life at home. In the city, she would never venture barefoot, much less walk the streets alone, nor did she ever think she would want to do those things until now. Engulfed by the carefree atmosphere, the dense loneliness of her breakup lifted from her heart. She breathed in the fresh Caribbean air and savored the warm gentle wind as it swirled across her cheeks. Perhaps the bartender had been right, she admitted, maybe she would find her true self in this paradise.

It didn't take long for her feet to dry, and she slipped her office shoes back on. Ahead, there was a flat-stone walkway that led up to the luxury resort. A brilliant bouquet of red and orange tropical flowers caught her attention. She couldn't resist and stooped over, ready to inhale the fresh blossoms. But the paver under her foot became loose sending her awkwardly forward off balance and wedged the tip of her low-heeled sling under the loose rock. In a split second, she lost her balance and envisioned herself with her face planted squarely into the oversized foliage.

Tess reached out blindly. Her hands grasped a large and gritty form. She clung tightly to the solid, protruding object, regaining her balance. Glad not to have nose-dived into the bushes, Tess looked up and her mouth gaped to see an oversized sculpture of a sea Neptune. Like the pillars direct lighting, the triton's naked porcelain body was illuminated clearly, detailing the intricate merman-like scales and partial covering just above the groin. The scantily dressed sculpture left little to the imagination and Tess quickly removed her hands from the stone's protrusion, which she realized had saved her from her fall. Tess glanced down the path and exhaled heavily, relieved that no one had seen her near disaster. Wiping the porcelain residue from her hands, Tess noticed the statue was at the entrance of the resort pool. Now composed, she stepped through the gateway.

The bluish-green water sparkled in the lighting. She admired the seashells and artistic scenes of mermaids and dolphins painted along the walls. Stretching across to the other side, the underwater art etched its way along, eventually meeting at a jagged rockface waterfall. The tall water feature spilled over its edges and into the pool below. Jungle leaves and bright red flowers cascaded down its sides.

"Wow! So, this is what I'm paying for, on my credit card," she said, twisting her lips. "It's even more beautiful than the online pictures."

The landscaped jungle and waterfall background surrounding the pool looked real. Its grandeur inspired her, and for a modest moment, she entertained the idea of going on an adventure tour, like what she had seen advertised in her hotel lobby. At her hotel, the bookstands were stacked full of mini-adventure brochures, promising a memorable excursion through the tropical forest. But the idea of mosquito infested jungles with over-sized spiders, and other unknown creeping things, made her shiver. She gave the poolside another look.

"I think I'll enjoy my outdoor adventure right here," she said.

Across the water she noticed two guests playfully splashing each other under the sprays of the falls. Tess stared at the couple. Like the lovers on the beach, the young woman giggled as her boyfriend wrapped his arms around her waist kissing her lips and pulling her body closer to his. Visions of Roger and his floosy flooded through her mind. Tess's smile quickly faded, and she looked away. The sting of Roger's betrayal surfaced. Visions of his piercing blue eyes played over in her mind. Tess slid her fingers down over her throat, pausing as they brushed over the silk buttons. Her hand lingered. The moist, sultry air engulfed her, and her lightweight blouse clung to her skin. Disenchanted, the image of Roger faded.

***

THE BEAT of Caribbean music echoed through the air. Tess glanced one more time at the Grand Simone poolside before she turned and headed towards the reggae rhythm. She followed the Tiki torches that lit the path along the way. Like the little cantina, the Simone's bar had a jungle appeal with vines twisting around each post at the entrance. She gaped at the large birdcage hoisted overhead with cackling calls from the flamboyant red, orange, and green colored birds. The bird's tail feathers protruded through the cage making it necessary to duck, avoiding their elongated plumes. Tess anxiously took a deep breath and stepped across the threshold.

Wooden planks lapped over the interior walls with nets draped across them. Glass bottles, starfish, and other sea-like memorabilia hung entwined throughout the netting, completing the pirate theme. She remembered a few of the articles she had skipped over on the computer before booking their getaway vacation. Travel advisories talked briefly about Belize and its early ties to piracy. Tess glanced around at the authentic looking décor and half expected 'ol Peg Leg, himself, to round the corner any minute.

The size of the bar doubled compared to the dingy pub next to her hotel. She understood, now, why the bartender had encouraged her to venture out and party at the Simone. The vibrant atmosphere lifted her spirits, making her glad that she stepped out of her comfort zone, even though she was alone. She would prove to herself and to Roger that he had been wrong about her and that she could be spontaneous and adventurous if she wanted to. And, she hoped, the Grand Simone atmosphere would be the perfect way to get started.

From over her shoulder, she heard a high-pitched voice call out her name. It vaguely sounded familiar. Tess looked through the crowded group of strangers huddled near the counter, but she didn't recognize any of them. *That's crazy,* she shrugged, *who do I know in Belize anyway?* She chalked the delusion up to all the new sensations that exploded around her. Her nerves fluttered like a field of butterflies and her shoulders tingled with anticipation. Working up her courage, she drew in another breath and scanned the lively room for an empty seat. None were available.

"Yoo-hoo!" a woman yelled.

Tess turned around. A small commotion stirred, and a round-faced woman wedged her way through the crowd. It was the perky tourist from the bus, the same one that pried into her relationship status. Tess cringed at the notion of explaining, once again, how she ended up in paradise single and alone. Glancing around the room, Tess looked for the nearest exit. It was too late; the woman slipped past the crowd and headed her direction. Tess waited, helpless as the rosy-cheeked woman traipsed over. The woman's hands were clasped around a large glass topped with fruit pieces and two pink umbrellas leaning haphazardly over the rim.

"Yoo-hoo! There you are!" the voice echoed again.

Tess watched as the woman pushed past the last few people gathered near the bar. Tess couldn't help but stare at the oversized earrings that swayed back and forth with each peppy step. A matching strand of beads lay bold across the plump woman's chest just above a sea of half buried cleavage.

"Hi there, uh...," Tess stuttered.

"Oh, I saw you coming down the path and I just had to come over and say, *Hello*!" the round-faced woman said.

"Well, that's so nice of you," Tess forced a smile.

"So have you found the one?" the woman asked.

Tess hesitated as the quizzical character wasted no time blurting her question. The blunt woman wrapped her bright colored lips around a straw protruding from her cocktail. She stared at Tess wide-eyed, and her cheeks sucked in forming dimples as she gulped down the fruit packed drink. Tess stared back at the large round eyes that eagerly waited for an answer.

"I don't know what you mean. Found what one?" Tess said.

The woman pulled the straw from her mouth and let out a bold laugh. The aroma of tequila and coconut swept through the air. Her short black hair bounced as she did a quick jig with her feet and fluttered her eyelashes.

"Oh, you are just so sweet, like an innocent vacation virgin! Honey, I'm talking about the one. You know, to let your hair down with," she said, twisting her lips. The woman tucked her chin and with her mouth slightly agape, she gave an exaggerated wink.

"Oh...," Tess laughed, "that...one! No, I haven't picked one out...," she hesitated, "but I'll work on it." Tess looked away and scanned the room for a distraction.

"Don't you worry, sweetie. A cute catch like you won't have any trouble finding a handsome stud," she said.

The woman gave Tess a sober nod. An awkward silence followed for just a moment as the curious woman looked down at Tess's blouse then back up. She contorted her lips and scrunched her nose. Tess arched her brow and glanced down at her blouse.

"Oh, Honey...do you mind if I offer a suggestion?" the woman asked.

"Uh...I guess not," Tess lied.

"Well, you might want to undo a couple of buttons," the woman nodded glancing down at Tess's silk blouse. "You know...," she leaned in close to Tess's ear and whispered, "just to advertise the merchandise a little, that's all."

Tess's mouth gaped. "Thanks, I'll keep that in mind."

The heavy beat of the music stopped, and the murmur of conversations filled the air.

"Ooh, the band must be on a break," the woman said, puckering her lips. "Good! It'll give us a chance to chat."

Before Tess could protest, the bubbly tourist grabbed her by the arm and the two women ducked under the overhang that led up to the bar. A couple of unoccupied stools sat at one end.

"Perfect! We can sit here and have a double Coconut Gyrator!" the woman beamed.

"A coconut what-ator?" Tess cringed.

The woman giggled, lifting her glass up. "One of these silly!" she said.

Tess placed a hand to her chest, "Whew, I wasn't sure what I had gotten myself into for a moment."

The two women laughed, with the bouncy tourist's voice carrying through the room. Tess didn't care. The colorful tourist's energy was infectious, and having a drink or two would be just the thing to get this vacation started. They took a seat on the unoccupied chairs. Moments later, a tanned bartender approached.

"What can I get you ladies?" he asked.

"We'll take two Gyrators...doubles," the woman giggled. "This is my friend, Tess." The woman leaned slightly over the bar and whispered loudly. "She's on a maiden voyage."

Tess shook her head. It would be of no use disputing the fact, and instead, she raised her hand in defeat. "Guilty!" Tess said.

The bartender gave her a wink, then turned to make their drinks.

"Is it really that obvious? What gave me away?" Tess asked.

In search of her own answer, Tess glanced down at her clothes. She overslept this morning back at her apartment. In her haste, she accidentally punctured her last pair of nylons with her fingernails. It was the third pair ruined by unintentional tears. Finally, she conceded, opting for bare legs.

Tess looked down at her feet. In hindsight, she thought, arching her brow, it had worked out rather well, at least for walking barefoot on the beach. She continued surveying her attire. The black skirt had a slit in the back and its snug fit showed off her curves. Glancing out at the other patrons, Tess scrunched her nose recognizing her business attire didn't have the same tropical flare worn by most tourists. But, in her defense, she hadn't known she would be running for the airport and jet setting off to Belize.

The skirt seemed a safe choice in case Roger decided he would shower her with roses and apologies. It wouldn't have been the first Monday she had received an apology bouquet. In the past, she would inevitably take him back. This time, however, she would have laughed in his face and thrown him and his would-be roses down the elevator, or at least that's the scenario she played over in her mind. Tess wasn't about to let him know how much his betrayal hurt her. And the sooner he'd see her uncaring about his lust affair, the better. She glanced around the room. Besides, the skirt made her feel sexy, and right now, it's all she had. Tess fidgeted in her seat, tugging discreetly at the hem as it inched its way up her thigh.

"Oh, honey, don't you worry, this place is loaded with shops. We'll find you some cute clothes tomorrow," the jovial woman said.

Their drinks arrived and Tess eagerly took a sip.

"Delicious! Is everything in Belize always so fantastic?" Tess looked around. "I mean, look at this place, it's like a jungle paradise. Those palm trees," she gestured towards the doorway, "I feel like Jane of the jungle. This is going to be a great adventure—I can feel it!"

"Well Sweetie, all you need now is Tarzan!" the woman said.

They both laughed.

"Hey! I just realized I don't know your name," Tess said.

"It's Connie," she grinned. "So, tell me, how is it that you ended up coming here by yourself, and in office duds and all?"

Her new friend took a sip of the frosty Gyrator with eyes focused.

"That's a long story. Let's just say I expected it was going to be a honeymoon, but it turns out he had another *honey*, and I ended up with the moon!"

The woman swished her hand through the air. "Oh, shoot sweetie, is that all? I thought you were going to tell me a steaming hot office romance, or something like you came out here with your sugar-daddy boss and his wife showed up instead story. Now that's something to get juicy over!" Connie nodded.

Tess frowned. "I suppose I'll just have to settle with boyfriend dumps girl for another girl, saga."

"Oh, honey," the woman's chest jiggled with her laugh, "that is tragic. But you know what they say, when you fall off one stallion, you just go find yourself another one and climb on!"

"Is that what they say?" Tess laughed.

"You bet, and once this music kicks in, we'll find you ...that *one*!" Connie gave another overly exaggerated wink.

The rhythmic rumble of drums echoed behind them. Seizing the moment, the two women clasped their drinks and turned to face the dance floor. Tess again situated her skirt, then tucked loose strands of auburn hair behind her ear. From the corner of her eye, she saw a black spot on her blouse near her shoulder. The dark image looked like a spider. It startled her and she quickly brushed her hand at it. She paused, then chuckled removing a tiny piece of a leaf that clung onto her shirt, a souvenir from the poolside, she assumed. She looked down over her chest and made sure no more critters were crawling in places they shouldn't. The lace of her spaghetti strap camisole peeked from underneath her shear blouse. Connie's well-meaning advice filled her thoughts. Tess ran her hand across the tiny satin wrapped buttons. She shrugged. *Why not, I might as well show the merchandise. I certainly wouldn't want to look like a virgin tourist.*

Connie glanced over, nodding her approval as she took a sip of her fruit-filled cocktail. Reggae music filled the room and couples flooded onto the dance floor.

Tess tapped her toes on the bar stool and twirled the pink umbrella in her drink. Vaguely remembering that Connie had ordered them as doubles, she sipped the coconut Gyrator, enjoying the soothing effect of the alcohol. Glancing around, she felt a pang of jealousy at the idea of Roger staying at the Simone with his new girlfriend. She glanced down, swirling the ice in her drink. A moment later, she took a deep breath, and let out a deliberate sigh. She would have preferred to put the whole incident behind her, but visions of her quarrel with Roger at La Maison flashed through her mind. His callous smirk burned in her memory. She knew then she had been played, used for her money, her apartment, and her connections to the elite and more sophisticated crowd. Yep, Roger was nothing more than a two-timing, free-loading deadbeat—plain and simple. Furrowing her brow, Tess vowed that the next man in her life would be self-supporting and honest. Connie gave her a nudge.

"Don't look now, but I think Tarzan just walked in."

Tess lifted her eyes glancing across the room. She took a long-drawn sip of the ice cool drink and surveyed the handsome stranger as he stepped onto the dance floor. Draped over his muscular forearm, a petite brunette, around Tess's age, sauntered past them. Tess watched the exotic looking couple. The dark-haired temptress's full figure stretched taught into the bodice of her sex-kitten garb. Tess sized the young woman up, taking another sip of the Gyrator. Jealousy pricked at the back of her neck.

"Ooo-hwee, must have been painful squeezing into that dress!" Connie nodded. "And check out Mr. Studly. Now if that don't say take me home tonight, I don't know what does!"

Connie let out an infectious giggle and sipped more of her drink. Tess redirected her attention, assessing the woman's partner as her eyes roamed over him, taking in every detail. His white shirt offset his Caribbean tan with sleeves snugged showing off his biceps. The etching of a tattoo peered from under the rolled cuff of the cotton fabric. In her experience, guys with tattoos were unpredictable. Clean cut and shaven, those had been the men she was drawn to. They were the ones to succeed and know what they wanted in life, she rationalized. Tattoos and piercings she would leave to the street vendors and artsy types. Roger, on the other hand, had been clean cut, no tattoos, and look where that had gotten her. She twisted her lips and shook her head attempting to get images of Roger out of her mind.

Tess sipped her coconut concoction and settled onto the barstool. The sun-bronzed dancer captured her attention. He was tall and, despite his hidden tattoos, he had confidence, like that of a businessman. He certainly, however, did not give the impression of being the managerial type. No, this was not a businessman, she rationalized. His chin looked too chiseled, and his five o'clock shadow was too thick to attend any corporate meeting. He didn't fit the rich philandering type either. There was, however, something about him. She couldn't quite put her finger on it, but certainly he intrigued her.

Drawn to their movement, she watched as he spun his partner around. His dancing skills were seemingly well developed, she thought, arching her brow. Intensely, the man pulled the woman close. Their bodies melded as one for a moment and then, with the deep beat of the music, he twirled her away only to have her saunter back. Caught in his trance, Tess watched him caress the young woman's body swaying with her movements.

"He definitely looks like he has done this before," Tess whispered.

Her words were more thought-like and she hadn't meant to say them out loud. Connie picked up the drink coaster and fanned it at Tess.

"I think the heat is gettin' to you girl, or maybe it's him swaggerin' that sexy pelvis like that! Ooo-hwee, but you're lookin' all flushed!"

They laughed and Tess pressed the back of her hand to her cheek and nodded in agreement.

"Maybe he is my *one*," she joked.

"Oh, honey, he is a handful! You best be careful with that one!"

Tess bit her lip and smiled. "Well, I suppose I'll be safe, looks like he's taken anyway," she said, wiggling her brow.

Avoiding more conversation on the matter, Tess turned her attention to the couple and hypnotically watched the good-looking stranger move across the dance floor. The way his skin glistened under the flicker of the yellow torches made her throat feel dry. She sipped her drink. Even in the dim light and a modest distance away, Tess could see his dimples crease along his jaw. As the charismatic local moved with his partner, his dark hair tumbled over his brow. Every detail about this mystery man fulfilled her romantic ideals—tall, dark, and delectable. With eyes focused, she took another sip of her drink and secretly envisioned herself running her fingers through the stranger's black wavy hair. She would then caress his chin in her hands and run her thumb over his perfect lips just before devouring them. Even with Roger her emotions hadn't stirred like they were now. She drew a breath and bit her lip. The background faces in the bar faded from her view and the conversations throughout the room sounded more like distant muffled chatter. Perhaps she should pinch herself, but she quickly withdrew that option. If it were a dream, the idea of waking up didn't sound appealing either. She wanted to see just how far this erotic dance pair would go. The dark-haired stranger spun the woman and held her tight. Tess's thighs tingled as she watched the couple and secretly wished it were her in his arms.

She noticed every flex of his muscles as he spun the woman and pulled her close to his chest. Tess downed more of the coconut Gyrator. His moves were gentle and effortless, as if caressing the woman, seducing her. Tess was hooked. She wanted that passion in her own life. Rhythmically, his pelvis pressed to the woman's thigh and, with his shirt half undone, Tess could see the beads of sweat as he turned and dipped the brunette slowly back. The young woman lay vulnerable in his arms. He lifted her, gently. Goosebumps quivered down Tess's arms.

"Whew! He is a hot one, I'll say," Connie said, fanning herself.

Tess remained silent as her gaze fixed on the enthralling couple. She watched, completely absorbed, as his hands gently caressed the woman's lower back. Tess imagined the sensation of his touch against her own skin. Then his lips brushed past the brunette's ear. The erotic stranger lingered with his face close to the woman's cheek. His lips moved, whispers of ecstasy, she imagined. The fiery brunette turned her head away. Tears glisten in the olive-skinned woman's eyes as the man wrapped his arms around her, swaying with the music. Tess nudged her friend.

"Doesn't look like she's into making out on the dance floor," Tess said.

"Well, I don't know about her, but I'd gladly take her place!"

Connie gave Tess a quick wink and the two women let out a devious laugh. The music drummed louder, and the beat quickened. Once again, she found herself staring from across the room. Then, for a brief, unexpected moment, the gaze of the invigorating stranger looked straight at her. Before she could look away, the curve of his lips lifted, forming a sly, teasing smile. Just as swiftly as the encounter had taken place, the brazen man looked back to his partner. A lump formed in Tess's throat, mortified that he had caught her gawking. She swiveled her chair around.

"He sure seemed interested in you, honey!"

"I must have looked like the pub creeper staring at him!" Tess said.

"Oh, it would take more than a look to be a creeper. Besides, there's no shame in watching, but man," Connie's eyes lit up, "there's some electricity out there. This is going to be one hot night, I can tell!" The bubbly faced friend fanned herself.

"I think I'll look elsewhere for my *one* and make sure he's not already taken. I've had enough of that for a lifetime!" Tess said.

She focused on the ice in her glass and sucked on the straw. The coconut Gyrator quickly disappeared followed by a slurping sound. Tess swiveled her chair back around scanning the room for her own unattached date. She looked past the dancers to the tables that lined the perimeter, but the music flared and, yet again, she found herself focused on the passionate couple. The brunette danced with renewed energy. She put her hands in the air, twisting like an Egyptian goddess and spun around into her lover's arms. Her willing partner groped at her waist pulling the vixen towards him. The olive-skinned woman leaned into his muscular build and the man lowered his chin. His mouth brushed over her skin. This time, Tess noticed, the woman didn't pull away. Instead, she threw her head back allowing him to run his lips down her neck.

"Don't look now, Connie, but I think they're going to do it right here!" Tess rolled her eyes.

"Well, it wouldn't be the first time!" Connie said.

"What do you mean?" she asked, trying not to care.

"Oh, just kidding, but that stallion," she paused, "he's been here before. I was here last month and, come to think of it, I think he was dancing with that same kitten." Connie sucked on her straw. "Like I said, you might have to wrangle that one in, if you want to ride him!"

Tess laughed, blushing. "But wait, last month you were just here and now you're back?"

"Yep, that's right," Connie said.

"Why do you come here so often?" Tess asked.

The woman fluttered her brow, smiling.

"You little she-devil" Tess said, leaning in and lowering her voice. "Do you come down here just to pick up men?"

"You catch on pretty quick," the woman clanked her glass to Tess's, "but really, it's not like that."

"No?" Tess asked.

"I thought I had found *the one* last time—we hit it off great. In fact, we even made plans to see each other when we got back to the States, too. Unfortunately, it just didn't work out," Connie sighed.

"I know all about that," Tess said, furrowing her brow, "things not working out, that is."

"Oh, I am a firm believer when you find that *one* you're supposed to be with, nothing will stand in your way!"

Both women nodded in unison.

"For me," Tess grumbled, "they always turn out to be Mr. Super Dud."

"Don't you worry, sweetie, your guy is out there, you'll see. When you least expect it, they come riding in on their big 'ol white horse staring you in the face. Trouble is, maybe you just haven't recognized it."

"Maybe," Tess's voice trailed.

She looked out across the dance floor and resumed watching the intriguing couple. The music's tempo changed, and the beat slowed. The tall stranger held his partner close. Tess again wondered what it would be like to be held by him. She couldn't help herself and she peered below the man's waistline sipping her double coconut drink. She pulled her gaze from his groin and glanced back at his face. Mortified once more, the stranger looked right at her. His lips curved, grinning, as if he expected her to leer. The man winked. Caught in the act, she spewed her drink, gagging. Tess spun her chair and gasped for air. Still choking, she set her drink on the bar. The glass teetered. Hastily, she steadied it with her hand and reached for her napkin to cover her mouth. She stifled back her cough.

"Gracious! Are you alright?" Connie asked.

The bubbly friend patted her on the back. Still gasping, Tess nodded, avoiding any further eye contact with the dance floor.

"Yes!" she blurted, "I'm okay. Just went down the wrong way."

Tess darted a look where the overconfident, local had been. Had he seen her make a fool of herself hacking and coughing? Moments passed.

Convinced he had moved on, Tess casually spun her chair around facing the dance floor once more. A twinge of disappointment nagged at her. The rogue dancer, the man she could not resist staring at, was now further across the room. This time, though, his attention was on his partner. She arched her brow, slightly displeased, and sipped on the remainder of her drink. Perhaps it was best to put the bronzed womanizer out of her mind. She looked around the bar, but her gaze settled back onto the dance floor.

Beyond the couple she saw two men sitting at a table along the bamboo perimeter. The men's clothing looked somewhat out of place with their tapered-leg kakis and elongated loafers. Brothers perhaps, or maybe a father and son? She wasn't sure. The man on the right facing the floor had a slight tint of grey at his temples. He was good-looking, neat in appearance and by the looks of the gold watch he was wearing, he most-likely had money. She couldn't make out the brand, but even from across the room the diamonds, which were faceted around the face of the band, glittered in the low-luster light. She had seen enough gold watches, Rolex, Cartier, and other high-end brands, worn by many of her clients, that she could recognize a good one when she saw it.

The two men were discussing something, and by the hard lines on their faces, the mood was intense. With one hand, the older-looking man held his drink, using his other to articulate the conversation. Neither seemed to care much about the music or the dancing, in fact, she speculated, the manner in which the grizzled-templed man leaned in, it looked like they were arguing. The younger of the two slumped back into his chair and drew a drag from his cigarette then jetted out his bottom lip as he blew the smoke across the table. His face looked out towards the dancers. With his mouth taut, he seemed intent, eyeing the brunette and her rogue partner. Agitated, the young man straightened in his chair, dousing his cigarette, and nervously stretching his forearms on the table in front of him. He clasped his hands and twisted his wrists.

"Looks like they've caught the attention of some men at that table," Tess nodded towards the dancers.

"They're a little difficult not to notice, if you ask me," Connie agreed.

Intrigued, Tess watched the younger man sitting behind the dancers. He stared at the olive skinned brunette and fidgeted with his drink. Clearly, the young man must have known the exotic woman on the dance floor or else he wouldn't seem so aggravated, she thought. Tess turned her attention back to the lovers. The brunette continued swiveling her hips and maneuvering herself around her partner. The music climaxed as the tempo of drums, flutes, and tambourines grew bolder—all wildly intertwined. With the crescendo near, the seducer pulled his prey close to his body. With skillful ease he caressed the woman's throat with his lips. Slowly he traced the edge of her breasts with his mouth and kissed her skin navigating back along her neck.

"Geesh!" Tess gasped.

The wild stranger brushed his lips over his partner's ear. Just then, a commotion stirred at the table behind the two lovers. The young man's drink toppled over. No one seemed to notice, and the music vibrated on. Eyes wide, Tess arched her brow absorbing the scene. She tapped her friend on the arm.

"Ooh, I think there's going to be a fight."

The slender-build man seated at the table, clenched his fists, and stood abruptly. Long, deliberate strides carried him swiftly across the floor. The sudden movement caused his bamboo chair to wobble precariously, almost tipping over. But, the older gentleman, still seated at the table, quickly steadied it. The young man's steps were full of purpose. His pointed Italian-like leather shoes, like those she had seen Roger wear, stood out among the flip flops and sandals. Tess watched, intrigued. The angered man shoved the woman's dance partner aside. He grabbed her by the arm and led her back over to his table.

"Whoa, looks like skank only goes so far," Tess scoffed.

A sense of vindication came over her watching their would-be love making succumb to an end. She continued watching the rogue dance partner, unmoved, as he tilted his head, then bowed slightly and kissed the woman's hand letting it slip poetically through his fingers. She half expected the rogue flirt to fight for the woman but that, she frowned, only happens in romance novels. Tess looked down at her drink and swirled the bits of ice. She sipped the watered-down mixture and glanced over at Connie.

"Can you believe that? She must have been that guy's girlfriend all along!"

"Oh honey, I could believe just about anything in this place." Connie's eyes lit up as she looked towards the entrance. "*Oopsy-doosy*! I do believe I just found my *one*!"

Tess chuckled at her friend. The stout woman quickly gathered her bright yellow oversized purse and turned to face the newcomer that just stepped into the bar.

"It's been wonderful talking with you, sweetie," Connie said. The bubbly woman gave her a wink. "Now, you watch yourself with that stallion of yours, he might just have a few fillies to chase off."

Tess turned and watched her new friend rush past. Giggles faded and the seasoned tourist headed the direction of the bald-headed man dressed in black with purple and grey pinstriped shorts. He wore a bright purple, short-sleeved, button-up linen shirt, offset by white loafers—most likely alligator, she imagined. Within seconds, Connie, in her bright yellow dress, scooted up to the oblivious tourist. Without hesitation, Connie locked arms with the man and right away Tess could see them carrying on in conversation. That poor sap hasn't a clue what's about to happen to him. Tess grinned and swirled the melting ice in her drink. She scooted back into her chair, straightening her skirt. Tucking her chin, she checked the buttons on her blouse.

"Oh, don't worry about me," she muttered. "I think I'll stay clear of Mr. 'ol slime bucket. Even Belize has...," her conversation with herself cut off as she lifted her eyes and stared across the room. As if a boulder had dropped, a pit slammed in her stomach.

"Roger!" she stifled a gasp. "Why you little snake!" Tess's cheeks burned hot. The mere sight of him made her blood boil. She could see it was the same blonde from the café. Sparkles glittered from the bimbo's neck and wrist. She glared, eyeing the dazzling accessories. She further huffed, noticing the gaudy diamond bracelet and thick matching necklace were complimented by a pair of over-sized diamond earrings illuminating the woman's face like a bedazzled neon sign. "Well, he always did like the finer things. I suppose at least she's got money." Tess smirked. "I'm sure he'll find a way to soak it from her, too."

Her heart ached. The intoxicating drinks, the seduction on the dance floor, and now the sight of Roger and his harlot overwhelmed her. She bit her lip, holding back her tears—the evening's events had been more than she expected.

"Pardon me?" a man's voice inquired.

Tess looked up. Their eyes met. It was him, the rogue stranger.

Chapter Five

Deception

THE DARK-HAIRED MAN LEANED his arm on the back of Connie's empty chair. The front of his shirt partly opened. Tess's eyes betrayed her, and she struggled not to stare at his bare chest. The essence of sweat and musk wafted past her nose with that familiar hint of coconut she encountered from the bartender earlier. Only moments ago, this stranger had practically seduced his dance partner in front of everyone and now here he was, just inches away, focused on her. Tess stared up at his deep brown eyes. They were dark and enchanting, as if luring her away. Her head swooned. From the tips of her breasts to the depths of her thighs, instinct betrayed her. Everything about him screamed delicious. But then she remembered his coy personality, how he had flirted with her while tantalizing his partner. The same Roger-like morals, she presumed. Tess pressed her lips tight, looked down at her drink, and circled the remaining ice with her straw. She sensed him watching her, his attention roving over her body. With a guarded poise, she raised her brow, turning to match his intrusive stare. Creases formed at the corner of his eyes as his smile broadened and his dimples deepened. God, could he be any more scrumptious? Every nerve in her body heightened and she struggled to keep her composure. She cleared her throat.

"Is there something amusing?" she asked, staring as coolly as her nerves would allow.

Her heart raced as her eyes traced over his mouth, her gaze descended, taking in the defined contour of his chin. The air became still and the voices around her blended into the background, muffled by the ringing in her ears as her nerves soared. She watched the corners of his mouth tighten, mocking her with his grin.

"You said something, I didn't quite catch it. Something to do with soaking it up, I think," he said.

His voice gave her goosebumps. For another moment, her mind went numb. He dipped his chin forward and nodded towards her drink.

"Oh, I was just...making a reference, that's all," Tess replied.

Get it together, Tess, she scolded herself. *He's just another Roger.* Roger! She had forgotten about him, momentarily, and glanced over at the two, still cozied next to one another. Tess scoffed then realized the swaggering stranger was still standing beside her, watching her. Roger's presence overshadowed the stranger's teasing eyes. He was no different than her extracurricular, duping ex! Her eyes narrowed. She still felt the man's cool stare, rudely ogling over her, his eyes dipping below her neckline. Did he think she was that easy? That he could discard one woman and saunter over to her and pick up where he had left off? She fumed at the notion and turned, facing him—catching a glimpse of his eyes. Tess ran her hand over the satin blouse buttons. Finding the closures still secured, her shoulders relaxed. Her cheeks blushed and she glanced around the room hoping to see Connie. Right now, Tess would have welcomed the interruption. From the corner of her eyes, she watched the stranger. He cocked his head to the side and continued ogling her. She could sense his gaze lingering over her thighs. The high-rise bar stool made it almost impossible to keep her skirt in place, and the slick bamboo seat only helped to inch the material higher. She tugged at the hem to no avail. Cornered, she lashed out.

"Do you often gawk annoyingly at women you don't know?" she snapped.

His lips curled the same sly smile. Her attempts to have him go away only seemed to encourage him more.

"Only the ones I find intriguing," he said.

His voice reverberated with a perfected suaveness. Rolling her eyes, Tess tried to appear disinterested. But the glow from the bar room lights shimmered in his beckoning, chocolate brown eyes. With only a glimpse, she knew it would be lustfully easy to lose herself in them. The tiki torch flames flickered with the breeze, and the light danced across his face. Beads of perspiration formed by the sultry Belizean air glistened along his upper lip. Tess fought back the emotional urge to devour them, caressing his face with her own lips, and tasting the sweetness of his skin. Suppressing the urges that welled like a volcano inside her, she looked past the stranger, darting one last grimacing glance over to Roger and his floozy.

"Someone you know?" he asked.

"No," she lied.

She cast another glance at Roger. Taking a deep breath and exhaling forcibly, Tess stirred the bits of ice floating in her drink, ignoring the unwanted conversation with the stranger standing next to her. Slurping noises echoed as she sucked in the last of her drink. She held her glass up to the bartender who gave her a nod. Moments later another Belizean Special with peach liqueur and blue rum slid in front of her. Without hesitation, the tempting intruder paid the tab.

"Allow me," he said.

His swift act caught her unprepared. "No, it's...I'm," she stammered, "really, I can get it."

"Nonsense, what sort of gentleman would I be if I didn't buy a beautiful young lady a drink?"

She raised her eyebrow, amused by his self-proclaimed pretense of being a gentleman, and responded with the least amount of interest that she could muster.

"That sounds like a line you use often," she said.

"So not only beautiful, but a bit feisty, too, I see."

Ignoring him, she looked over at Roger. Her unfaithful ex sat with his arm still wrapped around the blonde harlot. Tess could see them talking. She sneered at the occasional laugh erupting from the blonde tart, no doubt feeding Roger's enormous ego. Tess scowled, aggravated that Roger was still getting to freeload and enjoy the vacation that was meant for her.

"So, tell me," he said, glancing the same direction as Roger and then back to her, "are you here by yourself in Belize?"

Good question, she thought, and ran her hand across the cocktail napkin. Her fingers traced over the gold embossed emblem of a palm tree— another reminder of how exquisite the hotel was. Tess let her mind drift, wondering what the room, the one she and Roger had booked together, was like. If the pool and grounds were any indication, she imagined the suite would be just as breathtaking, at least twice as beautiful, and most certainly grander than her drab little fleabag of a spot near the other end of the beach.

She frowned and reminded herself that she hadn't come to Belize to reunite with Roger. The fact that he was sitting just a mere thirty feet away fondling some tramp, Tess decided, was not going to affect her vacation. Still, she also did not want to spend time with a known make-out artist, like the slimy, sun-bronzed gecko next to her. Intent on landing an insult and making the stranger leave, she spun her chair around to look him in the eye. But the

Belizean specials were affecting her judgement. She found herself unintentionally staring into his captivating gaze.

For a moment, she let herself bask in his magnetic crooked smile, and drank in his deep-set dimples, strong jaw, and irresistible dark chocolate eyes that captivated her intensely. Why did he have to be so lusciously attractive and impossible to resist? She hadn't wanted to feed his ego any more than she already imagined it was. But the foggy effect of the alcohol brought her guard down and her stare lingered. The open fold of his shirt caught her eye. Entranced, she could feel herself staring at his smooth and luscious physique. *No!* She scolded herself. No more vain, womanizing, Roger-type bad-boys. She cleared her throat and looked up at him ready to answer his question. But she couldn't form the words to explain why she was there. No matter what scenario she ran through her head, it all sounded pathetic and lame. Besides, she didn't even know him. And, from what she witnessed on the dance floor, she would only end up another notch on his booty call list anyway.

"No, I'm not alone. In fact, my boyfriend is here. I'm just waiting for him," she lied.

"Is that so?" He looked around the room. "I'd say he's taking a long time to get here, don't you think? Maybe you should call him, see if he got lost."

The stranger set his glass on the counter and Tess glanced at his reflection in the bar mirror. His relentless inquiries were becoming annoying. She watched as he ran his hand through his hair and leaned his elbow on the mahogany bar.

"Seriously?" she mumbled.

Tess narrowed her eyes—certain he was taunting her. The man leaned closer. The scent of tropical spice again filled the air. He did smell rather delicious, she mused. A tuft of deep dark hair tussled over his forehead and in a quick moment she envisioned herself again running her fingers through his luscious locks. This drifter tantalized her. He had a muscular build—not overly so, but enough that a girl could wrap her arms around and hold on tightly. His mostly unbuttoned shirt offset his bronzed skin, no doubt, she guessed, from hours under the Caribbean sun, which led her to wonder what sort of work he did. Maybe he was a beach bum? No, too much swagger, she decided. Besides, his clothes were too neat and his conversation overly confident with fluent sarcasm—it was annoyingly seductive.

Tess glanced over at the man's face as he turned towards the bar and ordered another drink. Narrowing her eyes, she pondered his personality. Even as he stood mocking her, he held a certain sensual and charismatic appeal. She wasn't sure that she wanted him to leave, but at the same time, she had just moments earlier watched him shamelessly ravage another woman. *No!* She again told herself. Tess peeled her eyes from his seductive physique, frustrated that her mind would betray her just because he was good looking. She had already made that mistake and wasn't about to sign up for it a second time. Scowling, she glared once more at Roger.

The stranger paid the waiter and turned back towards her. It was time to send this new arrival away and free his barstool up for a real chance at romance, she decided. She had already let one cheater get the best of her and she wasn't about to let it happen again. Tess squared her shoulders, but the drumming of the music started again. The room echoed as the drums and bongos thumped, sending deep pounding beats of reggae booming through the air. The foreign stallion lifted his hand and gestured.

"Shall we?" he said.

His eyes creased with his smile. She hadn't expected the invitation, and for an idealistic moment, she contemplated the indulgence but then quickly thought better of it.

"No, no thank you," she hesitated, "you're not my type."

Satisfied his ego had taken a direct hit, Tess turned around and faced the bar. She stirred the melting bits of ice floating in her glass hoping he would get the hint and leave, but a sideways glance proved he was still there. His expression looked even more cocky. She wrinkled her brow and tightened her lips, she had taken all that she was going to from this bothersome, overly-good-looking, two-timing seducer. But before she could land another insult, a voice interrupted.

"Tess?" the familiar tone paused. "Tess, is that really you?"

Her mind reeled. Oh, God! Not now, not here. She resisted the urge to slink down into her chair. It was too late anyway. Roger had seen her and the stranger. By the look on the stranger's face, she thought he was enjoying her discomfort a little too much. She glared at him before acknowledging her ex, then spun around.

"Roger!" she faked a smile. "What...what are you doing here? Are you staying here?"

"I was just about to ask you that same question, Tess," Roger replied.

"Well, since I had the ticket and the time...," she said, sarcastically.

"Wow...Tess, you came to Belize after all...I didn't think you...," Roger hesitated.

His gaze shifted to the man next to her. Roger arched his brow, darting a puzzled look back at her. *The nerve of him!* she screamed internally. *That he could carouse around with his pinheaded blonde, but that her coming to Belize was a shock, like she would just crumble to pieces because he left her.* Tess raged.

"Yes! Yes, Roger, I did...uh, huh...," she stammered. Before she could stop herself, she reached out and grabbed the stranger by the arm. "I...," she hesitated, "I mean, yes, *we* came. Me—him, us—yes, together."

She glanced at her captive—her eyes pleaded. For a moment, the stranger hesitated. He glanced at her with arched brow and slightly wide-eyed. But quickly he recovered. The crease in his brow softened and his eyes gleamed. A twinge of panic flittered through her gut as she watched his lips curl, forming the same sly grin she had seen from across the dance floor earlier. Like the seductive reggae rhythm, the man cadenced into character. He swiftly reached his arm around her waist and pulled her tight against his side.

"Yes, together," he looked into her eyes. "Isn't that right, darling?"

Tess's smile flinched as his hands held her secure. With their façade now set, she attempted to regain her composure. "Roger, I—I'd like you to meet an old friend of mine…"

Fear rushed through her sending prickling sensations to her temples. She turned towards her fake beau with wide eyes, searching the stranger's face and realizing she didn't even know his name. Her phony counterpart didn't miss a beat.

"Anthony!" He thrust his hand to shake Roger's. "And you are…," Anthony's words trailed as if interested.

"Roger," her ex retorted. Tess detected a flinch of jealousy darting across his face. Roger sized up Anthony and then turned his bewildered look back to Tess as if she should explain, but instead he continued. "Great," Roger shook Anthony's hand, "are you two staying here at the…"

"No!" Tess blurted. "Uh, I mean, no, we—we rented a room down the beach," she paused, surprised at how easily the words rolled off her lips. She dared to keep going. "It's really romantic, you know—bungalow—bed," her eyes widened, "huge bed!"

Anthony didn't resist, "Yes, that's right, *huge bed*."

Her fake boyfriend looked into her eyes as his hand slapped, slightly too hard upon her rump and followed by an advantageous squeeze. Tess jumped, swiftly sliding her hand down his arm, removing his palm from its lingered grope around her buttocks. With his hand now firmly gripped in hers, Anthony spun Tess towards the dance floor.

"Shall we, my dear?" Anthony's mouth curved, grinning.

"Uh…yes, of course. See you around," she forged a smile at Roger.

Anthony twirled her out onto the dance floor. A low chuckle vibrated from his throat.

"Aren't you the impudent one," he said.

Still smiling he raised their clasped hands nodding to Roger who watched with a pale look on his face. Anthony then turned his attention back to Tess and placed his free hand firmly along her back as he dipped her low. He leaned over, his face close to hers.

"No, it's...it's not like that," she fumbled for her words.

The stranger lifted her upright and spun her around. The motion thrust her into his arms. He held her close. The strength of his thigh pressed against her, and the warmth of his breath brushed across her cheek. Warm spiraling sensations raced throughout her body. She closed her eyes, as if in a trance, and envisioned their naked bodies entangled as they made love. The music stopped and the spell ended, leaving her head swooning and her heart beating rapidly. Out of breath she looked up at him, her arms rested against his chest. His lips curled, grinning—teasing her. She looked up into his eyes, their gaze met. Her body felt numb and ravaged at the same time. The Belizean cocktails had made her dizzy as the room began to spin. They stood embraced in each other's arms.

"I...I should go," she said.

Anthony slowly released his hold. Fully into his role, he took her by the hand and led her from the dance floor. From the corner of her eye, she could see Roger glance over, watching them as Anthony led her from the dance floor and out onto the path.

Chapter Six

Turning Tables

A DOOR SLAMMED. TESS WINCED as the echo reverberated from the hall. Pangs of last night's aftermath pierced her temples. Her fingers gripped the flimsy pillow, and she pressed her face deep into its scrawny polyfoam form. It was no use. Heavy footsteps, doors thudding and roll-away suitcases clacking down the hallway penetrated the thin walls. She rolled over. Her head throbbed in seismic motion. The morning light filtered into the room and the eager sunrise seeped through her eyelids.

She would have groaned if her throat would have allowed it, but instead, she groped for the water decanter next to the bed. Her hands rummaged blindly over the bedside table, knocking the plastic wrapped cup onto the floor. Defying the early hour, her eyes strained to open. On one elbow, she propped herself up and grasped the slender pitcher. Water sloshed onto her upper lip as she drank straight from the container. The sandpaper-like dryness of her mouth stuck to the glass carafe as she gulped it down. Like a sponge, her throat greedily absorbed the stale water. Tess groaned, thankful to lick her lips again. The stillness of the room gave her a chance to slow the spinning in her head.

"Well, Tess...," she chided herself, "you might need to re-think those Belizean Gyrators."

The room spun like a slanted carousel. She slumped back onto the pillow, closing her eyes. She would need to pace herself if she were going to enjoy the remainder of her vacation. She recounted last night's events, which were hazy at best. Visions of the bubbly woman played through her thoughts and the aftertaste of peach flavored beverages drifted across her taste buds. Tess hiccupped. Hypnotic, dark-chocolate eyes wandered into her memory like a dream. She recalled a teasing crooked smile, and the scent of tropical spice. The wispy vision brought tingles to her thighs. Then Roger's face flashed through her mind and doused any sensual desire. Tess groaned as visions of Roger sitting with his blonde bimbo slammed through her thoughts. The rest of the evening's history fluttered by vaguely.

"Ugh, glad to be rid of you, Roger, you two-timing snake!"

Like a bass drum, her head pounded. The faint sound of bells chimed from across the room. She recognized its familiar cadence.

"Who would be calling me this early?" she grumbled.

Carelessly, she placed the carafe atop the nightstand. It teetered and the contents slopped onto her wrist. Tess steadied its base while the phone continued to chirp. She scanned over the tiny room and tried pinpointing the cellphone location while guessing the possible caller. *It must be Roger!* Her eyes brightened, at least to the degree that the dull pounding in her brain would let them. But in the same instant, images of their parting dinner and his egocentric remarks filtered through her mind. She would never go back to him, not now, and especially not after seeing him all over that platinum floozy.

"Why do I care what he wants?" she said.

Another muffled chime sounded, resurrecting her hopes while conflicting with her emotions. Maybe he's decided to leave that snipe of a booty-call. Images of Roger's disbelieving gaze played over in her thoughts. He wanted her back. She had seen it in his eyes as he watched her walk away. Now, he's calling to apologize, to admit that he was wrong. Her mind surged and adrenaline sparked through her veins.

She flung the dull duvet aside and stumbled her way across the room. The persistent ringing of her cellphone echoed sharply in her hungover state. Certain the room was swaying, Tess reached for the table. Without warning her toe caught the edge of the chair. The less than sturdy rattan toppled over, sending her crashing to the floor. Gravity plunked her onto her knees. Tess winced at the unexpected pain and looked out across the room where the ringing continued. But, like a replay in slow-motion, her mind decelerated, and for a moment she disregarded the phone. Is this what I want? What should I say? He had been so cocky with his new minx, his new money source. She took a deep breath. No, she wouldn't give him the satisfaction. She would be in charge of her destiny, not Roger. But still, a twinge of revenge flirted at the tip of her thoughts. Maybe, she cajoled, I'll let him think there is a chance. She ambled across the floor ignoring the angry throbs from her toe and the pangs of her rum induced headache. Parting the cushions lumped on the floor, Tess surged over them. Uncovered, the phone's melodic tone heightened, momentarily. She grasped the slender cellphone and plunged her finger across its face, swiping at the lighted button.

"Hello!" she blurted.

The phone went dead. She had missed the call. Tess lay on the floor and groaned. Pushing herself up, she looked around the tiny room. As if a cyclone had ravaged through the small abode, Tess raised her brow surveying the disarray. The cushions lay dislodged, tossed about from their original places. Another chair lay flipped over next to the bed. For the first time since waking, she took a clearer look around. Tess sat on the floor rubbing her foot, still sore from its run-in with the chair, and continued the disheveled room's assessment. Besides the worn-out duvet she had tossed aside, the rest of the covers had been pulled off the bed, draped mostly onto the floor. Her shoes and clothes were flung about sporadically, like a trail of breadcrumbs. She shivered and looked down at her attire, or rather lack thereof, wearing only her bra and matching panties. With the pillow still clasped in her hand, the importance of the phone call diminished.

"What happened to my room?" she paused. Like a firework exploding, the remainder of the evening poured into her lucid mind. Now she remembered the chocolate parfait eyes. She bit her lip. "Anthony!"

Sensations lit across her breasts. She remembered leaving the Grand Simone and the walk along the beach, taking off her shoes and the thrilling sense of the warm, tiny sand crystals that filtered through her toes. The events of last night revealed themselves more. She remembered their facade, Anthony pretending to be her boyfriend, and Roger's blindsided expression. Tess smirked delighted by the blow to Roger's ego.

She smiled, recalling their playful splashing in the waves, and Anthony's laughter as he mischievously splashed her back. She recalled the way he had looked at her and the seawater-soaked blouse that had clung to her skin. Then she remembered stumbling and Anthony catching her, his hands wrapped around her waist. Tess gripped the pillow tight and pulled it close to her chin. She remembered his touch and the warmth of his breath and how he had escorted her to her hotel. Tess pressed her hand to her forehead as her face blushed. Her veins pulsated. Images of her room key falling onto the floor just outside her door and Anthony retrieving it swept through her thoughts. The vague memory cast through her mind. She remembered how skillfully suave he had been, swiftly using his foot to open the unlocked door, sweeping her into his arms and carrying her over the threshold. Tess sat up and darted a look back at the bed half expecting to see him lying there, grinning.

"Oh, thank God *that* didn't happen!" she muttered, relieved that no one was there. "Just forget about him, Tess. He's no better than Roger—a complete flirt!" she huffed.

The chime on her phone sounded once more—whoever called had left a message. She arched her brow. Roger never liked to leave messages. He always said they were too impersonal.

"Well, I suppose there's a first time for everything," she said and quickly played the message.

'Good morning sleepy head! Just wanted to call and see how it's going over there. Have you run into 'ol numb nuts yet?'

Tess chuckled, disappointed yet relieved that it wasn't Roger's call that she had missed. Instead, it had been Molly. Just hearing her friend's voice made her smile.

"Oh Molly, you're such a comedian. Wait, how did she know Roger was in Belize?" Tess wondered.

Tess listened as Molly's New York attitude rang through.

'Yep, that man is a real snake. If you ask me, he did you a favor dumping your butt. Anyway, after you left, I closed down your computer and saw the seating change come through in your email. Your cheap-ass old boyfriend upgraded his ticket to first class. Sorry, kiddo, he's slime through and through. And from the looks of it, he put all the charges on your card.'

"That money-hungry bastard!" Tess fumed.

'Also, the rest of your itinerary popped up and I thought I'd remind you about that tour doohickey-ma-bob, that you and 'ol pretzel face booked,' her message paused, *'some boat ride thing-a-ma-jig, probably trying to be all romantic and stuff. Anyhow, it's on that paper I printed before you left.'*

Tess could hear Molly grunt, that deep grunt she made whenever someone she didn't like was in the room and she had to endure their presence, for the time being. Molly's tone turned mischievous as the message continued.

'It would serve his wily ass right if you beat him to it! You should go and enjoy the afternoon with that cabana boy snorkeling half-naked in the ocean instead of 'ol numb nuts.' Tess laughed as Molly's message kept going. *'Just a thought, after all,'* Molly's voice continued, *'he may have gotten the room, but you can have the adventures!'*

Tess flopped into the only upright wicker chair. In her hungover state, she had forgotten about the boat cruise. Deep in thought, she chewed her lip. Roger insisted on booking that tour. He even made the arrangements himself.

"Good 'ol Molly!" Tess smiled.

Molly was more than a co-worker and Tess knew she could count on her. She contemplated the boat reservations. A quick twinge of excitement slipped across her mind and a little rivalry nudged at her. She hadn't considered herself the jealous type, but Tess was certain Roger's platinum fish of a girlfriend's figure would turn some heads in a bikini. Tess's eyes narrowed at the vision of the blonde piranha and her glitzy jewels parading around the tour boat. A devious smirk crossed her lips as she contemplated a plan. She would love to see Roger's jaw drop when he found the boat had already left without him. Their afternoon lust-fest ruined!

Tess glanced down at her phone. "What time is it? Seven O'clock! When were they supposed to be there?" she muttered out loud. Rummaging through her bag, Tess found the crumpled itinerary that Molly had shoved into her hands before she left. Her eyes widened. "Eight O'clock!" Tess sprang from the chair. She ignored the shards of pain from last night's indulgence. "I can make it! I'll show that two-timing prick just how adventurous I can be!"

***

"YES, MISS, right away. Is there anything else I can bring you?" the indifferent voice waited on the end of the line.

"Aspirin, I'd like a couple of aspirins if you have them," Tess said.

"Yes, of course, miss. I'll have them brought up right away."

"Thank you," she said.

The conversation was quick, and the desk clerk seemed agreeable. After all, tourists are forever forgetting things, she rationalized. Tess jumped into the shower convincing herself the extra few minutes would be worth feeling human again. Like the room, it was no surprise that the water pressure flowed haphazardly in the wimpiest stream. She soaped her skin but, uncertain of the water and the chance for a good rinse, she held off on shampooing. Besides, in a few hours, she'd be snorkeling in the deep blue ocean.

Tess dressed quickly in the only clothes she had brought. The wrinkles in her skirt and the stench of stale seawater on her blouse made her cringe. Looking at herself apologetically in the mirror, she mustered a pep talk.

"It'll just have to do," she told herself.

She searched under the bed for her shoes. A soft rasp sounded on the door. Tess slipped her patent leather heels over her foot and winced having forgotten about her stubbed toe. Hopping on the less painful foot, she ambled over to the door. As promised, the bellhop presented the items. She thanked the young steward and closed the door. First things first—she grabbed the bag and tore open the red and white package of aspirin. Dumping out the two tablets into her hand, she swallowed them down, or rather attempted to do so. The pills caught mid-way. Her dry throat gagged on the chalky texture. Tess leaped across the bed, grabbed the decanter, and swallowed a chug of stale water. The aspirin slid down leaving its sour taste behind. She let out a slight burp and the essence of coconut and peaches wafted past her nose. The taste made her shudder—another reminder of last night's Belizean Specials. Tess fanned her breath and scrounged through the toiletries for the trial size toothpaste at the bottom of the bag. She tapped her phone and glanced at the time.

"Forty-five minutes! I need to get going."

On her first day of arrival, the young bellhop pointed out the direction for the boat dock as part of the hotel's amenities. She could make it if she hurried and still have time to shop at one of the local stores Connie had told her about. Her mind drifted to Connie and the bald-headed tourist. She briefly wondered how that had all worked out. Another glance at her phone and Tess grabbed the toothbrush, squeezed out the green flecked gel, and stuck it in her mouth. No time to use the sink, she resolved, and grabbed her purse and cellphone, then bolted out the door.

Her feet skipped down the stairs and she practically ran up to the front desk, her toe finally forgiving her. The same reserved man from yesterday greeted her.

"Good morning, miss," he said, eyeing her frazzled state. "I trust you found everything satisfactory last night?"

His eyes diverted back to the computer screen beneath the counter. By the man's dry composure, Tess figured he had seen every guest scenario possible; and the only indication of emotion she detected on his stone-like face, was a slight arch to his eyebrows. She took the toothbrush from her mouth and held it in her fist.

"Yes, thank you," she replied. There was no time for polite chit-chat if she was going to get to that boat before Roger. She thought it best to get right to the point. "Bathing suits," she blurted. "Where can I get a bathing suit?"

"Yes, miss. A bathing suit," he paused. With no raised reaction, he snapped his fingers. The bellhop hurried over. "Miguel, I want you take Miss Martin to the Shoppe's Argant."

The boy nodded and, unlike the clerk's slow methodical response, the youngster trotted out the door ahead of her. Tess followed after him, noticing he wore the same clothing as yesterday, white cropped linen jodhpurs and an oversized tunic top. His bare feet navigated the stone path and soon the trail widened. A small row of shops lined the area. The boy ran up the small landing in front of a two-story mercantile brightly decorated in artistic murals. Connie had mentioned a bi-level café and souvenir shop with authentic works of art. The bubbly friend had said the locals have truly captured the Belizean folklore and tropical love in their work. *This must be the store,* Tess told herself.

Deep green vines grew up on the sides of the stucco exterior. Blooms of yellow, red, and orange flowers dotted the wall like a painting. She paused for a moment, running her hand over the texture. She had never seen anything so simple yet so beautiful, too. The vines wound their way up the side and along the thatched roof where more bright blossoms bloomed. Belize certainly did not lack for color, she smiled, mesmerized by its beauty. The smell of fresh baked muffins and the familiar aroma of rich dark coffee carried through the air. Her stomach let out a low rumble. She would make it a point to grab one of the warm biscuits before she left.

"Thank you, Miguel. I think I can take it from here," Tess said.

The boy's face lit up when she called him by name. He nodded and waved as he ran back in the direction of the hotel. Tess pushed open the bamboo door and stepped inside the curious store.

Along the wall hung every color and shape of bathing suit a tourist could want. Tess beamed. By the looks of it, she hadn't been the only traveler in need of one. There were souvenirs, as she had expected, and rows of sunglasses, as well as an endless supply of tanning oils. Scanning quickly for the items she would need, Tess also noticed local crafts, including some vibrant woven handbags along the back wall. She would rummage through them later if she had a few extra minutes, she decided. Eying a small display of women's sandals, Tess made her way through the store. The sandals were tucked under a table, loaded full of T-shirts with tourist-like drawings such as, *I Love Belize,* with a bright red heart in the middle. Not exactly the style of clothing for an afternoon cruise, she thought. Tess quickly looked around and found a pair of tortoiseshell framed sunglasses with amber lenses. She figured the brown tones would go well with her fair complexion. Next, a rack of bright colored sundresses caught her attention. This section of clothing was more like what she had hoped to find. Like Molly had said, a credit card was all she needed. The impulse to leisurely shop was tempting, but for now, she'd have to focus. There would be ample time to browse when she got back this afternoon.

"I'll just get a few things, enough to get me through the next few hours," she whispered, pragmatically.

Tess quickly flipped through the bright colored fashions, admiring the array of sunset-gradient-oranges, blue tones, and yellows. But it was the red vibrant flowers that swirled with lime green vines and colorful sea-blue background that caught her eye the most. She paused at the three-piece sundress. It had a bikini halter top with a shear removable peplum ruffled over the midriff. A soft cotton skirt wrapped around the waist, which looked like it should be worn low, over the hip and tied off to the side. A matching bikini bottom hidden within the skirt was also part of the ensemble. It, too, had shear ties that would show off her smooth skin. She raised her brow at a self-preview of how she might look lounging at the poolside and liked the eye-catching movement the ruffles made. Surely, this would attract some attention. Maybe even Roger would have a twinge of jealousy seeing her surrounded by the Grand Simone's eligible bachelors. And, she rationalized, it would be versatile. A swimsuit and sundress all in one, a perfect wardrobe choice for any would-be tourist about to embark on an afternoon boat excursion. Echoes of Connie's advice flittered across her mind.

"This will definitely show off the merchandise," Tess giggled.

The clerk approached her, smiling. "Would you like to try it on?"

In any other situation she would have taken the opportunity to do so, but given her time crunch, she glanced at her phone, she'd take her chances with the fit. Besides, she was sure the ties would adjust, even for her unproportioned self. Tess pointed to the wrap and its blue tropical flower print.

"It's beautiful. Are the flowers native to Belize?" she asked.

"Yes," the older woman replied, "it is called Coral Hibiscus. It is said to bring good fortune to young maidens." The matron took it from the rack; her movements flowed gracefully as she gently laid the garment on the counter. "My grandmother once told me that a woman who wears the hibiscus will find her true love."

"That's a pretty amazing flower," Tess said.

The clerk smiled. "Grandmother was a wise woman. They say that the young virgin will be blessed with courage."

"Ah, well, I don't know about the whole virgin part, but the rest of it I could certainly use," Tess smiled at the clerk. "I think I'll take it, and...," she laid her other purchases on the counter, "I'll take these as well." Tess piled a pair of sandals, the tortoiseshell sunglasses, suntan lotion, and a colorful handwoven purse she found at the back of the store, onto the counter. The scent of fresh baked bread wafted past her nose. Her stomach groaned. "Oh...and a biscuit would be great, too."

The woman nodded. Within a few moments Tess stepped out of the doors of the little shop and tipped her new sunglasses over her eyes. She had slipped off her heels for the more comfortable sandals and stowed her shoes and the rest of her purchases in her new purse.

"That's got to be a new shopping record!" She slung the handmade strap over her shoulder and took a bite of the fluffy biscuit. "Mmm, like heaven," she murmured and devoured the rest. Her eyes widened as she glanced at her phone. "Fifteen minutes!" Tess panicked. "I've got to get to that boat before Roger!"

Punctuality was not Roger's strong point and, as with most appointments, he could be counted on being at least ten minutes late, if not more. Still, she'd rather be well on her way and out to sea by the time he arrived at the docks.

Tess hurried, making her way down the narrow side street and thankful for the shortcut the store clerk had told her about. Ahead, she could see the marked sign pointing her to the beach. She rushed down the path. Immediately she could see boats moored at the tiny dock not far away. Adrenaline, like that of a thief before a heist, speared through her body. The idea of bandits and capture, images from the articles she had skimmed over, briefly flickered into her mind. Her stomach churned nervously. *You've got this,* she told herself. Whether or not she believed it, she didn't take note. Rather, she continued down to the pier hoping the trembling that was working its way into her shoulders would subside. She feared her over-anxious nerves would take over and her legs would turn to jelly, collapsing—giving Roger the opportunity to sail away with his rich girlfriend. But the want for revenge, payback for his betrayal, was unexpectedly exciting, almost criminal, she smiled. With newfound energy, she sprinted towards the water.

***

A SMALL, thatched kiosk stood at the head of the dock. Nailed to the bamboo post hung a signboard with names written in neon chalk. *Diving Kays* labeled across the two columns, *Private* and *Group Tours*. She gulped as her eyes scanned over Roger's name listed near the top. A handsome attendant sat on a wicker stool. His skin glowed from undoubtedly countless hours of basking in the Belizean sun. Tess found herself gawking longer than expected. She liked his red swim trunks and their floral design, most likely hibiscus she determined, remembering the store clerk's lore of the magical flower. His thin cotton tank top stretched snuggly across his physically fit pectorals and Tess found herself lost for words as she drank in his Caribbean magnetism. For a split moment, she entertained asking him to go with her. Molly would surely have approved.

"May I help you?" the man said, smiling.

Tess pulled the itinerary from her newly purchased purse and handed it to the captivating attendant. "Uh...yes, um...I have a reservation for Mar...," she paused, "I mean Van de Camp," she pointed to Roger's name written on the sign.

The man slid his finger over the wooden clipboard in front of him. He lifted his head and their eyes momentarily met. She smiled hoping he wouldn't see the blood pulsating through her temples or hear the deafening pounding of her heart, which she was certain might seize at any moment. He smiled and shifted his gaze back to the list.

"Ah yes, a private tour, and...," his voice deepened, "a special request for the *Charisa*, I see."

"Yes!" she nodded, not sure of the significance his tone indicated.

For a moment she thought she'd given herself away. That somehow the attendant knew she was lying. But, she contended, it wasn't really a lie. She had paid for it using her credit card, even if Roger was the one who made the reservation. The attendant glanced up and looked around; he raised an eyebrow.

"It says here the reservation is for two. Will anyone else be joining you?" he questioned.

She sensed a hint of suspicion in his tone. Her heartbeat continued to rampage. She was never good at being deceitful and for a brief moment she wondered what the inside of a Belizean jail cell would look like. The blood rushed to her face. Surely, she could muster enough courage to douse any suspicions that she was hi-jacking the tour from her two-timing ex-boyfriend, who, she reminded herself, could at any moment walk in on her attempt and thwart her plans. Pressing down the material of her sundress, which had protruded slightly from her purse, Tess shifted the strap on her shoulder and looked the attendant in the eye.

"No," she said, enjoying the facade, "I'll be going alone. Besides," she added, "I'm what you might call, the adventurous kind of girl."

The man nodded, "Very well. I suppose it wouldn't matter if you left a bit earlier than scheduled either," he paused, his eyes met hers, "do you have any objections?"

"Yes!" she blurted. "I mean no! I mean that would be fine, earlier, yes, that would be great."

"Well then," he handed her a ticket, "you can give this to the steward on board. The *Charisa* is in the last slip on your right. Enjoy your cruise," he said. His eyes gleamed as he nodded towards the end of the dock.

"You have no idea just how much I will," she said, muttering under her breath. Tess took the ticket, flashed him a smile and headed down to the pier.

***

THE MAN at the kiosk watched Tess as she made her way to the boat. He placed a sign on the counter that read, *Closed*. He gestured across the way where two figures stood waiting next to a battered fishing boat. Upon his signal, the two men pushed their oversized dinghy into the water, pulled the start on the motor, and sped away.

Chapter Seven

Out to Sea

THE MARINA BUSTLED WITH TOURISTS. Tess's heartbeat thumped at the base of her throat. She didn't dare glance back to the shore. If she saw Roger, she feared she may not have the nerve to keep going. That idea alone caused her feet to move quicker. She made her way through the crowded dock. Her pace rushed, not quite a jog. She shuffled to the side, nearly running into a young couple that stopped along the railing with their arms linked around each other sneaking a kiss while they waited among the other tourists standing in line. Children squirmed while moms and dads patiently adjusted their life jackets. Others, ready to skip the formalities, jumped up and down on the wooden dock pointing out the brilliant-colored parrot fish swimming near the shore.

There were boats moored closely to one another, some towering, dwarfing the smaller crafts. She pushed through the last cluster of sun-tanned guests. A large yacht waited at the end of the pier. Any thought of Roger disappeared as she gaped at the beautiful vessel. Bold letters outlined in gold paint spelled its name, *Charisa.* Like Cinderella in her fairy tale, Tess beamed—her carriage awaited.

Gleaming in the sunlight, the enchanting yacht looked almost out of place compared to the other smaller charters. There were ropes and bumpers that squeaked against the boat's hull as the floats moved up and down along the pier. The clear water lapped against the weathered dock which contrasted dully to the shimmering glow of the *Charisa.* The polished yacht, thirty to forty feet long, she guessed, bobbed gently. Its narrow bow and sleek sides gave it an agile appearance. Conversations and noise from the tourists faded behind her—everything was going as planned.

A gentle breeze wisped past her and like a warm tropical kiss, the wind brushed over her lips. She tucked a loose strand of hair behind her ear and felt the hot sun on her face. Tess adjusted her newly acquired sunglasses, inhaling deeply, and settling the jitters in her chest as she hid behind the amber lenses. Tess smiled knowing Roger wouldn't be sailing on her dime today. *Sorry, Roger, this time I'll be getting the gem,* she whispered to herself.

Venturing up the small ramp that led up to the yacht, Tess peered over the railing. The spotless deck sparkled like a well-cut diamond in the morning sun. A small table held refreshments, and a bottle of champagne chilled in a silver ice bucket as droplets of moisture slid down the metal container. Her mouth watered. Beside the sparkling wine stood a tall crystal carafe filled with a juicy orange liquid—mango, she guessed. She licked her lips savoring the anticipation of a tropical mimosa.

A slight pang pricked at her forehead, a reminder of last night's indulgence. *I'll have to pace myself this time,* she told herself. Next to the drinks, a fresh fruit tray sat on the table, her empty stomach rumbled. The earlier bite of biscuit had worn off, and Tess was eager for more sustenance.

As if on cue, a casually dressed man appeared onboard the yacht. She smiled and the man held out his hand.

"Allow me to introduce myself," he said. "My name is Rolan, and I will be your captain this afternoon."

Tess nodded, gripping his hand firmly as he helped her aboard.

"Is anyone else accompanying you, miss?"

"Uh, no," she stuttered, "just me. My...my friend had a little too much excitement last night. He wasn't feeling very well this morning."

The captain furrowed his brow. Tess saw his jaw stiffen as he glanced past her looking towards the dock, expectantly. He must have known the reservation was for two, she worried. The blood rushed to her cheeks. The captain looked down at the weathered dock and then back to her. Again, her heart raced fearing he would see through her lies.

"Perhaps you would prefer to wait until he felt better? I'm sure we could reschedule," the captain politely encouraged.

"No, he...he didn't want me to miss out on this adventure, he insisted I go on without him," she looked past the skipper. "Wow, this is nicer than I expected!"

The man nodded, "Yes, she is state of the art."

"Oh, state of the art?" Tess tried to change the topic and sound knowledgeable, but this was the first charter she had been on, and by far the nicest vessel.

"Well, if your friend insisted...," he said.

"Yes, he just said to go on without him," she said.

The man smiled. "Well then, we should be off."

Tess smiled back, relieved not to have the conversation about Roger anymore. But the captain's thick accent intrigued her. It seemed familiar, Russian, perhaps. Roger's voice sounded Russian at times, she recalled, especially when he was irritated. Tess shrugged and pushed her sunglasses on top of her head. With the frame secured by her auburn hair she looked around.

The foreign captain fit the exquisite craft's profile. She guessed his age to be around the mid-forties. She sensed him watching her and turned to face him. For a moment, he held her gaze and an awkward silence hung in the air. Tess's cheeks flushed. The sternness of his jaw softened, and the corner of his eyes creased slightly. His mouth curved into a wide grin.

"The *Charisa* is among the finest yachts," his foreign English broke the awkward moment. "She is forty-four feet of sleek thunder and boasts many comforts a guest of *your* excellent quality could want. You may have noticed," he said, nodding towards the helm, "she has an upper deck where you may find the cool air of the salon more suitable should the heat become too much."

Tess raised her brow, noticing the narrow staircase leading to the upper deck. She could sense the captain watching her. Reaching up, she slipped the sunglasses back down over her eyes, concealing her anxieties behind the darkened lenses.

"Ah, a salon, yes, I might like the idea of having my nails done."

The captain chuckled. She knew somehow, she'd given herself away, that her ignorance of boats had slipped out. He gestured to the back of the boat with the array of food and drinks.

"You'll find everything you need has been provided."

"Mmm, the food looks delicious," she replied.

Eager for a distraction, she helped herself to a skewer of fresh mango and melons. The captain popped the champagne and filled a crystal flute with both the bubbly wine and the mango juice. He nodded and handed her a drink.

"Thank you," she sputtered through bites of food and happily sipped the concoction.

The tangy drink went down easily. The captain placed the carafe back on the table and a gold Cuban linked wristband slid from under his sleeve. Her eyes, still hidden behind the auburn lenses, surveyed the flashy jewelry. She wasn't sure of the brand, but she had seen enough high-end pieces to know it was expensive. There was something about this captain, she tucked her nose deep into her glass and inhaled the flavors of the fermented juice. Whatever it was, she concluded, it would just have to wait. For now, she would breathe in the fresh air, lounge richly on the deck, and enjoy the fruits of her bounty—Roger's booty call sailing trip!

Tess sipped more of the mimosa as she watched Rolan. He turned slightly and his white linen shirt, mostly unbuttoned, revealed a bronzed and slightly hairy chest, laden with gold chains. The thick style matched the bracelet she had seen just moments earlier. Judging from his tan, she was sure he'd spent a great deal of time sailing under the Caribbean sun, an experienced seaman, no doubt. Her shoulders relaxed a little.

Tess's knowledge of watercrafts ranked zero on a scale from one to ten—one if she considered the dinghy at the YMCA where she'd taken lifeguard training. It was the summer following graduation, her mind drifted. Passing the class would surely get Tommy Thompson's attention, or at least she had hoped it would. Tommy, an exceptionally good-looking, lean, six-foot tall, athletic build guy, was in her swimming class. He had golden brown hair and when he tossed his head his hair flowed like a surfer. The dimples in his cheeks offset his sparkling blue eyes. Other than an occasional wink that would make her knees weak, Tommy Thompson didn't know she existed. The fruitless attempt at the lifesaving course also failed miserably and, if it hadn't been for Ben Whitley, an all-star athlete, diving under the water and propelling himself sternly under her bottom, jetting her out of the water like a dolphin, she may never have made it atop that rubber raft. No, she glanced around the *Charisa*, her sailing experience was minimal, at best, and when it came to boats, especially vessels of this caliber, she wouldn't have a clue how to run it.

"Ahem." Rolan bowed slightly, his hand extended directing her to the stairs below. "The stateroom is right this way. You can stow your things there if you'd like."

Tess was eager to change into a more tourist-like attire, but something just nagged at her. She hadn't noticed anyone else on board. Surely, she reasoned, there would be more than just herself and the captain.

"Is there anyone else on board? I hadn't noticed," she tried to sound nonchalant.

"Yes, my first mate is also on board, you'll meet him soon. He's making some," the captain paused, "preparations for our departure," he smiled. "I assure you, miss, you are in capable hands."

She was glad for the assurance and headed below, excited to view the rest of the vessel. At the base of the steps the room opened into a small, private, luxury lounge. Along the yacht's mahogany trimmed wall was a fully stocked mini bar. A tiny port window funneled the sunlight through its tempered glass and the filtered rays bounced off the crystal wine flutes that sparkled throughout the cozy space. There was a small sofa tucked snugly along the opposite side. She ran her hand across the loveseat and continued the few steps further to the stateroom. Like the rest of the craft, the room boasted smooth polished walls. The deep swirls of the woodgrain accented richly throughout. *Roger sure picked the most romantic tour boat, I'll give him that,* she noted internally.

Tess opened the door to her room. A king-sized bed capitalized on the cabin's modest space. Oversized pillows supported a silver tray offering two mints wrapped in foil. A matching satin coverlet tucked over the edges and draped just above the side rugs. To the side of the bed was another polished door, slightly narrower. Curiosity got the better of her as she tenderly opened it. A petite private bath sparkled before her. The sweetness of her pirated spoils fluttered in her stomach. Tess grinned deviously. "Thank you, Roger!" she said.

Alone in the room and eager to change, she slipped off her stale office attire and put on the newly purchased sundress. Tess reached for her bag, stuffing her worn clothes into it, but at the same time, the engines roared. The motion unsteadied her, causing her to fall back against the bed, flinging off her tortoiseshell sunglasses and landing them beside her. The churning of the water slapped against the sides of the yacht. She gripped the bathroom door handle with one hand and slung her purse, attempting to land it on the hook next to the doorjamb but missed. She bent to retrieve the bag, along with the scattered clothes, but the jouncing motion thrust forward sending her into the mahogany wall. Tess steadied herself and, rather than attempt a third time to clip her bag to the peg, she turned to the cabin door, collected her balance the best that she could, and climbed the steps.

Squinting at the bright sun, Tess slipped on her polarized lenses salvaged from her recent fall. She brushed her hair back with her hand and hesitantly looked around. A medium build attendant stood at the helm, the polished wheel firmly in his grasp. Tess sighed heavily, relieved the boat had not run away like she had imagined. The man turned his head, nodded, and grinned, exposing a black hole where a tooth had once been. His hair, while not overly long, was pulled back into a ponytail, a common style she had noticed among the locals. She gathered her sea-legs and walked over to the back of the yacht. Briefly, she took a second glance at the man's face. There was something familiar about him, she pondered for a moment, unable to recall where she had seen him.

The yacht cadenced smoothly through the water and the warm salty air whipped at her face. Rolan stood alongside a glass table at the stern of the boat, his eyes dipped. Tess noticed him staring, ogling at her neckline. She adjusted the ties of her flowered top sundress. Rolan grinned. A nervous lump thickened in her throat and Rolan shifted his eyes, nodding the direction of the helm.

"That is my first mate, Sergey. He knows his way around the reef best."

She glanced back at the attendant who smiled his familiar toothless grin. Rolan paused and raised his brow.

"I, on the other hand, prefer to find my way around other, more delicate things," he chuckled.

Tess blushed, but before she could protest his coming on to her, the captain filled another glass.

"We'll be heading out now. It should be a couple of hours before we reach our destination," he said.

His voice was pragmatic as he set down the juice decanter and offered her the drink. As before, his smile softened and the tenseness in her shoulders dissipated. She returned the smile tentatively and rationalized, the Caribbean, after-all, was the land of sun and love, and flirting seemed to be customary. She took the glass from his hand and sipped the sweet beverage. Once again, the glint of the sun reflected off the band around his wrist. Casting her eyes sideways, Tess looked over the rim of her tipped glass. This time she recognized the timepiece. It was a Cartier. She had seen a few of her clients wear the expensive piece. The full-face diamond facet was distinctive to its brand. She wondered how a captain of a chartered tour could afford such an expensive and elegant wristwatch.

Tess could never justify the cost to wear such a lavish piece of jewelry. But it came as no surprise that one of her most recent clients, Mr. Becker, boasted several times about his fine taste in men's fashion. He had gone on to say that a real man of wealth and stature would only wear the best, which he declared to be a Cartier. Truthfully, she mused, if the thing could keep time and looked nice, that was good enough for her. She remembered trying not to gasp when the client told her what he had paid for his fashion statement.

Roger had always been fascinated with the stories about her clients and their wealth. He would intently listen to the details as she would relay them to him over dinner or just idle conversation. That was one of the things that had drawn her to him, she realized, his attention to details and his endless knowledge of the finer, more expensive things.

In the beginning of their relationship, Roger had acted as the perfect boyfriend, always interested in her galas, and attended all of her grand openings following a client's renovation. Like a scene from a love story novel, he would come up behind her, wrap his arms around her waist and whisper in her ear. He jokingly told whimsical stories of the wealthy attendees. This tantalizing game, she remembered, always pointed out the clients that Roger believed would spend the most money, no matter what the cost and he encouraged Tess to mingle with them. *'To secure them as future clients,'* he would say. Tess admired his remembrances of conversations, always paying attention to her, earnestly interested in the progress while she worked on the client's project. The sloshing of the waves brought her out of her daydream. Tess arched her brow. Until now, she hadn't realized that Roger had always been right about her clients and which ones were the wealthiest and most likely to spend top-dollar to get what they wanted. Tess sipped her champagne and looked over the glass rim. Rolan stared at her.

"What's our destination?" she asked.

With his wine glass in hand, he motioned across the water. "We'll be heading out to the Blue Hole," he replied.

"Sounds intriguing, what is it?"

"It's a reef in the middle of the ocean. Well-known for snorkeling."

"Is it far?" she inquired.

"It's about forty miles offshore..."

"Forty miles!" Tess interrupted. Her eyes widened. "I'm up for snorkeling, but forty miles, isn't that a little excessive? I mean, since it's just me, we don't have to explore too far away."

"No worries, I assure you it is quite a smooth journey. If the wind or sun gets to be too much, you can sit inside where there is air conditioning," he motioned above. "The upper salon has a full view, you can take in the sights, perhaps see a school of dolphins."

She realized that the salon Rolan had mentioned earlier was not for hair or nails. Her cheeks blushed and a quick glance at Rolan's face affirmed he knew how unfamiliar she was with maritime life. She glanced back to the shore.

The warm air swirled and the morning breeze wisped at her hair and rippled across her skirt. She tucked the stray auburn strands behind her ear. It was true the distance to the reef made her uncomfortable, but she also got the impression that the pocked faced captain was a little too interested in her as well.

"It's too bad your *friend* couldn't make it," Rolan cut in. "Please," he lifted the iced beverage to her, "relax and enjoy your cruise. I guarantee you are in good hands."

She glanced up at him. Somehow, she doubted the captain felt troubled at all about Roger not being there. Stepping over to the railing, Tess held the long-stemmed glass in her hand. As she sipped the mango cooler, she wondered if it had been a mistake coming out there alone. Briefly, Tess argued with her conscience that her imagination was working overtime and reminded herself that she ventured to Belize for a vacation, to let her hair down and to enjoy life. She looked around at the lavish surroundings and watched the rippling waves fade into the distance. The pampered ambiance surrounded her as she smelled the faint tropical sweetness in the air. The effects of the mango mimosa warmed her cheeks and relaxed her anxieties. Tess squared her shoulders, pressed her lips firmly and nodded in agreement.

"Lead the way, Captain!" she said.

Toasting her glass to his, Tess gulped the contents down, delighting in the visions of Roger left standing on the dock. After all, she stifled a belch, it's a *tour* boat. The company wouldn't allow anything bad to happen. With that, she settled into the soft cushions, rested her head against the seat and closed her eyes. The smooth cadence of the yacht and the morning mimosas lulled her as dreamy images of Anthony flickered across her mind.

***

FROM THE port, the white caps of churned water trailed the sporty yacht. Roger clenched his fists as he watched the *Charisa* speed away. The blonde sidekick stood next to him.

"Hey, where are they going? I thought you said we were going for a ride!"

Chapter Eight

Traders

THE DULL ROAR OF THE ENGINES woke her. She hadn't meant to fall asleep. The stranger from last night at the bar, her faux boyfriend, had consumed her mind while she napped. She sat up smoothing out her flowered skirt and looked over to see Rolan at the helm.

"I must have dozed off. I didn't get very much sleep last night," she explained.

Rolan pulled back the throttle and the boat slowed. Tess yawned.

"Are we there?" she asked.

He pointed past the boat. "Yes, you see that dark shape that circles around?" he said.

Holding her hand up, she blocked the sun's glare and looked beyond the yacht's bow. A large dark circle formed just beneath the water's surface.

"That looks like a big reef," she said.

Tess looked out across the waves, disappointed that there were no other boats nearby. Far off in the distance she could see tiny specs of what looked like sailing vessels, but here, at the Blue Hole, they were alone.

She wrinkled her brow. "I thought you said this was a popular diving spot."

"It is. We've arrived earlier than most," Rolan said, matter-of-fact like.

He shut off the motor; the air stilled. Only the soft sloshing of the waves sounded alongside the sleek yacht. The snorkeling cruiser bobbed gently with the breeze. Tess tucked another rogue strand of hair back behind her ear, then slid her sunglasses atop her head. The water was indeed a deep blue color. Unlike the sandy shore near the hotel, here there was no beach. Only the underwater shadow of the reef stood out. Looking over the edge of the railing, Tess glanced over at Rolan with her brows arched and wondered about dangers lurking beneath the surface.

"It looks deep. What about sharks?" she hesitated. "I mean is it safe?"

The corner of his eyes creased as he chuckled. "Nothing to worry about, I assure you. Sergey knows this reef well."

She felt somewhat childish for worrying about the possibility of sharks, but this was her first time at sea and thought it best to find out before jumping in. And truthfully, the idea there might be dangers in the water had never fully occurred to her before now. She was still uneasy even though Rolan assured her that all would be fine. Tess fought back the growing urge to have the captain turn the boat around, retreating back to shore and to the safety of her hotel. Her shoulders tensed as spikes of adrenaline subconsciously filled her veins. *C'mon, Tess,* she encouraged herself, *you've come this far, don't back out now.* Inhaling deeply, the tension building in her shoulders subsided.

"I suppose it would be rather daring to be the only ones in the water. When will the other charters get here?" she asked, hoping the idle conversation would take her mind off her growing thoughts of dangerous life forms swimming beneath them.

"The others will stop along the way, at different snorkeling locations first." He looked up at the sun and then back to her. "I would say they will make their way here within the hour."

"Will we be stopping at other locations, too?" she asked hesitantly.

"But of course! You will not be disappointed. Before long there will be more boats and the fish will scatter some. But because we're here now, you will have the ocean to yourself. I'm sure you'll find many colorful species along the coral. Sergey will show you."

Tess gulped, looking out over the railing and into the enticing aqua colored seawater. Closing her eyes, she took a deep breath. *You've got this,* she convinced herself. Taking the opportunity to float along with puffer fish and yellow striped sea bass could make the trip worth the risk, if any. Her fears melted and she found herself anxious, eager to snorkel in the clear blue water. She would prove to herself, and to Roger, that she was capable of adventures. And what could be more spur-of-the-moment than jumping into the middle of the ocean forty miles from shore? She quickly pushed any negative feelings aside and looked over at Rolan. As if he anticipated her acceptance, he gestured towards the back of the boat.

"Sergey will meet you at the stern and have your gear ready," he said.

She glanced over to Sergey who nodded and smiled his toothless grin, he then lifted a seat cushion next to the swim deck and pulled fins and dive masks from the concealed bins. Tess inhaled deeply, suppressing her nerves and the fluttering of butterflies within her gut. Slowly, she exhaled, releasing her breath along with the tension that had built up in her shoulders. Tess looked up at Sergey.

"I'll be right back," she said.

Tess skipped down the flight of narrow steps and latched the door to her room. A quick rummage through her tote, which still lay on the floor from when she lost her balance, produced the two-piece hibiscus print bikini, the remaining part of her sundress ensemble. Tess recalled the graceful woman at the store and the folklore tale of the enchanted blooms.

"Let's see if I find my true love today," she laughed lightly.

If nothing else, she thought as she held the swim garment up to her, it was a cute suit. And while she had her doubts that she'd find *Mr. Right* in the middle of the ocean, she considered it possible that she could attract a wealthy tourist back at the Grand Simone. Images of the adorned pool and its tropical allure splashed through her mind. She eagerly anticipated another eventful evening at the five-star hotel; surely her odds were better there than at her own subpar lodging.

Tess fastened the straps that crisscrossed the top together and tied the soft material at the nape of her neck. The bottoms had the same pattern and tied snuggly at both hips. She looked at her reflection in the full-length mirror that was fastened to the back of the bathroom door. Turning to the side and getting the full image of herself, she shrugged contently, pleasantly surprised at the suit's perfect fit. Next, she pulled her hair up into a ponytail securing it with a band. Her fair skin, she hoped, would be protected from the intense sun under the water. She lacked the pigment for a deep tropical tan, the fate of most red-haired women.

Back home there wasn't much opportunity to be outdoors in the sun anyway. Meeting deadlines and accommodating client's schedules often took her into the late evening hours. Weekends, however, she set time aside and tried to encourage Roger to take up golf with her. But he always had a rehearsal or would just forget to show up. She spent one Saturday afternoon hitting a bucket of balls by herself. Still looking into the mirror with her fair skin reflecting back, Tess frowned at the memory. With each swing, she had envisioned Roger's face, smacking the tiny white orbs high into the net. Her memories dispersed and she focused on the present—and her future. But, as she stared at her reflection, a knot tightened in her throat. The night at the restaurant and Roger's harsh words rushed back into her thoughts and she cast her eyes downward. There were so many signs, she paused briefly pressing her lips and shaking her head. *Be brave, Tess, you can do this,* she whispered to herself.

She straightened her shoulders, as if headed into a business meeting, and exhaled deeply. Excitement and energy revived through her veins. *You won't ruin this for me, Roger Van de Camp, not this time!* Casting a final glance, she gave herself a reassuring smile, ascended the elegant mahogany staircase, and stepped out onto the deck where Sergey waited for her.

***

THE STEADY motion of the waves relaxed her as she lay floating face down in the Caribbean waters. This was her first snorkeling adventure and figuring out the snug fit of the mask took a little bit of work. Sergey did his best, and within the ten-minute snorkel crash course, she had successfully sealed the rubber contraption to her face and managed several breaths through the snorkel tube, which allowed air in but sealed the water out. Sergey floated with her until she could breathe steadily. It didn't take long, and she gave him the thumbs up, ready to venture.

The reef was enormous, and the sea life hovered near the coral edges. Just as Rolan had said, shoals of fish swam alongside her. Some dared to get close enough that their fins tickled her thigh. Sergey swam off to the side and just ahead. She was glad to have a little distance between them. Earlier, onboard the *Charisa* and after she had emerged from below deck, Sergey waited at the swim deck for her but had changed out of his knee length khakis to the skimpiest swimsuit she'd ever seen on a man. Perhaps it was the latest style in Russia, or maybe Belize, but it was all she could do to stifle a laugh. The lack of his covering left little to the imagination, and Sergey, she noticed, was very well equipped. She had quickly diverted her gaze only to unintentionally look right into his steel grey eyes. Wryly, he smiled, which immediately told her he was very much aware of his gift. Not wanting to send any misconstrued messages, Tess decided a little distance on the surf would be a good thing.

The sky was vibrant, and the sun filtered through the Caribbean waves illuminating the clear aqua water. Sea urchins along the colorful reef gently swayed with the motion of the current. Blue Angelfish, with their puckered lips, made her laugh but she was careful not to break the seal of her mouthpiece to her skin. She glanced off to the side and watched another tiny school of narrow-shaped fish move quickly out of Sergey's path. Their movements synchronized, like choreographed swimmers. She paused and watched them shimmer in unison. Slippery Dicks! That's what they are, she realized. Her past client, a retired marine enthusiast with a flair for the eccentric, insisted on having a gigantic aquarium built into his grand foyer and given his naval sense of humor, told his wife he would fill the tank with the odd little fish. She remembered the wife bellowed in return that she'd be sure to serve them as appetizers if he did such a thing. Tess wondered if the wife had made good on her threat. The cigar shaped performers darted off in a new direction.

A cloud of bubbles brushed over her shoulders. Distracted by the small, silvery creatures, Tess had drifted close to Sergey. He was now only a few feet ahead, motioning toward a different coral cluster—at least that's what she guessed. The taste of saltwater and the pangs of her snorkel learning curve remained fresh in her mind. She kicked forcefully to his right, maintaining her distance. She didn't want the flip of his fin to dislodge her mask and make her swallow the nasty-tasting seawater.

Gliding past the pink and blue hues of the reef, Tess could hear the static-like noise coming from the fish nibbling on the coral—the bigger the fish the louder the crunching. A shadow caught her attention. The shriveled, narrow face of a creature slithered quickly, reversing into its hole. The eel's black phantom-like shape, speckled with white dots and bulging large eyes, disappeared into the darkened coral den. It most definitely wasn't the prettiest creature she'd seen. She scrunched her nose at the ugly thing then took a moment scanning the area before convincing herself that no other creatures lurked nearby. She continued exploring, being vigilant for any other dark shadows lurking within the reef.

The Caribbean seawater swished warmly across her legs while an entourage of Angelfish faithfully swam by her side. The small fish seemed indifferent to her presence or the fluttering of her dive fins. Her body floated weightless along the coral's edge and her snorkel mask was clear, allowing her to see a good distance through the water. She took deep breaths at the surface and then plunged her face into the sea, kicking her legs swiftly and propelling herself down under the water. The special snorkel allowed her a few moments to explore deeper before resurfacing for another breath. Tess continued to dive and resurface again for as long as her breaths could last. The vastness of the ocean dwarfed her body, a mere speck in its immensity.

An ominous shape suspended in motion caught her attention. It was large and moved eerily across the dark coral gateway to the Blue Hole site. Even underwater she felt her hair stand on end. Tess shuddered. Like the wrinkle-faced eel earlier, she realized there were other, more dangerous creatures inhabiting the reef. Quickly, she glanced over to the familiar pink coral beds. They were further away than she had expected. Realizing she had drifted over the deepest part of the sinkhole—a bottomless cavernous abyss, a sudden bout of lightheadedness swept over her. The protection of the coral reef was gone. Tess panicked. Immediately, she brought her knees up high to her chest and kicked out feverishly, stretching her arms and paddling quickly to a more secure area near the coral. It would be best to admire the unknown sea creature from a distance, she decided, and to not lose sight of her guide.

Tess stayed closer to the surface, limiting her brief dives, and regaining her confidence. Another school of bright yellow and blue striped fish caught her attention. She put her fears aside and enjoyed the curious Parrotfish and the graceful gliding of the Blue Angelfish swimming alongside her. More yellow and black Reef Butterflyfish also joined in. Every time she surfaced for more air; the little creatures would be waiting beneath her. She enjoyed their company. Her favorite ones had protruding eyeballs and puckering lips—a constant state of pouting. They made her smile. She lost herself in their cuteness and reached out to touch them, but they dashed away. Moments later, they would appear beneath her and resume swimming back and forth.

Suddenly, another large, dark shadow glided over her. Unlike the recent encounter moments ago, this one was closer. Her heartbeat quickened, and she could hear rhythmic beats thumping through the current. At first, it felt like it was her own pulse reverberating in her chest, transmitted through the water. But then she realized it was something else, vibrations caused by an unseen force. Fear paralyzed Tess as she envisioned an enormous beast closing in on her. It had to be gigantic, her mind raced. The thumping sounds enveloped her, adrenalin surged through her veins, and she flailed her arms and kicked her legs wildly.

Her thrashing dislodged her mask and the salty ocean water rushed across her face. She inhaled from the snorkel but it, too, had filled with seawater. Barreling for the surface, Tess breached the surf like an uncoordinated flounder, flying crazily over the waves. Choking and gasping for air, visions of an enormous shark grotesquely chomping at her flesh flooded through her mind. Her hands pulled at her disheveled hair, clinging across the mask—her vision obscured.

Tess kicked hard to keep afloat and grasped the mask from her face. Blinking the saltwater out of her eyes, she looked about, ready to face the danger that most certainly loomed nearby. But as her thrashing stopped, there was only the muffled sound of an engine overhead. She squinted up at the clear blue sky. A small airplane flew over. The same familiar dark shadow again rippled over the waves. She cleared her mask, threw her head back, and bobbed on the surf. Exhausted and embarrassed she laughed, relieved it was only a small plane and not a dreaded shark coming to devour her. Tess took a moment and collected her composure. The plane had been extremely low. Maybe it had been an island tour, she shrugged. At the hotel lobby, she had seen brochures on airplane tours that flew out to the Cays along the coast.

Although calmer, she could still feel the jittery pangs of her nerves. Tess scanned the waves in the direction she had last seen Sergey. It struck her as odd that he would leave her, in the middle of the ocean, alone. Sure, she realized, it wasn't really an emergency, but...after all, it could have been a shark! Sergey was nowhere near, and certainly not there to protect her. Continuing to look out over the surf, Tess caught a glimpse of Sergey's fins steadily churning the ocean water, heading back to the *Charisa*. The small plane disappeared into the sunlight. Tess pressed her lips and furrowed her brow. She would be sure to let Sergey know exactly what she thought of him and his guiding abilities. He'd be lucky if another tooth didn't get knocked out of his mouth, she fumed.

Tess straightened her mask, blew the water from the snorkel, and headed straight for the yacht. But Sergey's strong legs propelled him further and further away. She focused on the *Charisa*, which was drifting. For every stroke she made, the yacht floated more out of reach. Her imagination kicked in and she let herself think that Sergey might have seen a shark and had left her to face it by herself! Adrenaline spiraled up her neck. That's why the plane flew so low, to warn her, she thought. She panicked and kicked harder; each stroke more determined to get herself back to the yacht.

Sergey was still out of sight. Only her small blue and yellow harem faithfully kept pace with her. But quickly, they too dropped back and swam in the other direction. She put her face into the sea and windmilled her arms pushing faster through the water. Moments later she could see the yacht's hull with its dark blue stripe painted just beneath the water line. Relieved, she put her hand out and glided until she held the swim ladder in her grasp. With her mask still fixed to her face, Tess stretched her foot out searching for the step. A shadowy figure stepped towards her. The glare of the sun and the condensation on her mask blurred her vision. She tugged at the rubber edges pulling her gear off then sat on the landing. Her chest heaved out of breath as she looked up. Sergey leaned over her. Fresh beads of seawater rolled down his chest as he held out his hand.

"Here, take ahold," Sergey said.

"Why did you leave me out there?" Tess fumed.

Her legs trembled, unaccustomed to the ocean workout. Images of her extreme self-defense class flashed across her mind. It was one of those fliers from the coffee room and Molly had convinced her, *'You never know when you might need to make a few moves in this urban jungle!'* The fact was Tess had found herself enjoying the four-week, physically challenging course. The instructor even said she was his star pupil. The memory quickly dissipated, and she could taste the bitter salt of the ocean, no doubt from the gallons she ingested getting back to the *Charisa*. Speed swimming had taken its toll and she held on to the railing, catching her breath.

Glaring at Rolan, she waited for an explanation, but before anyone answered her, he turned the switch and the engines started. Without warning he pushed the lever, giving it full throttle. Her legs wobbled. She stumbled back onto the swim deck. Her heart leaped to her throat as she watched the water churn beneath the roar of the motors and visions of her body flailing overboard rushed through her mind. She screamed and reached for the metal bar next to the landing. Tess held the banister tight. She turned and glared at the captain, who was ignorant of her almost detrimental fate.

"Are you crazy? What the hell are you doing?" Tess shouted.

"Get her below!" Rolan growled.

"What's going on?" Tess cried out.

"Nothing to be concerned about, I assure you," the captain said. Rolan's Russian accent bellowed over the roar of the motors.

She watched as Rolan turned the wheel hard and the boat swayed. Struggling to gather her balance, she held tight to the railing and peered beyond the bow. A reflection glistened out in the distance.

"What is that…is that a boat? They're coming straight at us!" she yelled.

She stared, helpless at the craft heading fast towards them.

"Pirates, miss! We've got to outrun them," Rolan shouted back.

"Pirates! Out run them, seriously? What do they want? I mean, we don't have anything, do we?" she said, bewildered.

The image of the captain's expensive watch flashed across her mind. Then she looked at herself, scantily clad in a tropical bikini. Rolan nodded to Sergey.

"Take her below, see that she stays there," he demanded.

Bewildered, her mind raced at the situation, like being in the midst of a bad dream, only this dream was happening right before her, and it was real! Sergey shoved her down the steps to the stateroom and pushed her through the doorway. She turned and faced him. He grinned as he reached his hand out, his eyes dropped across her cleavage then back to her face. Tess glanced at his wrist noticing a tattoo wrapped around his arm—it looked familiar. Her eyes lifted and met his steel hard scowl. The look on his face frightened her as he pulled the door shut and the latch clicked. It all came rushing back, the man, the tattoo…it had been him, the angry man at the bar. It had been Sergey at the Grand Simone. He had been the one who almost knocked over the table and the chairs and had taken the flirtatious brunette by the arm, forcing her from the dance floor. And now he was here, sailing on the *Charisa*, an attendant on her cruise. The blood drained from her face and a sickening knot formed in her throat. She pulled on the handle. It would not budge. Sergey had locked her in. She beat on the door with her fists. The louvered slats bruised her hands.

"Let me out! You can't keep me in here. People will know I'm missing!"

Any hope for rescue sank like an anchor. No one knew where she was, there would be no one looking for her and especially not out in the ocean forty miles from shore.

Chapter Nine

Rendezvous

TESS LEANED AGAINST THE CABIN door. "You can't keep me locked in here!" she shouted. The roar of the engines drowned out her calls. Her mind reeled. "What if it really is pirates—what then?" she said, horrified.

Tess bit her lip. She heard stories about young women being kidnapped on cruise ships, but she didn't think they were true. Certainly not here in Belize and especially not on a chartered boat—*her* chartered boat! There's got to be a way out. Looking around, she scanned the small room for an exit. Tess spotted the port window next to the bed.

"There! I'll break the glass and...," her voice trailed.

It was no use, she realized. The thick glass would be impossible to break and even more impossible to fit through the small opening—not to mention the vast ocean on the other side of the glass. Suddenly, the boat surged, turning hard to the left and thrusting her sideways. The unexpected motion threw her off balance, causing her to shuffle across the hardwood. The strap to her woven purse slipped onto the floor, coiling itself around her ankle. As she attempted to move, the remainder of the bag caught on the edge of the bedpost. The momentum of the engines and the capture of her foot sent her toppling across the room, landing hard against the bathroom door. It slammed shut. She winced as her shoulder wedged into the wooden trim, bouncing her head off the dark mahogany slats. Letting out an agonized groan, Tess slid her hand up to rub her forehead. As her fingers brushed across the door handle, something small and slender slipped from the bathroom door lock. It clanked as it hit the floor. Looking down, she saw a small brass key lying next to her foot. Without hesitation Tess grabbed the key.

"Oh, God, thank-you, thank-you!" she said. "Please work, please work."

She turned to the cabin door that Sergey had shoved her through and put the small key into the lock. With eyes closed, Tess turned the key. With a click, the lock released, and the door swung open. Tess scrambled up the stairs and peered out onto the deck. The engine roared then quieted as the motor shifted into idle. Gliding forward, the boat slowed, its bow settled onto the water. With only the low rumble of the idling engine, Tess could hear the agitated waves lapping against the yacht's sides. But there was another sound growing louder. It was the robust throttle of an approaching boat. Without warning the thunderous roar of the opposing boat's engine deafened the air, sending a mammoth wave over the side of the yacht, drenching the back of the *Charisa*. The cascade of water splashed hard onto the deck. Tess gripped the banister and leaned back just out of striking distance. Sergey rushed towards her, but the wave knocked the vile backstabber off-balance, sending him toppling over the edge and into the sea.

Serves you right, she smirked. But the triumph was short lived. The loud roar of the attacking vessel approached for a second hit. Her nerves stood on edge as the roar of the speedboat charged straight for them. Tess peeked around the corner, crouching out of sight. With Sergey cast off into the seawater, the deck was empty. She looked around but Rolan appeared to be gone, as well. Tess chewed her lip. She wondered if both the Captain and Sergey had fallen overboard. Anxiety flared within her, sending a surge of queasiness to her stomach as she dreaded the possibility of facing vicious pirates alone. Out of nowhere the rogue motorboat swished into view. Tess ducked. Her heart raced, fearing the *Charisa* would succumb to sea-wielding guttersnipes. She shuddered at the thought and ran her hand down her throat, glancing down at her attire. Meeting up with ocean thugs in her skimpy bikini would be a terrible idea, she gulped. She scuttled down the stairway and bolted back through the cabin door. Grabbing the crumpled sundress, Tess quickly put it on. Frantic, she grasped her handbag, still lying on the floor from its lost fight with her ankle. As if it could protect her, she held it tight to her chest, then darted back up the stairs. Just as she reached the opening, another mammoth wave cascaded over the yacht. A direct hit! It happened so fast that she didn't have time to take cover. Her hibiscus sundress, now drenched in seawater, clung to her body.

She sputtered and wiped her hand across her face. The saltwater burned her eyes as she blinked hard, peering from the steps. Hoping to get a better view, she leaned up against the wall. But the sun's bright rays glared across the wet, glistening deck. With her hand over her brow, she squinted. This time she could see Rolan, he held a long gaff in his hands as he leaned over the railing. His clothes were drenched by the harassing boat. Most likely, she guessed, Rolan was retrieving his first mate from the ocean. But then she realized that Sergey had fallen at the back of the boat, not up front. She observed more intently as she noticed Rolan jostling the pole clumsily in the water. Near the bow, a package floated, bobbing with the waves. The turbulent water made it difficult for Rolan to snag it. One thing was for certain—it was not Sergey he was after.

"What are you doing?" she shouted.

Rolan ignored her. Tess stood on her toes, trying to keep an eye on the package and Rolan, while still keeping her distance. After her ordeal with Sergey shoving her below, Tess wasn't sure about the captain anymore either. The object bobbed closer—she could see it more clearly now. It had the shape of a small beer keg. Perhaps a party boat lost its cargo, she guessed. But there weren't any other boats around other than the pirate boat and the airplane, too. Her eyes widened and a sickening pit formed in her gut.

"Are those drugs?" she blurted.

Rolan paid no attention to her. *Of course!* It made sense, she nodded. There wasn't anything worth value on the yacht. The pirates must be after the container. They must have been waiting for the plane and now the *Charisa* was in their way. She sighed, relieved at knowing that Rolan was trying to help her, and Sergey, too.

Rolan continued navigating the pole just missing the floating canister. He twisted and jabbed the gaff for what seemed like an eternity while she stood in disbelief, not knowing what to do next. Finally, Rolan snagged the package. She wasn't sure the little container held any contraband, but the captain, she noted, seemed convinced it was worth the effort. Rolan hoisted the treasure on board. A twinge of compassion flashed through her mind, recalling Sergey going overboard. Tess realized that she may have misread Sergey's actions and that he might have been concerned for her safety, too. Sergey had only shoved her below to keep her safe, to protect her from the approaching thieves, she reasoned. She glanced at Rolan who was fully engrossed in his mysterious cache.

"What about your first mate? He fell off the back of the boat," she yelled.

Tess pointed in the direction where Sergey had splashed overboard. But Rolan didn't pay attention, nor did he answer. She glared at him, furious that he would be more concerned with a floating keg, which was most likely filled with illegal narcotics, than to rescue his own man tossed into the sea by the pirate's deliberate wake. And, for all either of them knew, Sergey had drowned.

The roar of the rogue boat grew louder as it barreled on a collision course for the yacht. Tess looked up; her eyes widened. This time, the bow headed straight for the *Charisa*. Rolan stood holding the canister in his hands. He glanced out at the fast-approaching boat. Frenzied, he spun around and barked orders to Tess.

"Hit the throttle!" Rolan bellowed.

Tess jumped to the helm following Rolan's orders. There were levers and buttons plastered across the dash—green, red, solid lights, and other blinking ones. But they were all foreign to her.

"Which one is the—?" she looked up. To her horror the impending clash was mere seconds away. "Look out!" she shouted.

The sleek power boat veered and careened towards them with its bow lifting out of the ocean. Tess screamed and held the wheel firmly. The boat slammed into the yacht flinging the keg from Rolan's grip and sending it back into the churning water. Staggering, Rolan regained his balance, then reached behind his back and pulled out a gun. Tess gasped as Rolan aimed towards the pirate boat. The waves bobbed violently, and a loud bang pierced her ears. Her mouth gaped as the bullet missed. Rolan aimed for a second shot, but this time he stumbled, and the hard soles of his loafers slipped on the metal gaff lying on the wet deck.

Tess watched the scene unfold as the captain's arms, along with the gun in hand, flew up into the air. A broad, dark figure onboard the speed boat slung a rope with a grappling hook. The line wrapped over the yacht's railing. With agile form, the crook leaped over the banister and barreled into Rolan, knocking him down. The firearm slid across the deck, landing next to the helm. The captain lay heaving from the blow and the rogue villain turned towards her. Tess gasped.

"*Anthony?*"

Her face paled in disbelief. She glanced down at the gun that had slid to her feet. As if time slowed, she shifted her gaze to Rolan, then back to the provocative dance partner. Last night's memory-flash quickly faded. She stood staring at the two men in front of her, bewildered. But then her eyes narrowed, realizing the events she had just witnessed.

"What the hell! What are you doing?" she glared.

She watched as Anthony's jaw tightened. With his nose flared and his lips curled, he stared back at her.

"What am I doing? What the hell are *you* doing here?" he demanded.

She darted a look at Rolan as he lay on the floor recovering. Like a dream in slow motion, reality unfolded. Her chest felt heavy, the thick air and humidity smothered her. Her ears rang and she staggered to the helm, steading herself. *This isn't real, it can't be real,* she told herself.

A light breeze rippled over her wet clothes reviving her senses. She stood, regaining her composure. From the corner of her eye, she watched as Rolan shifted a cautious glance at the intruder then back to the weapon that lay just out of his reach. Her heart leaped into her throat as Rolan dove for the pistol. Anthony sprang after him. The two men once again entangled in a struggle. First, Anthony sat atop Rolan. They wrestled across the deck, grunting. Next, Rolan gained the upper hand. But in one swift motion, Anthony grabbed the gaffing pole lying on the deck and thrust the bar to Rolan's throat. Tess watched helplessly as Rolan strained to hold the pirate back. But Anthony overpowered him and shoved his elbow into Rolan's jaw. The commotion continued.

Tess stood frozen as she watched Anthony overtake the captain. Bits and pieces of yesterday's encounter filtered into her mind. If she had known he was a tropical gangster, she would never have talked to him last night. Oh, God, she winced. She had even used him to pose as her boyfriend tricking Roger. Her mind whirled. He had been so dashing, his lips so gentle.

Goosebumps trickled up her arm as images of his warm breath taunting her neck reappeared.

Snapping out of her dream, she twisted her lips, hardening her gaze at the two brawlers. Looking down at the deck, Tess picked up the gun. It was heavier than expected. She'd never held a gun before and certainly never to apprehend a thief or a pirate. The black steel was cold in her hands despite the heat radiating from the sun. Wrapping both hands around the handle, Tess squared her shoulders and put her finger through the loop.

"*Stop!*" she yelled.

But the men continued to brawl. She closed her eyes and squeezed the trigger. The jolt of the weapon jarred her whole body, and the blast pierced her eardrums. A shard of polished wood splintered where a bullet hole marred the deck between the two brawling men. Both men jumped to their feet, their attention now on her. Holding the gun firmly, she pointed it first at Anthony and then at Rolan. Anthony held up his hands. The sun blared down, and her palms began to sweat. Tess shifted the heavy weapon between her grip and clutched the gun tighter.

Cocking his head, Anthony nodded to Rolan. "If you're going to shoot somebody, shoot him," he said.

Her eyes narrowed, unamused at his pirate-like savviness. Rolan labored out of breath. Holding up his hands, he gestured towards Anthony.

"No! He's the crook, shoot *him!*" he said.

Her ears still rang from the earlier gunshot. Confused, Tess didn't know who to believe. Never would she have ever seen herself in such a predicament, miles from shore and no one to help her but the pistol in her hands.

Like a pendulum, Tess pointed the gun barrel first to Anthony and then to Rolan. Who could she trust? Surely, Anthony couldn't be, her thoughts paused—his eyes were so incredulously seductive. Pressing her lips tighter, she continued pointing the gun at Rolan.

"Somebody better tell me what's going on," Tess demanded.

Rustling noises from the back of the boat distracted her. Tess glanced behind her, taking her eyes off the prisoners for just a moment. She gasped, relieved to see Sergey climbing out of the water. He sat exhausted on the swim deck. She quickly turned back to the men, but it was too late, Rolan leaped for the weapon, knocking it from her hands. The pistol slid across the deck. Anthony grabbed Rolan by the shoulder, spun him around, and landed a powerful blow to the captain's chin, knocking him backwards. Rolan staggered as his loafers slipped on the disheveled fruit scattered across the deck. Losing his balance, he tumbled over the railing and splashed into the ocean. In the same moment, a cold, wet arm thrust around her neck as Sergey grabbed her from behind. His forearm squeezed firmly across her throat. Instinctively, Tess grabbed Sergey by the arm, adrenaline surging within her. She twisted his wrist, and in a panic-fueled move, flipped him onto the deck. Her eyes widened.

"It really works!" she said.

Astonished, she quickly looked over at Anthony. His brow arched and a broad, quizzical smile widened across his face. Anthony threw back his head, reeling in laughter. Sergey lay on the floor, unconscious. Tess felt a twinge of guilt but not for long. Her brow narrowed.

"Why did you grab me and not him?" she glared at the unresponsive Sergey.

Tess sensed Anthony watching her and turned to meet his eyes, her scowl deepening in displeasure. She noted, with a mix of irritation and resignation, that her unamused expression only seemed to amuse him more. His laughter faded, yet his crooked smile told her he was still thoroughly entertained.

"Why, Tess Martin, you managed that quite splendidly!" Anthony smirked.

"I...I didn't mean...," she stuttered, then narrowed her eyes. "Wait, how do you know my last name?"

She was sure she hadn't told him. But then, she snorted, her mind was still foggy about all of the details of last night and this morning, especially waking up with most of her clothes off. The blood rushed to her cheeks. Anthony waited for an answer. Creases formed at the corner of his eyes and his upper lip lifted wryly, almost laughing, as he gleamed at her.

"You told me," he said, curling his lips more. "But you forgot to mention you were a Jujitsu princess."

She huffed and sensed he was purposely holding back. Sergey moaned and Tess glanced over at him lying on the floor. Arching her brow, and satisfied at her attacker's condition, she turned her attention back to Anthony, unconvinced at how he knew her last name. It nagged at her.

"I told you my name? When did I tell you that?" she asked. It was the first rule of bar hopping, not to give out your last name or your real phone number.

He shrugged. "Does it really matter? Perhaps you can ask your friends."

Anthony nodded to Sergey, still crumpled on the deck. Bending down, Anthony picked up the gun and tucked the weapon into the front of his pants. She couldn't help but notice how his shirt was partially opened from the earlier brawl on deck. Tess tried not to look where he tucked the pistol, but it was too late. She caught a glimpse of his bronzed skin and the outline of his muscles leading down to his groin. For a moment, Tess gawked then quickly averted her eyes. Missing details from last night flickered through her mind. She remembered standing on the beach with Anthony by her side and the rush of warm waves that had splashed across their feet. More vague images flittered into her memory, like how he had taken her chin into his hands and tilted her face towards his. She recalled how her fingertips had brushed across his chest and how she had looked into his chocolate brown eyes.

Tess gulped as she cleared her mind and regained her senses in the present, to the here and now on the *Charisa*. Anthony took the gaff and pulled the box from the ocean. She silently scolded herself as tingling sensations quivered through her inner thighs. Agh! He was so incredibly sexy! She bit her lip. *Seriously, Tess,* she scoffed, *pull yourself together.* Anthony set the box on the deck and flipped up the latches, opening his treasure.

"What are you doing? Is that why you're here?" she fumed.

He ignored her.

"You really know how to pick 'em, Tess," she muttered under her breath. "Are you just going to turn away from me and pretend that I'm not here?" she demanded.

"Now that's an interesting choice of words," he said with his back still turned, "it seems to me you were doing some pretty good pretending last night."

Pressing her lips tighter, she ignored his sarcasm as she peered over his shoulder. Several white plastic bundles were piled together. Anthony quickly closed the case, carried it to the railing and untied the rope binding the two boats together. With nautical ease, he slung himself and the baggage over the edge, landing onboard the long, narrow bow of the speedboat.

"So that's it? You have your drugs and now you're leaving?" she asked.

Anthony didn't reply. Her heart raced and her shoulders tensed. She didn't want him to leave her alone with Sergey knocked out on the deck and Rolan floating somewhere nearby, maybe even dead, she thought. She looked around the disheveled *Charisa*. The overturned table and the once carefully laid out fruit were now strewn about all over the deck. The mimosa carafe lay shattered, its beautiful crystal broken into pieces. Her moment to delight in the stolen spoils of Roger's snorkel adventure had turned into another disaster.

She gazed back over to Anthony as he reached for the ignition key. Tess held back tears that welled in the corner of her eyes. Anthony paused and took a deep breath. He looked out towards the open sea. She also turned her gaze to the tropical azure waters—no one else was in sight. Shifting her focus back to Anthony, Tess could see him glance down at the dash, as if contemplating his options. His jawline tightened as he simultaneously hit his fist hard on the steering wheel.

"Seriously?" he murmured.

Anthony ran his hands through his thick wavy hair as he turned and faced the ocean once more. Without a word, he spun around and with athletic ease he once more climbed onto the long bow of his boat. From there, Anthony jumped back onto the *Charisa* and lashed the rope over the railing. His swift behavior startled her as she took a step backwards. Her foot stumbled on the polished fruit tray, causing her to lean hard against the helm. With her hands and elbows braced behind her, Anthony leaned in close. The salty oceanic fragrance blended flavorfully with his tropical musk sweat. The alluring fragrance filled her senses sending tantalizing sensations rushing from her breasts to her thighs. He lowered his head and looked her in the eyes.

"What the hell are you doing here?" Anthony asked.

His breath was sweet but his tone harsh. She squirmed, fearing the anger in his voice. Tess turned to avoid his accusing glare and pushed herself away. She gathered her composure, taking a couple of steps aside but then spun to face him. The embers of fear sparked into rage, and she let him know it.

"Me? I could ask the same about you! How—how did you know I would be here?"

She sniffed, wiping the back of her hand across her cheek and catching the slow drop of a tear.

Anthony glared at her. "You—here, how the hell would I know you were on some date with Rolan? Or is it customary for American women to throw themselves at notorious drug lords?"

"Date!" her mouth gaped. "Thank you very much, but this was supposed to be a snorkeling adventure, not some...," she looked around the deck, "adventure with disaster!" Tess tightened her jaw, threw back her shoulders and walked over to the edge. Her eyes caught a glimpse of the retrieved box. "And, if you didn't come here to rescue me, then why are you here?" she asked. Tess turned and searched his face for the answer, but she already knew. "Who are you?" Tess pointed over at Sergey still lying on the floor. "And who are these guys?"

Anthony furrowed his brow ignoring her question and instead looked beyond her.

"Well? Are you going to tell me?" she asked, glaring at him.

Anthony yanked at one of the fender ropes next to the railing. The knot released without hesitation. He strode over to Sergey, who now stirred behind her, and bound Sergey's wrists with the cord.

"I'd love to sit here and chat with you about your *adventures*," he gave her a swift smile as he yanked the knot tight, "but I have better things to do, sweetheart."

"So, you *are* a pirate, and don't call me sweetheart!" Tess bantered.

With Sergey secured, Anthony walked over to her. Again, he leaned in closer. His warm breath brushed across her cheek. Tess's heart quivered.

"Right now, *sweetheart*," Anthony mocked, "we need to get out of here before Rolan's men come to the rendezvous."

"Rendezvous?" she asked, raising her brow. "What rendezvous?"

"Yes, rendezvous. I suspect this one," he paused, "to meet the buyers for those packages," he continued and glanced down at her, "...and any other merchandise they were bartering for," he said, matter-of-fact like. She followed his stare and pulled at her dress; her breasts pressed against the thin wet fabric.

Tess stood on the deck looking over the rail where Rolan had gone overboard.

"Oh God, I'm the merchandise, aren't I?"

The dimples along Anthony's jaw twitched. "Look," he coaxed, "we haven't got much time. Are you coming or not?"

"I can't go with you. You're a...a pirate," she said. But she knew her words sounded hollow even as she said them. She pointed to the stash of bundles. "How do I know you won't try to sell me to the highest bidder like...," Tess nodded, looking over to Sergey, "like him?"

Anthony scoffed and freed the rope from the rail. He turned towards her—his eyes glistened. "For one," he grinned, "you're not my type!" And with that, he jumped back onto the waiting boat and started the engine.

A flashback to the bar crossed her mind. "Oh!" she huffed.

Anthony chuckled softly, which infuriated her even more as she clenched her fists.

"Are you coming with me or are you staying here?" he asked.

She hesitated. The thought of Sergey and Rolan groping at her made her shudder. But the idea of blasting across the ocean with this arrogant stranger from the cantina didn't sound incredibly wise either. Tess looked about the yacht and then out to the water. Neither option appealed to her. She squinted up at the sun that glowed in the late morning sky. Like a suffocating blanket, the heat wrapped around her. She had almost been traded at sea. Had it not been for Anthony though, she shuddered, not wanting to think of what might have happened.

"Suit yourself," Anthony retorted.

The sleek boat idled, pulling away from the *Charisa*. Fear and anxiety swept over her.

"No, wait!" Tess shouted.

She grabbed her purse still hanging alongside the helm and flung it into Anthony's boat. He gripped her arm, and she stepped on board. The engine roared as they sped away.

Chapter Ten

The Getaway

THE SUN BLAZED OVERHEAD AS the engine churned through the water, propelling the sleek sports boat across the ocean. Tess's auburn hair, unleashed in the open air, whipped across her face as the vessel sliced through the waves, making their swift getaway. She ran her hand over the loose strands, clearing her view as she glanced back over her shoulder. The *Charisa* had faded into the horizon.

Ahead, the vast blue of the ocean sparkled like crown jewels. Not another boat was in sight. Tess stood next to Anthony; one hand gripped the dash while the other held fast to the brim of the windshield. Her heart raced, matching the rhythm of the waves. She glanced discreetly at the stranger next to her. His face was taut, etched with intensity, as he maneuvered the boat through the water, the hull leveling over the crystal-blue sea. Her thoughts wandered, retracing the moments that unfolded. Had it not been for the gunshots, being shoved below deck, and a bundle of narcotics stowed away beneath the helm, yes, if not for those things, the scene might have been romantic, straight out of a novel.

There were no words spoken as they sped away, distancing themselves from the *Charisa*—further from the hotel and further from the marina. Contemplating her next move, her mind shifted to last night's encounter at the bar. Her thoughts roved over Anthony's tantalizing demeanor—his suave, textbook-like tactics were cliché, she surmised, like those an overconfident criminal might utilize.

Her experience with the illegal side of life also rated zero on a scale from one to ten. Outside of Roger's recent two-timing indiscretions, she had considered herself a good judge of character, avoiding the darker life. But this man, or pirate, Anthony, if that really was his name, she didn't know anything about him. The previous evening he'd been so quick to come to her rescue, to play the role of her boyfriend. Her smile faded as she recalled the long-legged brunette and the agile stranger's groping hands. *Keep it together,* she told herself.

Tess's mind spun, reeling from the unexpected predicament she had stumbled into. Now, fleeing across the Caribbean, the aqua waves parting beneath the boat's bow—she stood alongside him, a man she knew nothing about. Suspicion gnawed at her, second guessing her decision. Maybe it was reckless, even dangerous—but there was no turning back now. One thing was obvious, she pressed her lips tight, she had no doubt he worked for the Belizean cartel. The term had been on the news—tales of organized syndicates heavy into narcotics, weapons, or whatever else drug people were involved in. Her heart raced at the idea.

The boat continued blazing through the waves as the ties to her top fluttered in the wind. Tess looked down at her flower print skirt. The hibiscus blooms rippled against her—oblivious to their role of island folklore. The idealistic legend had missed its mark today, she frowned. Tess brushed over the soft material with the tips of her fingers. *What have you gotten yourself into?*

The unspoken tension shattered as the outboard motor sputtered. The bow dipped and the behemoth wake swelled, threatening to flood over the back.

"Damn, not now!" Anthony's words broke through the hostile air. He looked down at the gauges and pulled at the throttle. Tess glanced at the motor. The high whir of the engine popped. She then looked over to Anthony. "Here, take the helm," he ordered.

Grabbing her hand, Anthony placed it on the wheel, then strode over to the engine compartment. Before she could protest, she found herself steering the vessel as it chugged laboriously ahead. She'd never steered a boat before and glanced down at the dash. The smooth mahogany finish was like polished marble in her grip. She found it exciting and considered that the expensive shellac was not the typical finish found on most boats owned by thieves. The notion crossed her mind that at least she had chosen a guy who was doing well at his work. Tess quickly scoffed at the idea.

"What's wrong?" she asked, turning to watch him. The wheel shifted and the back of the boat swung hard to the left.

"Keep your eyes in front of you!" he scolded.

She jerked the wheel back.

"Your buddy, Rolan, seems to have hit the intake line with one of those bullets meant for me," Anthony retorted.

Tess remembered the gunshots back on the yacht. "Is that a bad thing? I mean, will it still work?"

With his head tucked under the lid of the motor, Anthony muttered out loud, "Looks like we'll have to change our plans."

Tess arched her brow. Plans, were there actually plans ahead of her? "And what plans are those?" she inquired.

"Well, it doesn't matter at the moment," Anthony replied.

She watched him as he looked out over the aqua blue water, then swiftly lifted one of the cushions that lined the immaculate cruiser. Anthony took out a long metal bar with a small propeller-like object attached to the end.

"What is that?" she asked.

"In simple terms, it's a trolling motor. We can hook it up to the battery," he paused as he unwound the cables, "it should get us to shore."

The small motor looked incapable, even to a boating novice like herself. "Is that standard equipment? Or just drug dealer issue?"

He glared at her. "Does it matter?"

"No, I suppose not, but will it work?"

"Do you have a better idea?" he said.

Tess looked back, this time taking care not to twist the wheel. The engine spat and whirred as a cloud of smoke spewed. The white churned water from the propeller surged and the boat stopped.

"That's not good. We'll have to turn the motor off and let it cool down," Anthony said.

"What about Rolan's men?" she asked, looking through the hazy puff of smoke. Behind them all she saw was the blue water and the sun shimmering on the waves. No assailants were chasing them, at least not that she could see. She let out a deep sigh and the tension in her shoulders faded.

"We should be okay. We were making good headway before now," Anthony assured her.

He turned his attention back to the out-of-commissioned motor. She watched him, impressed by his indifference to their predicament and, that among other talents, such as dancing and smuggling, he also appeared to be mechanically inclined. His head disappeared into the motor cavity. A few moments later he emerged holding wires in his hands.

"This should get us to one of the islands not far from here."

"An island," her eyes widened, "like a deserted island?"

She didn't like the sound of that. Stranded with a drug smuggler was the last thing she wanted.

"Something like that, yes," he grinned. "The Caribbean is full of small uncharted islands. Rolan won't be looking for us there. They think we've gone inland by now anyway," he paused as he connected the last few wires. The electric motor twirled feverishly.

"It works!" Tess chimed.

"For now, at least," he glanced at her and then back to the trolling motor. "The current is going against us right now. We'll be lucky to make it to the island before the battery runs out."

"What then? How will we get back?" she asked, panicked.

He brushed past her and took control of the wheel. When she abandoned the *Charisa* and stepped onboard with Anthony, in her mind she believed he would take her back to her hotel, or at least back to the city for help. But now, with a broken boat and their destination pointed in the direction of an unknown island, Tess wondered if she would be going back to her hotel at all. What reason would he have to take her back to safety, to the authorities? A shiver crawled up her spine, and a queasy flutter churned in her stomach. Yes, why would he help her? The gravity of her situation pressed down on her like a capsized boat plummeting fast. She stepped back from the helm and bumped into the leather passenger seat. The adrenaline from their plight on board the *Charisa* was wearing off and she found her legs weakening. With the soft cushions pressed to the back of her knees, she sank onto the bench. Tess hadn't realized how exhausted she had become. Still, she wanted to know his intensions.

"You are planning on going back, aren't you?" Tess asked.

"Planning? It would seem that both of our plans have changed."

He stared at her and for a moment she lost herself in his mysterious and captivating eyes. Feeling the blood rushing to her cheeks, she looked away. She hadn't charted her next move far enough beyond her descent from the

Charisa, and the realization that she had stumbled into something more treacherous than a little revenge on her ex-boyfriend, hit her like a tidal wave. She was at the mercy of this man to take her back to her hotel, and right now, it didn't appear to be his priority.

"You can't keep me..." she paused, "I mean there will be people looking for me. The hotel will know I've gone missing. I'm sure they'll call the police and..."

"Do you think I give a damn about you and your hotel or who might miss you?" he said.

Startled by his tone, she stared at him, his back still facing her. Until now, the idea that he might kidnap her hadn't earnestly been a concern. Roger would wonder if he didn't see her around, wouldn't he? And Molly would be suspicious if she didn't get a text or a call and would certainly want the details describing the bliss of stealing the snorkel cruise away from Roger and his blonde tease.

The high pitch whir of the little propeller hummed feverously, but without the more powerful engine, the sleek craft moved sluggishly through the water. Her head throbbed. Too much had happened. Tess wanted to be back at her hotel and the safety of her room. She looked back over to Anthony—maybe she could reason with him.

"I won't say anything about the drugs, or the plane, or..." Tess pleaded.

"I'm not going to hurt you," Anthony interrupted, his voice softened, "you have my word."

"But what does that mean? Where are we going?" she asked.

He didn't answer. Instead, Tess noticed his cheeks flinch as his jaw tightened. She decided not to push his patience. She believed him when he said he wouldn't hurt her, but there were questions still to be answered. For now, though, she would wait. Once her feet were back on land, that's when she would reassess her options.

Tess eased back into the seat. Her predicament surreal, she looked out at the faint colors forming on the horizon—the afternoon sun would soon be setting. The seriousness of her situation weighed heavy on her mind, but one thing she knew for certain, she was grateful Anthony had helped her escape. Tess wondered about Rolan and Sergey, she shuddered as to what might have happened if Anthony had not shown up. Glancing up at him, she reflected on the temptress from last night, and the captivating dance that had drawn her to Anthony in the first place. Even then, Tess admitted, she had seen a good side to him; after all, he did help her trick Roger, and played the part of her made-up lover.

Her mind drifted as she remembered the touch of his skin against hers. Tess imagined her hand stroking his bronzed cheek and his five O'clock stubble passing roughly over her fingers. Chills ran down her arm. From the moment he jumped onboard the *Charisa*, it had been like a switch sending waves of lust throughout her body. He aroused her curiosity and had awoken her desires more than any other man had ever done before. No, she decided, he wasn't ruthless, but could she trust him with her life, she wondered.

The wind picked up and the waves jounced the sleek boat. Her leg slipped, scraping against the yellow case, the same package Rolan had fished out of the ocean. The sight of the box brought her back to reality and the dream-like adventure of sailing away with her rogue pirate diminished. Her situation stood clearly in front of her. *Get a grip, Tess. This is no place for you and the sooner you get away from him, the better off you'll be.*

***

TESS WATCHED Anthony closely. She chewed the inside of her lip, recognizing she needed a plan. She looked down at her brilliant-colored purse. The zipper had parted. Of course! Her eyes brightened. My cellphone! She could text Molly and get help. She glanced up at Anthony, his back still facing her. Tess stretched out her arm and reached for the woven bag, but it was tucked too far under the dash. She shifted her view between the pirate spoils and the pirate himself. Her mouth taut, she focused on her target and slipped her leg under the dash, inching her foot slowly over to the limp purse. Finally, her toes reached the bag, and she looped her foot through the thick strap. The handbag shifted. Tess froze, glancing up at Anthony, who thankfully hadn't noticed her movement as he continued navigating through the waves. She slid the purse over to her seat; glad the soft material hadn't made any noise sliding it undetected across the small deck. Her adrenaline pumped like a firehose through her veins and the beat of her heart drummed into her ears. The shoulder bag would be in plain view if he turned around, she cringed and stealthily reached inside hoping not to make any sudden movements. Her fingers rummaged silently through the bag.

"You've gotten quiet," Anthony said. "What are you scheming up now?" He looked over his shoulder.

Tess yanked her hand back to her lap. "Nothing—I...I mean like what? I...I'm just trying to take all of this in."

Her gaze dropped to the open purse, and she could see the edge of her smartphone sticking out. She looked from her purse back up to him. Too late, Anthony yanked the pouch away.

"Give that to me," he demanded. "After your episode on the yacht and bullets circling my head, I think I'd better make sure you don't have anything else in there to cause problems."

"Me, like I'm the one that's caused all the problems?" she fumed.

Tess lunged, grabbing at her purse. But Anthony jerked it away. Her wrist wove through the straps and twisted the material which dumped the contents, along with her phone, onto the deck. Anthony looked at the device and glanced over to her.

"Ah," he smile with his crooked grin, "planning to make a phone call, I suppose?"

"What if I were?" she taunted.

He knelt and picked up the phone then tucked it into his pants pocket. He quickly inspected the spilled contents and stuffed them back into the bag.

Tess held out her hand. "I'll take my purse, thank you!"

Anthony chuckled and waved his finger at her. "I think it's best if I hold on to this for now. No telling what ideas you might have."

She glared at him. The nerve he had, telling her what to do. Hot tears flooded the corners of her eyes.

"What about you? You're the one stealing drugs from," she paused, and turned away, "well, from Rolan."

"Ah, yes...," he said, tucking her purse under the dash, "and what exactly is your relationship with the duo Russian team?"

"My relationship?" she spun around. "What makes you think I have any relations with those two?"

She glanced at him. Of course, looking back she chided herself for not realizing things were not as they seemed. Getting on the yacht wasn't the best decision, she knew that now. She had let her desire for vengeance and her double-crossing of Roger blind her to the obvious. She frowned, Rolan and Sergey, the only two attendants on board, Tess scoffed and shook her head, twisting her lips at the flashback. The way Rolan had greeted her, how he had looked at her and the expensive watch that slipped from his cuff—they were all signs. She had ignored the warnings, or rather, she didn't want to see the truth, just like she ignored the mass of red flags with Roger. Her guilt sank deep into her stomach.

"I should have known," she murmured, not realizing the words came out.

"So why were you there?" he asked, his face hardened, waiting for an answer.

"I...I don't know. I guess I just didn't want Roger to get the best of me."

She again glanced down at the detailed dash. The honey-colored wood with dark accents gleamed on the expensive looking boat. Probably stolen, she guessed.

"Tell me about this Roger, have you known him long?" Anthony asked.

"Long enough to want to forget him," she said, glancing up at Anthony. There was a flicker of surprise in his eyes. His probing seemed more like a confirmation rather than a question. She sensed he was keeping something from her. "What's with all of the questions? Why do you want to know?"

Shrugging, Anthony turned back towards the bow. "No reason. Just wondered how it was that you were on that boat with Rolan and his cousin, that's all. In my line of work, you can't be too careful. It's not often that I come across someone tagging along, as you say, innocently, at a drop zone."

"Cousin? You mean Sergey and Rolan are related? And I certainly didn't know it was a drop zone boat tour. Besides, all I wanted to do was to get even with my ex, that's all." Tess sank deeper into her chair.

"Get even? How did you get on that boat?"

"Ah, well, that was Roger's idea, the boat ride, that is."

"Roger?" Anthony said.

"Back home we were dating, well that was up until a few days ago when he decided to break up with me."

"Hmm, why did he break up with you?" Anthony cleared his throat. "I mean, you're an attractive woman, why would this...," his lips curled as he continued, "this Roger guy want to dump you?"

Tess scowled. "Thanks! That's kind of harsh," she paused, "and shallow, don't you think? Of course, a guy like you wouldn't have any idea about..."

"What do you mean *a guy like me*? Like what?" he interrupted her.

"Well, I doubt you've ever taken the time to be in a relationship, that's all."

"Ah, and now you think you know all about me?" Anthony jeered.

"I mean, you were all over that…that hip swinging flirt." Tess fired back.

She watched his jaw tighten and his gaze harden. Tess was certain she had hit a nerve.

"Hip swinging flirt?" he repeated with flared nostrils. "And you are an expert on people now? Now that your Roger has dumped you for another woman you think you're entitled to lay judgement on others?"

"Hey, I didn't say he left me for another woman, and besides, you certainly seem to know how to fondle your way around the dance floor!" she scoffed. Tess could feel her cheeks burning. Frustrated, she looked away. Her jaw tensed thinking about Anthony with that shapely woman. But Anthony erupted in laughter, and she turned, glaring at him. "Oh, it's funny? You practically made love to that woman, and in front of her boyfriend!"

"What woman?" he asked.

"*What woman*? You had your hands all over her and now you don't even remember her? You know the one, that brunette. I mean…," Tess pressed her lips together, "you two didn't seem to care who was watching."

"If that's what you consider making love," he paused, "no wonder your Roger, or whatever his name is, dumped you."

"Oh!" she fumed.

"Since you seem to know all of the details, I'd say you were enjoying it. Do you always like to watch, Miss Martin?" Anthony taunted.

"Stop! How do you know my last name?"

"Every dutiful boyfriend should know his own girlfriend's name, don't you think?"

He had left her with no argument. She did beg him to play the part last night and it had worked, together they had made Roger jealous. A flash of the two of them, Anthony's thigh pressed up against hers, flickered through her mind. Her face flushed, tantalized by the memory, but quickly she pushed her feelings aside.

"Ok, yes! I appreciate that you stepped in and…and…" she stuttered.

"And played the part of your boyfriend so that you could make Roger what's-his-name jealous? It must have been painful seeing him with his blonde girlfriend so soon after being dumped," Anthony jested.

"Please stop saying that word!"

"And what word are you referring to?" Anthony countered, arching his brow.

Tess grumbled, clenching her fists. "He didn't dump me...we just broke up, that's all," she paused and looked over at him. "Why did you do that?"

"Do what?" he asked.

"Pretend to be with me."

Anthony smiled and sized her up. "How could I refuse? A beautiful tourist grips me by the arm and asks me to make love to her?"

"I didn't ask you to...," she hesitated and wondered for a moment what Roger must have thought. First, the shock of seeing her at a bar in Belize and, secondly, a charming local draped over her arm. Tess glanced up at Anthony. "Oh God...I told him about the bed."

"Yes, as I recall," he toyed, "now let's see, how did you describe it?" Anthony paused intentionally. "Oh yes, it was a *huge* bed."

Tess hung her head. "I've got to quit drinking those fruity drinks!"

Anthony chuckled.

"Stop, it's not funny," she said.

"I would agree those Belizean Specials may have gotten the best of you. You were rather..."

"I was what? What happened last night?" she asked, searching his face.

His eyes brightened and his gaze drifted over her. Running her hands across the loose ties of her top, Tess closed the view to her cleavage. Her heartbeat skipped and her mind drifted back to this morning and her disheveled hotel room. All she had on when she woke up was her bra and panties. Her mind raced. The details of last night were cloudy at best. She remembered seeing Roger, and somehow Anthony was there. Tess stared up at him. She lost herself in his dimples that formed along his face and down to his perfect, juicy lips. A flicker of last night's events flashed through her mind, and she remembered the soft brush of his lips over her mouth. Tess groaned. Was she so drunk that she had propositioned the one man in the entire resort who had shamelessly thrown himself at vulnerable women? She felt the blood drain from her face.

"We didn't," she looked at him, her gaze sincere, "well, you know."

His eyes glistened. "Are you asking me to kiss and tell?" Anthony asked.

"Now you're teasing me," she said.

"No," he paused and stared out across the bow, "we didn't."

Tess sighed heavily.

"Well, I'm glad to see you're so relieved," he said.

Before she could say anything more, he pointed ahead of them.

"There! Do you see that land about a quarter of a mile out?"

Tess squinted seeing the small landscape ahead. "That doesn't look very populated," she said.

Anthony aimed the boat towards the small blurb out across the water. The tiny electric propeller whirred noisily as the boat turned.

"Will it make it? It doesn't sound very promising," she said.

"Here, take the wheel, and keep it straight."

Tess wanted to protest but Anthony swiftly scrambled to the back of the boat, lifting the engine cover. With an arched brow, Tess twisted her lips. The little motor, with its undersized blades, looked too small for their boat. Just then it squealed its last breath and the over-worked prop stopped.

"Damn!" Anthony groaned.

Her eyes widened. "What? Are we stranded?"

"Well, that's it. We'll just have to hope we're in the right current."

"Right current?" Her heart raced. "What does that mean?"

"Don't worry," he said, "we pirates know how to work the sea."

Gazing across the water, the small land mass quickly came into view. Tess could see palm trees dotted along the shoreline. A breeze wisped gently over them carrying the rich scent of the nearby island. She looked at the beauty surrounding her—the aqua water and the reddish-orange hues glowing on the horizon. Tall palm trees swayed in the distance, accentuated by the sky's vibrant tropical colors. Ironic, she mused, the scenery could easily have been on a postcard—a Caribbean vacation getaway.

***

SOON, THEY neared the island. Tess looked down through the clear water. The sandbar extended far from the beach and ahead the weathered ruins of an old dock rose from the waves. She scanned the coastline for signs of hotels and safety but, to her dismay, there were no cabanas or flickering torches. No chaise lounges or people playing along the seashore, only the decaying remnants of the old pier leading up to the isolated beach. Far from civilization, and on a deserted island with a drug smuggler, her hopes faded. Shivers cascaded down her arms as a chilling breeze of reality fell over her.

Chapter Eleven

Island Refuge

ALONE IN THE CARIBBEAN WITH a man she hardly knew, Tess watched as Anthony stepped into the shallow seawater. He skillfully pulled the out-of-commission boat up to the shore, tethering the bow to an old piling buried in the sand. The amber color in the sky had dulled, and the sun hung low on the horizon. Nightfall would arrive within the hour, and the chances of getting back to her hotel anytime soon were slipping away.

Tess glanced around at her surroundings, her gaze shifting to Anthony. The evening hue glistened on his bronzed skin, she stared at him as perspiration beaded across his lips. He didn't look like a drug runner, or at least she didn't think so. His shoulders were broad, and his hands were strong—she had noticed his steady grip when he helped her from the *Charisa*. The gesture had taken her by surprise; it felt confident, like a gentleman's gesture rather than a drug smuggling criminal's act. Not that she had much experience comparing the two professions, she mused. There was something else, deeper within him—his eyes held a sense of honesty and kindness in them.

Anthony was different, not like Rolan or Sergey. Those two were definitely not who they said they were. Just the thought of the callous marauders caused her eyes to narrow and her mouth to harden. In the wake of the chaos on the boat deck, Tess realized without a doubt that both Rolan and Sergey were part of something far beyond her understanding. Rubbing her neck, Tess ran her hand down her throat, swallowing hard. She recalled Sergey's ruthlessness as he grabbed her from behind. If Anthony had not shown up—Tess shuddered at the thought. Glancing over the bow, she watched him. Anthony's back was still turned towards her. A mild, evening breeze swept across the water lifting strands of her auburn hair that lightly whipped across her face. She tucked the loose curls behind her ear and continued studying him.

Anthony turned, rummaging through the rear compartments. His half-unbuttoned linen shirt rippled in the wind. She couldn't help but wonder about him and how it was that, once again, this rogue drug dealer—or whoever he was—had rescued her, perhaps even saved her. That alone, she thought, defied her definition of outlaw.

The remains of a neglected dock lay in ruin—splintered and scattered across the shoreline. Barefoot she jumped out of the boat. With each step, the water filtered away, as the white sand glided, like smooth, silk sheets under her toes. The sand, still warm from the sun, soothed her feet and she was glad to be on land once more—even if it was in the middle of nowhere.

It had taken what seemed like hours to ride the current to the island. She sized up the narrow coastline. Besides the scattered forgotten dock, a few scraggly palm trees dotted along the dense brush just beyond the beach. Nature's call had been triggered by the jouncing of the boat, and Tess scanned the area in hopes of a bathroom.

"Uh…I suppose it would be too presumptuous to think there are any restrooms here, right?" she asked, wrinkling her nose at the odds.

"There's an old outhouse," he pointed off to the right, "but you might be better off to use the more natural setting behind those palms next to it," he gestured to a small hedge of bushes. "Less chance of snakes."

"Snakes!" she gulped. "Out here?"

Anthony laughed, "They are more afraid of you than you are of them, I assure you. But they do like to coil themselves up during the evening and that old privy surrounded by those ferns just might be a good resting ground for them."

Tiptoeing, Tess navigated her way in the direction Anthony had pointed. Brushing back some oversized palms, she stepped over thick, waxy branches that covered the faint outline of a path, or at least where one had been once upon a neglected century ago. After a short jaunt up the narrow trail, she arrived at what looked like an old wooden shack covered in vines. An over-sized cobweb hung across the dark, hollow opening where a window had once been. She shook her head at the uninviting shanty.

"Yeah, forget that," she muttered.

Tess glanced around and took another look back towards the water. She could just make out the beach and the top of Anthony's head. Convinced the crude foliage concealed her, she stepped into the brush and settled on what looked like a safe enough location. Rustling sounded from the trees behind her. Visions of snakes crawling about made the hair on her neck stiffen and her heartbeat pounded. Quickly, she finished her business and rushed as fast as she could down the path leading back to the beach.

Stampeding like an out-of-control elephant, Tess crashed through the jungle. Finally, she burst through the brush, her crazed momentum stopped just short of colliding with Anthony, unaware that he was there. The commotion must have taken him by surprise, too, because she noticed his eyes—wide like a plate of oysters and his body rigid, as if ready for battle. For a brief moment, he shifted his gaze beyond her, then back, all the time sporting a quizzical arched brow. Chuckling under his breath, the tenseness in his jaw subsided as he turned back to the boat.

Now, with a sense of safety on the beach, her racing pulse gradually calmed. She swiped her hands across her somewhat disheveled clothes—just in case she had picked up any crawling creatures from the overgrown path. Tess plucked a few leaves out of her hair, regaining her composure as she casually walked the remainder of the way to the shoreline. Looking beyond the scattered pilings, Tess noticed a dark, large tower nestled amongst the overgrowth.

"What is that building over there?" she asked, pointing.

Anthony looked up then resumed his work with the engine. "It's an old lighthouse."

"It seems odd to have a lighthouse out in the middle of nowhere."

"The military used this place years ago," he grunted as he investigated the engine compartment.

"Military out here? Why?" she asked.

"Well, if you must know, they used it to keep an eye on...," he paused and looked up at her, "let's just say cargo."

"You mean drugs, don't you?" she said, placing her hands on her hips.

"You can relax. They've abandoned this place a long time ago. Except for a few noisy monkeys and an old airstrip, there's nothing else here."

"It seems like they may have left too soon," she grumbled.

Tess threw a glance his way, expecting to provoke a reaction. But he remained engrossed in the engine, oblivious to her sarcasm. She grew tired of watching him work on the motor, and with his attention distracted, she decided to explore the beach, an inviting backdrop to weigh her next move.

An overturned palm tree lay ahead of her. She walked over and wiped the loose sand off before sitting. It was only the second day of her whirlwind vacation. No one would really know she was missing. Roger certainly wouldn't care about her, not while he had his little platinum-haired diva, she scowled. And Molly would probably think she'd spent the night with the cabana boy or something.

"Nope, just alone with some stranger running drugs through the Caribbean and stranded on a deserted island. Nothing unusual about that!" she muttered.

Like the old dock boards scattered across the beach, so was her mind. She wasn't sure how she should feel about Anthony—if it was good or bad being alone with him. On one hand, she rationalized, he had rescued her, but on the other hand, she paused. *What other hand?* She covered her face and shook her head. *A rational person would know that this is crazy! Tess, get it together,* she scolded herself.

Looking up, Tess wiped back tears that formed in the corner of her eyes. The stars shone faintly as the sun began to set on the horizon. A tiny sand shrimp tickled her toe, and she quickly swung her feet up onto the log. Tess looked down at the little creature, cradling her knees safely out of its reach. She tucked her legs further under her chin. The air was warm, and the sound of the waves echoed as they lapped onto the beach. This place, she sighed, had a way of letting you forget reality. She shifted her gaze and watched as Anthony tossed the rag aside. He was looking for something and rummaged through the compartments only to slam one shut and then another.

"Damn!" he said.

"What are you looking for?" she yelled.

"If I had something to plug the hole, I could wrap the pipe and nurse the engine back to the mainland."

"Why don't you use a piece of wood or something?" she asked.

"It wouldn't hold; needs to be flexible."

She nodded. A moment later she sprang to her feet. Trotting over to the boat, she climbed on board. "I think I have something, but you'll have to give me my purse."

He looked at the bag shoved under the dash and glanced back at her. "Ah, besides a closet ju-jitsu, now you're a marine mechanic?"

She shot him an unimpressed glance and pierced her lips tight. "Well, I don't see that you have many options," she said.

"Can I count on it not being any sort of weapon?" he mocked, stepping aside.

She laughed quietly then hopped through the windshield bypass and stood next to the helm. "No guarantees, but you can look for yourself."

Anthony retrieved the handbag. Tess eagerly took it from him and unzipped the inside pouch. Rummaging through the bottom of her purse, she pulled out an unopened package of gum. She had almost forgotten about her last-minute purchase at the little shop earlier that morning. Anthony raised his brow.

"What?" she smiled, "I didn't have toothpaste and figured this would come in handy."

Tess ripped open the wrap and handed him a piece. It was an awkward moment while they vigorously chewed the gum. She finished first and spit the gooey glob into her hand, holding it out. Anthony took the gum from his own mouth and wrapped it with hers. The sticky mess stuck to her fingers and then to his.

"This just might do the trick," he said.

Anthony went back to the engine. Encouraged, Tess watched him work with the glue-like mass. She wasn't sure but it looked like he stuffed it into the hole and then took a rag and wrapped the pipe. He walked back to where she stood and turned the key. A couple of grinds and the engine turned over. It sputtered but continued to idle. Tess glanced at him, grinning.

"Well done," he nodded.

She beamed and looked out across the scenery before her. Part of her was sad they would be leaving this deserted place. Given any other circumstance she would have wanted to be here, to sneak away with a lover.

Turning, she watched Anthony as he placed the cover back over the engine. Her eyes roved over his body, and she reminisced how he had caressed her on the dance floor just the night before—his hands gliding over her skin. The images ended as Anthony turned off the motor. The floodgate of reality rushed through her mind and a dreaded pit of hopelessness sank in her gut.

"Aren't we going to go back?" she asked.

"Not tonight. We'll have to wait for the tide. We'll only be able to idle the motor and we'll need the current to help push us in."

"But we need to get back, to the hotel," she looked around, "it can't be safe out here. What if Rolan…"

"Relax. Rolan and his men won't be looking for us in the dark and," his eyes dropped over her, "you don't really have any other choice, do you?"

She knew he was right. He was her only option at the moment. Besides, she didn't even know where they were. Tess slumped into the seat.

"We're going to sleep on the island?" she asked.

"No. It would be best if we slept in the boat," he grinned and pointed to the trees, "you might end up with an unwanted bedpartner if we don't."

The sun had set, and the dusk light cast shadows along the beach. She gazed along the shoreline and noticed a dark, animal-like creature scurry up one of the palm trees.

"What are they?" she asked.

"Island monkeys, mostly known for their loud voice, but they have been known to be aggressive, especially during the mating season."

Tess stared in the direction of the little critters; her eyebrows arched. She wasn't sure if he had told her this to keep her from running away or if the hairy beasts might actually be vicious.

"Oh. Is it mating season?" She looked over at him, daring him to answer.

His eyes met hers. "Yes," he said.

An awkward silence fell over them. The moonlight glowed across his face, and flecks of perspiration dotted along his lips. A surge of warmth filled her, and her thighs tingled. Anthony's voice interrupted the moment.

"I'll sleep on the bow," he gestured, "you'll find the seats make quite the comfortable bed."

"Oh," she said, brushing her hand over the pillowed cushions. "Of course."

***

THE CLEAR sky filled with stars that cast a shimmering light across the water. Wadding up her purse, Tess tucked it under her head. The tanning oil, shoes and crumpled clothes poked into her skin. She tucked her knees close and wrapped them with her skirt, it comforted her. The evening had been surreal. Anthony lay only a few steps away, a stranger, yet she felt a connection with him. She found herself in deep thought. For the first time in what seemed like forever, a sense of excitement and relief swept over her. And for now, at least for the time being, the stress of her life lifted. But her sense of peace quickly faded, and she knew this lifestyle would never be her reality. It was a fantasy that couldn't last.

It would be absurd to think of herself with him. Her lips twisted, frowning. No, what I need is not here, the sooner I get back, the better. *But how?* she asked herself. Her thoughts turned to her cellphone. If she could get to it, now would be the opportunity to send Molly a message. But what would she say? Would she call for help to be rescued from this man who sparked her inner emotions? Conflicted, the moments passed. Slowly she sat up and looked over where Anthony lay. His arms folded behind his head as he leaned against the windshield facing out to the beach. The pocket with her cell phone bulged open and Tess could see its silvery case shimmering in the moonlight. Perhaps she could reach it without him knowing. Doubtful, she conceded. Most-likely, she imagined, he slept with one eye open. Besides, maybe she wasn't sure she wanted to be rescued, not yet.

It wouldn't have to be her forever life, but there was something about this stranger. He had intrigued her sense of adventure. Looking up at the star-lit sky, she wondered what kind of life he really lived. Her focus shifted to the box pulled from the water. Anthony stirred. Quickly, Tess sank back down into the cushions and again looked up at the stars. Her mind drifted as she wondered about the stowed away package and the rogue man that saved her. *Who are you?* she said to herself.

Overwhelmed with exhaustion and her eyelids heavy, tonight, she decided, she would not dwell on it any longer. Tomorrow, as she gazed over to the bow, everything would become clearer. Tess took a deep breath, rolled onto her side, and closed her eyes.

Chapter Twelve

The Village

TESS STIRRED. THE MORNING SUN beamed its warm rays across her face as she nuzzled further into her makeshift pillow. The distant echoes of waves lapped against the boat. With eyes closed, her mind wandered. She dreamt of Anthony beside her—his alluring dark eyes pulling her in. She traced the contours of his lips, her fingertips brushing over the stubble of his chin. His face leaned close to hers. Her senses ignited as his hot breath caressed her skin.

Aroused, she moaned at his touch. A hand patted her on the head and a pungent smell filled her nose. In an instant, the desires of her dream shattered, her eyes sprung open. Tess screamed. The wrinkled face of a curious monkey stared back at her. She sat up, wiping her cheek where the hairy baboon had licked. Laughter echoed from the beach. Wide awake, Tess turned, glaring at Anthony who doubled over in dubious laughter. The ape screeched as it scampered across the jumbled boards. Leaping onto the sand, the creature disappeared into the trees.

"Very funny!" she said.

The beast's stench lingered. Tess shuddered as the rickety remains of the dock bumped the sides of the boat. She looked out at the white sands stretching down the shoreline, a slight lace of foam rippled onto the beach. As the tide came in, Anthony secured the boat closer to the shore. The surprised creature, with its curiosity piqued, had not strayed far from the sandy shore to reach the boat. Tess's gaze surveyed the area, making sure no other beasts lurked nearby. She marveled at the early dawn, watching the island's silhouette emerge against the brightening sky. Anthony's laughter dwindled into a stifled chuckle as he approached the boat. In his arms, he carried an array of fruit. Tess cast an unimpressed scowl towards him.

"Good morning. Care for some breakfast?" he gestured.

Still shaken by the unwanted creature's touch, she peered over Anthony's shoulder—her eyes alert in case the hairy beast might return. But the sweet smell of the fresh mangos floated through the morning air and her stomach betrayed her with low rumbles. Giving up her guard, she looked over the delicious crop. Creases of laughter still lingered on Anthony's face. Before she could protest, he handed her the delicacy. Again, her stomach grumbled. She hadn't eaten since yesterday, and only a couple of bites on the *Charisa*. The meager snack had worn off hours ago. She took a piece of fruit and held it to her nose. Tess breathed in its sweet flavor.

"I don't think I've ever smelled anything so fresh!" her eyes glistened. Biting into its vibrant orange-red flesh, the satisfying juices tingled across her tongue. Licking her lips, Tess savored the nectar. "Mmm, this is delicious."

Tess's gaze lifted to Anthony. His eyes sparkled like sun-kissed dewdrops in the morning light. The remnants of her anger ebbed away, and she put the episode of the smelly ape aside. The morning sun glowed across the hillside filtering through the palm trees. Like a scene from a travel brochure, the jungle stirred brilliantly to life. Birds filled the air with their calls and the vibrant shades of flowers, concealed by last night's dusk, now dotted the tree line with vivid hues. It was like nothing she had seen before, truly, a tropical paradise. More curious eyes looked out from the trees.

"I doubt they've seen many people," she pointed.

The smaller of the monkeys scurried down the trunk. The larger one displayed its disapproval, chanting until the littlest baboon climbed back to the branch. The young ape settled next to the bigger one which kept an eye on her and Anthony—foreign beach intruders trespassing onto their exclusive oasis.

"We'd better get going while the mainland's shore is still sleepy." Anthony said, untying the boat.

"No, wait! I'll only be a moment," she said.

"Suit yourself, but you might want to make it quick."

She looked in the direction of the dilapidated bathroom. There were fewer palm trees near the old shanty which she decided would mean less chance of a curious monkey. That gave her some relief as she looked down at the shoreline where a group of the little beasts had gathered. A monkey scurried up the base of a tree, rejoining its mate. At least they seemed afraid and wouldn't bother her, she hoped. Her earlier encounter had no doubt awakened the rest of the jungle and now, it seemed, all eyes were on her.

"If they'll just keep their distance, I'll keep mine," she muttered.

The trail was covered with more foliage than she remembered from last night. A cold, moist vine startled her as it caught onto her sandal and wound itself around her ankle. She reached down and untangled her foot. Leaves rustled beside her, and she glimpsed a fleeting shadow moving nearby. She gasped but the creature disappeared under the oversized fern before she could get a good look. Anthony's warning about snakes played over in her mind. The hair on her neck stood rigid as she glanced around. This would be far enough, no sense risking a snake bite by going any further, she thought.

Relieved, she started back down to the boat and brushed back a palm leaf hanging low along the trail. Her hand wisped across a cold, thick, scaly lump. She quickly let go of the branch. The waxy frond flung back into her face and a bug-eyed lizard, its body stretching nearly a foot, fell at her feet. It landed with a thud. Its green molted form wriggled past her and disappeared into the foliage slithering its tail behind. She jumped, screaming. With her adrenalin charged, Tess bolted straight for the shore. In a blind reckless panic, she pushed past the thick underbrush and unknowingly stepped off the path. Branches—dense with leaves and dangling vines, surrounded her. Fear and anxiety raced through her mind filling her head with visions of the yellow-eyed, tongue gushing critter chasing after her.

Tess headed the direction she hoped would lead back to the beach. Through an opening in the thicket, she could see Anthony a short distance down the hill next to the boat. She dashed down the hillside, her legs running as fast as they would go. Her arms stretched out in front of her dodging through the jungle brambles.

She was careening too fast down the slope. A thin stand of trees blocked her path. With her hands held out in front of her, she blazed through the saplings, dodging past their fronds. She could still see Anthony a short distance ahead as she scrambled between the leafy branches. Tess tried calling out, but a thick, sticky web clung across her face and before she could wipe it away, she partially inhaled it. The web lodged in her throat. She choked and gasped, groping at the stringy web that still stuck to her mouth and draped across her lips. Imagining herself laden with over-sized tarantulas crawling up her skirt, her adrenaline shot through her veins. It was more than she could bear. Tess screamed as loud as her lungs would allow.

With new energy, she stretched her legs into a full panicked run. The closer she got to the beach the more her screams suppressed into muffled hollers. Her leaps turned into hysterical stamping as she wiped her hands feverishly across her body, swiping away any possible waxy-legged beastie from her clothes. Tess wiggled and hopped with one last shuddering dance pulling the sticky spiderweb from her mouth and hair.

Making her way closer to the shore, she could see Anthony, who jumped into action, tossing the nautical rope onto the piling, and pulling a gun from his waist. His jawline tensed as he looked past her, ready to take on the imminent danger. Allowing herself one more uncontrollable flutter, which included the stamping of her feet and another wild brushing across her sundress, Tess pulled more of the stuck-on spiderweb from her lips. The furrowed lines on Anthony's brow softened and creases formed at the corner of his eyes. His protective readiness gave way to loud boisterous laughter as he put the gun back in its place. Embarrassed, Tess jumped into the boat, flinging herself into the seat. Anthony ran his hand over his chin and chuckled.

"It's not funny!" she glared.

He looked over at her. His eyes widened. "Hold still!"

"What? What is it?" she panicked.

She jumped up looking down at her shoulder. Clinging to her hibiscus print dress, a giant spider reached out its spindled leg as it crawled closer to her neck. She shrieked and jiggled, again uncontrolled. Anthony flicked his hand and knocked the critter away.

"It's gone!" he said.

Her breaths came in quick, shallow gasps. Trembling all over, she watched the eight-legged beast as it landed on the craggy dock and scampered up the pier. Wrapping her arms around herself, she shuddered. It was more than she could bear, the furry ape, the sloth-like reptile that flung from the branch, and now the gangly legged creature. She looked up at Anthony and burst into tears.

"I want to go home," she sobbed. "I don't want to be here anymore. I shouldn't have come to Belize, to the hotel—the cruise. I should have stayed home. Roger...," she paused hiccupping, "he's such a jerk."

Her chin quivered as tears slid down her cheek. Tess looked at Anthony. His dimples pressed deep into his face, and she could see his expression soften.

He held her gaze then reached out and pulled her close to him. Tess didn't hold back. She sobbed uncontrollably. With her arms to her sides and her face buried against his chest, she let herself cry. Anthony stroked her hair and wrapped his arms around her. The bristles of his unshaven cheek and the musk scent of his skin pressed against her. His rogue, jungle cologne filled her senses. In his arms, the worries of the island disappeared, and she could feel his heart pulsating as he held her close. His lips brushed softly next to her ear and his deep voice whispered sending waves of desire throughout her body.

"You'll be okay—I won't let anything happen to you," he said softly.

Her tears slid down onto his shirt. She lifted her head, gazing into his eyes, and in that moment, he leaned in, covering her lips with his. It was as if time stood still and the chaos of her ordeal had ended, a moment of escape. She gave in to his kiss, pressing her mouth hard to his. Her thighs tingled at the raw taste of his sweet lips and the firmness of his mouth covering hers. Anthony's hands caressed her body. Their mouths parted and his tongue explored over hers. Passion boiled through her veins as her fears melted in his embrace. She leaned into him, desire murmuring from her throat. Then, just as suddenly as the passion had swept over them, Anthony abruptly pulled away.

"I'm sorry, I shouldn't have done that," he said.

Spinning around, he grabbed the rope from the pier and shoved the bow away from the beach. The boat bobbed in the surf as Anthony stood at the helm and turned the key. The low sputtering idle of the engine sounded.

"We can run it at half speed. With the help of the current, we should be able to make it," he said, avoiding eye contact.

With eyes wide, she stood next to the helm and looked over at him. He stared out towards the water. Her cheeks burned red, realizing how foolish she had been. Of course, she rationalized, what was she thinking? Did she really think that Anthony would run away with her? She shook her head. What kind of life could they have, traipsing through jungles running from authorities, from Rolan. The sound of the engine hummed louder, and Anthony pushed the throttle part way. Without uttering a single word, Tess gripped the wooden dashboard. Her eyes focused on the dawning sunrise, and she put her foolish notions aside.

***

BEFORE LONG, the mainland beach lay ahead of them. Other than the low rumble of the compromised engine, the ride had been uneventful—neither had spoken of the kiss. Soon her nightmare would be over; she would find the authorities, tell them about Rolan and Sergey and get back to her hotel. Then, she would see about changing her airplane ticket and leave her tropical vacation disaster earlier than planned. The sooner she put this place behind her, the better off she would be.

In the distance, Tess could see the faint dots of what she guessed were hotels along the beach. Anthony directed the boat away from the crowded resorts until they came to a narrow passage. It didn't bother her that they would land in secret. She wanted Rolan and Sergey to pay for their part, but Tess looked over at Anthony, his gaze intent on the river channel ahead, she didn't want Anthony mixed up with the police. She had decided she would tell the authorities that Anthony had seen the struggle onboard the *Charisa* and stopped to help her. Of course, she wouldn't mention the package of contraband, at least not for now.

The entrance to the channel narrowed and the jungle thickened around them with sweeping branches and waxy palm leaves that hung low, just above the water. She held out her hand and ducked, avoiding the dense foliage as the boat made its way upstream. As the low hanging fronds swept over them, she remembered seeing a map of Belize, compliments of the airline. The thematic foldout, with highlighted illustrations of natural landmarks and recreational routes, had shown several river channels that twisted their way deep inland. The narrow passage, she assumed, must be one of those waterways.

The morning air was still, and the thick jungle brush muffled the sounds of the motor. Only the slight hum of the engine and the slow sloshing of the waves echoed around them. Anthony pulled back the throttle lever and the boat crept even more silently as they made their way upstream. The thick, sweet fragrance of tropical greenery, with the undertone of enriched earth, lay heavy in the humid air. The further inland they went, the sweeter and thicker the landscape became. It was as if the jungle were swallowing them whole with a breath mint in its cheek.

"Where does this go?" she asked, breaking their silence.

His eyes looked straight ahead. "There's a village not far from here."

His voice sounded hollow, no longer the low tone of assurance he had whispered to her on the island. She furrowed her brow. Tess was certain by his indifference that he had put their kiss out of his mind. *Of course, what did I expect? A man like Tony...*she bit her lip and looked up as if he might have heard her thoughts. *Tony,* she liked the shortened name.

Holding back the overhang of thick palms, Anthony turned the boat into the overgrowth along the bank. The cruiser glided through. Tess continued to watch him as he shut off the engine, coasting onto the muddy shore. The leaves along the bank encompassed the boat, obscuring it from view should anyone pass along the waterway. Anthony stepped out onto the bow and leaped to the bank. He tied the rope around the base of a tree that angled over the water. Glancing around the area, he turned towards her.

"We're here," he said.

"Where is 'here'? Are we going back to the hotel?" she asked.

She stared at him and waited for an answer. But instead, his face hardened, and he brushed past her. Her cheeks burned hot. Tess grabbed her purse and scrambled from the boat looking through the dense leaves. Ahead, she could see a faint pathway leading into the brush. Traipsing once more through the creature-infested jungle made her eyes widen.

"Where are you going?" she insisted. Still, he ignored her. "I won't go another step until you tell me where you are taking me," she said, slinging her bag over her shoulder and crossing her arms.

"Suit yourself," Anthony retorted, continuing on.

She glanced at the unfamiliar surroundings and mulled over her options. Everything looked the same. Without the sun overhead she had lost her bearing and didn't know which direction they faced. On the boat, she knew they had traveled north, away from her hotel. Adrenaline raced up her arm and she arched her brow. She could run from him now that she was on the mainland. But just as quickly as her blood surged, her shoulders slumped back to reality. Here, among the thick brush, she had no idea where she was or which way to go. Tess turned around, full circle. Visions of freedom dissipated. It would be useless to pretend she could find her own way back.

"*Urrr*...let me put my shoes on," she grumbled.

Tess reached into her purse and removed the dainty sandals she'd purchased for her cruise. The straps were thin with a wider band of leather for her toe and the other two straps stylishly wrapped around the ankles. On the beach, going barefoot had been okay. But walking through the jungle, she found there were more prickly things to look out for. She brushed away a twig sticking to her heel, then situated her woven bag over her shoulder. With a defeated sigh, and her feet protected as best as she could, she pressed her lips firmly and followed after him.

Along the beach, the sun shone out across the ocean making the views bright and warm. But here, in the cover of the jungle, the morning light sparsely shone under the canopy of leaves and the air was more stagnant. The tips of the leaves brushed against her bare legs. Determined to avoid another wispy web she extended her hand, pushing aside the fronds. She decided to pay closer attention to the ground and carefully navigate around the vines that lay across the path. Anthony's strides were long. Tess quickened her steps to keep up.

The shrill pitch of a bird startled her. Tess looked up into the trees. Sitting high up on a branch was a big, colorful bird. Its large beak overbalanced its small, black body covered in brilliant orange and black feathers. The vivid colors stood out among the green jungle background and its round glassy eyes watched them.

"Is that a Toucan?" she said.

Anthony didn't answer. Tess continued on as another flock of colorful birds suddenly fluttered high into the branches. She found herself engrossed, watching their kaleidoscope of colors flying through the trees. She had never seen such dazzling red, orange, and yellow plumes before. Their long sweeping tail feathers disappeared into the trees. Tess could hear their chirps echoing, most likely broadcasting her and Anthony's arrival.

Finally, the trail opened up. A small hut sat at the edge of the clearing where a thin faced man sat on the porch. His neck stiffened and the curious man watched her and Anthony closely. Within moments he jumped down and pointed a gun towards them.

"Anthony? That you, mon?" the man asked, squinting.

"It's me," Anthony replied.

"What the hell, mon? Where you been?" His brows arched as he shook Anthony's hand. The man's smile faded, and his eyes darted quizzically over to Tess and back to Anthony. "What she doing here?" he asked.

"It's a long story," Anthony said, dryly.

"What 'da hell, Anthony, 'dis not what we planned for! You were supposed to get 'de package. Dat is all, mon!"

"Tell me about it, I didn't want her here anymore than you!" Anthony said.

Tess glared at the stranger, then back to Anthony. "Could you please stop talking about me as if I'm not standing right here?" Tess put her hands on her hips, glaring at the man. "And who the hell are you anyway?" Her gaze shifted to Anthony. "When are you going to tell me what is going on?"

Any earlier romantic ideals she had about Anthony were gone now. It was as if the kiss on the boat had never happened. Her face flushed with anger as she realized she had allowed the tropical surroundings to influence her, giving in to her raw desire. Biting her lip, Tess shook her head, disappointed in her lack of self-control and yet another foolish mistake. It was obvious that Anthony didn't care about her. And he certainly didn't see himself running away with her, as she had let herself believe. No, all he cared about was his precious package, his drugs. To him, she gathered, she was just another score he hoped to notch on his Belizean, drug-wielding belt, and that, she scowled, certainly wasn't going to happen now!

Anthony ignored her as he turned to the stranger. "Rolan and his men have branched out. They seem to have stepped up to...," he stopped mid-sentence then wrinkled his brow casting a sideways glance in her direction.

Her mouth gaped as she placed her hands on her hips. "Excuse me! What was *that* look for?"

The gun wielding man shook his head, disapproving. He paced a few steps and turned back to them. With his lip curled, the man leaned in close to Anthony. "So? You should have let it be and not bring her here! Do you realize how 'dis will affect us now? You could have blown 'da whole thing! It's too late now. 'Dey will look for you," he lifted his hand that still held the gun and pointed Tess's direction, "and 'dey will come for her now, too! You know 'dis, right?"

"Yes!" Anthony pushed past him. "The package is on the boat, and the girl stays." He took Tess by the arm. "You had best come with me."

She dug her heels into the soil and yanked her hand free. This time, she wanted answers. "No! Tell me who you are," she demanded.

"Like you said, a pirate, remember?" Anthony sneered.

"What do you mean a pirate? Do you work for somebody? That man..." she looked back, "is he your partner?"

Anthony stepped past her and stopped. The tension hardened on his face as he spun around. Without uttering a word, he held out his hand and motioned for her to come with him. She glanced up at him, contemplating her choices.

"Look, we need to leave now! I can't tell you everything. You just need to trust me," he insisted.

His voice was stern but the crease in his brow softened. For a moment she saw the familiar look in his eyes, the one she had seen just before he kissed her. She gazed ahead of him towards the dense brush. The idea of wild creatures and unknown thugs lurking in the jungle was more than she was willing to manage on her own.

"Fine!" she huffed. "Lead the way."

Chapter Thirteen

A Celebration

STAGNANT AIR HUNG THICK AND humid in the mid-morning temperatures. The shear material of her three-piece sundress clung to her skin as beads of perspiration trickled down her neck. Avoiding eye contact with the dark-skinned man, who had made it abundantly clear that her presence was unwelcome, Tess followed after Anthony. To make matters worse, she realized, he also would have preferred she remained captive on the *Charisa* with Sergey and Rolan. Looking back over her shoulder, she made sure they were alone.

"Who was that man?" Tess asked, annoyed.

Anthony didn't respond. She wondered if he had heard her or if he was just ignoring her. Tess felt a familiar slithering sensation at her foot. Glancing down, she noticed a willowy vine wrapped around her ankle. Simultaneously, she stumbled forward, and the ground rushed to meet her. Her arms flailed out, catching herself against the rough trunk of a palm tree. Anthony spun around and stopped. He glared at her. Tess arched her brow as she straightened her worn skirt. With her head held high, she readjusted her shoulder-bag then motioned him on.

"Are you going to tell me who that man was?" she asked.

"His name is Devon. He's a local that lives here with his family," Anthony replied.

"It seems he does more than just live here," she said, rubbing the fresh scratches on her leg. "Why does he need a gun? To shoot people that try and steal your drugs?"

"No. Only red headed tourists poking around where they don't belong," he retorted.

"Very funny," she smirked. "You said that you were here to help them. What kind of help is it to bring them contraband fished from the ocean?"

Again, he ignored her as she hurried to keep up. They walked past another little hut and continued through the grassy opening where other bamboo-like structures stood in the distance. The closer they got, the more she realized they were coming into some part of a village. They walked past the small shelters and ahead she could see another tiny building situated further back. Tess noticed that it looked more like a storage shed rather than livable space.

"We can stay here," he said.

"As good as any place, I suppose," she said, eyeing the crude hovel.

Anthony walked up onto the porch landing and entered the hut. Tess followed but hesitated at the doorway. A faint fragrance, like fresh blossoms, filled the air and she noticed a small, wilted bouquet of flowers tucked through the wooden slats. A twine ribbon wrapped the stems together. The décor seemed odd for a bachelor's place, she mused, and peered inside.

The furnishings were simple. A cut-out window with a drop down covering made from palm tree fronds allowed light to filter into the room.

The modest shack was bare except for an old rattan chair and a wooden table that sat in the middle of the floor. Against the wall she saw a thick woven bamboo-like mattress. Tess set her purse down on the table, brushed her hand over the woven chair and turned towards Anthony.

"How do you help them, what is it that you do?" she asked.

Her gaze followed him as he stepped over to the window. Anthony pulled back the fragile curtain and looked out. It was unclear if he was looking for someone or perhaps making sure they were alone. He spoke without looking at her.

"Devon and his family are poor farmers. They live outside of the city, away from men like Rolan who steel their daughters, their wives, and enslave their children."

Tess couldn't believe what she heard. "So, you're like some *Robin Hood-type* guy that takes from the rich and gives to the poor?" she asked, half serious.

He let the curtain fall into place, Tess stood watching as he walked back over to the doorway. Anthony stretched his arms up over the threshold of the open door and stood with his back to her looking out. When he finally spoke, his words were abrupt. "Devon's family are good people; you'll be safe here."

He lowered his arms and turned to face her. His expression appeared dull, and even his eyes conveyed sadness. Only the tautness of his jaw let her know his sincerity. "I need you to stay here—I'll have to make arrangements," he said, matter-of-fact like.

"Arrangements," she paused, "what sort of arrangements are you talking about? When can I go back to my hotel?" She searched his face for an answer. "I am going back to my hotel, aren't I?"

Anthony looked troubled. "Yes, of course. But it's complicated," he said.

"Complicated? How is it complicated? Just tell whoever it is that you stopped to help me. Tell them that you were just out boating and..."

"Tess, you're safe, I promise. Just stay here and don't leave the village. Devon may seem rough, but he will make sure that nothing happens to you."

***

SHE STEPPED out onto the bamboo porch watching Anthony as he walked through the clearing just beyond the village huts. A small group of women along the path walked towards him, opposite where she and Anthony had arrived. They held what looked like baskets on their hips and a couple of children ran on ahead. Tess watched as Anthony stopped and spoke with one of the women. Wrapping her arm around the post, Tess looked on, curious about the strangers. Anthony turned, pointing in her direction, then turned back to the group that had gathered around him. She could see the women more clearly now, their faces earnest as they listened.

One of the women stood out more than the others. She was petite and had a streak of silver hair framing her face. Tess guessed the woman to be older than the others in the group. The mature woman glanced over at the hut and then back to Anthony. Tess wondered what Anthony would say about her. Would he tell the truth saying he kidnapped her out on the ocean? Or would he make up some story of a lost tourist in need of help? The older lady nodded her head. Anthony turned briefly and looked in Tess's direction. For a moment, their gaze met. Then, in an instant, he spun and hurried away. The village lady rushed over. Her feet were bare, but her steps were agile as she swiftly walked up the wooden stairs. Her brown face, weathered by the sun, beamed with a welcoming smile. Tess let out an anxious sigh.

"My name is Rubi. An'tony has 'tod me 'ju are his friend, 'jes?"

Tess raised her brow and hesitated. Her attention drifted to the clearing, but Anthony had already disappeared into the jungle. Was Anthony her friend? It was a question she hadn't considered. He had rescued her from the *Charisa*, and she had spent the night with him under the stars. And, of course, there was the kiss this morning. But then, Tess twisted her lips, Anthony still held on to her cellphone, obviously he didn't trust her. She had given up on being able to use it—most likely there was no service anyway. She looked down at the woman eagerly waiting for her reply.

"Yes, I am his friend," Tess smiled.

The old woman beamed and set her basket down motioning towards the fresh delicacies.

"He has 'tod me about 'jor troubles. 'Ju must be hungry, and such an ordeal. Please, have som'ting to eat."

Anthony, confiding the truth to this woman, surprised her. Whoever Anthony was, Tess realized, these people respected him. And, he did say that Devon would look out for her. She shuddered at the image of Devon waiving his gun in the air. She didn't trust him, at least not completely. But, she rationalized, Anthony did, and for now she would trust Anthony. After all, did she have a choice? Taking a deep breath, Tess turned her attention to the rosy-cheeked woman.

"Yes, it has been an ordeal and yes, thank you, I am hungry." She reached into the basket and picked out a soft green fruit.

Rubi smiled. "Come," she said, "we visit 'wit 'da others."

The energetic woman took Tess by the arm and led her through the small village.

***

RUBI INTRODUCED her to the other women who lived in the tiny village. From what she gathered, they were living quite primitively, and the jungle provided all they needed. Rubi mentioned she did not like the city. She said the people were too busy and there was too much corruption. Tess mulled over what Anthony had said – *'men like Rolan stealing their daughters.'* Had Rubi also been a victim, and did she lose family to those tyrants? Tess caught herself staring at the old woman's wrinkles. Around her eyes there were creases that deepened when the woman smiled or laughed. She noticed deep, bold lines on Rubi's forehead, like that on a face aged by worry, or worse— lines formed by grief. Her heart sank and a hard knot formed in her throat. Shivers cascaded down her arms to think of such harm coming to these welcoming and friendly people. Tess's eyes brimmed with tears. Rubi caught her staring. The gentle woman reached across the table and squeezed Tess's hand. The old woman's infectious smile beamed. Tess relaxed and put feelings of Rolan and any thoughts of menacing drug runners aside, and allowed herself to enjoy, for now, the company of new friends.

The women in the village varied in age from Rubi—who Tess guessed was in her mid-fifties, based on the grey strands accenting her petite face—to the young school-aged children, although she wasn't sure they attended any formal teaching. The younger children's faces smiled brightly as they invited her to pick flowers along the grassy edges of the area. Tess eagerly joined them.

It didn't take long before their baskets were filled with the colorful blooms. Rubi took her by the arm and led her, along with the other women, to the center hut. It was an open structure with four posts that supported it. They all sat around the long table centered underneath the thatched roof. The older girls braided necklaces and soon all were adorned with beautiful Belizean leis. It amazed her how many different plants bloomed in the jungle. Brilliant colors and sweet fragrances surrounded them. A shy round-faced girl held out a yellow flower. Tess noticed it was the same flower as printed on her sundress.

"For me?" Tess smiled.

The girl nodded. Tess tucked the flower into her hair. The little girl smiled wide and hugged her. The gesture took Tess by surprise, but she welcomed the embrace.

The day went by quickly and Tess enjoyed the women's company. In all, there were about fifteen women in the camp. Each went about their chores as well as Tess who, under the helpful guide of Rubi, helped prepare the baskets of fruit and other foods that were set aside. Devon kept to himself, lurking along the outer perimeter as if expecting others. She hadn't realized how long Anthony had been gone until she noticed a motion from the corner of her eye. Looking over, she saw Anthony walking back into the village. One of the young girls stood with a bouquet and ran to him.

"An'tony!" the little voice called out.

The dark-haired girl put her arms around Anthony's neck and kissed his cheek. Relieved to see him again, Tess watched as he embraced the slender girl, leaning down to kiss her forehead. The young girl held out the flowers with the twine dangling from the stems. Anthony took the bouquet in one hand and lifted the girl up with his other arm. An unexpected warmth roused through her.

Anthony glanced in her direction and their eyes met. Butterflies flittered in her stomach. Her cheeks blushed, radiating—like the heat from an untamed flame. Tess fought back her desire to run to him, to be the girl he wrapped his arms around. She diverted her eyes, then blinked and looked back towards him. Their gaze met again. He set the young girl down, never breaking his captivating stare. Her heart pounded as his long strides carried him across the grassy opening. The sun peered through the trees glistening onto his bronzed skin. Like the first time she had seen him staring at her from across the dance floor, Tess could sense the deep intensity of his gaze.

That moment, at the Grand Simone, had seemed so long ago but she reminded herself it had only been a day. And now, he was here, no brunette in his clutches, just her—here with him. Anthony strode up to her, confidence exuded from his very being, feeding the sensations welling up within her. As if he knew her thoughts, he smiled warmly.

"Well, I see you've gotten a taste of village life," he said.

He lifted the braided necklace from around her throat. The warmth of his hands brushed along her neck, and his gentle touch ignited a tantalizing fire throughout her body. Her legs weakened, and she was grateful to be sitting.

"Yes," her words choked. "Rubi has been a wonderful host."

"Life in the village is different than your hostile pace at home, no doubt," he said.

"Mmm, yes," she agreed.

She turned her attention to the tropical setting. Small blooms of red and yellow dotted the thick brush of the jungle landscape. She could taste the scented dew that swirled in the breeze. Tess savored the sensations. Unlike the full blaze of the sun at the ocean, here the sun filtered through the palm trees cooling the air and the birds cooed high in their branches. It was a paradise, or what she imagined paradise might look like. She drew in a deep breath and turned to face Anthony.

"You were gone quite a while, where did you go?" she asked.

"I've made arrangements for you to travel back to your hotel in the morning," his voice trailed.

Her heart sank, disappointed to leave. She knew she would have to go back but she hadn't expected to feel this way. The idea that she might never see him again overwhelmed her. She remembered the touch of his lips and the rush of his breath against her cheek. She wanted him more than any other man she had ever known. But how could this work? How would they live? Her head began to spin. But, as quickly as her mind flooded with images of wrapping her arms around him, she scoffed at herself and her unrealistic ideals of romance. Anthony was not interested in her. She remembered how he had pushed himself away this morning when he could have taken her right there at the beach. No, if he had any feelings for her, he wouldn't let her go.

"Oh, the hotel, yes, that would be good," she paused, "we both need to get on with our lives," she said, and watched him straighten his shoulders.

"You can report the incident when you get back to the city. I'm sure they would be interested to know about the threats to our unescorted tourists," he said.

"What about you? Where will you go now…I mean now that you won't have to drag me around with you?"

He smiled as his dimples set deep into his chin. "I think it best not to discuss my plans. The police sometimes frown on such things."

"Of course, I didn't mean to imply that I would tell them where you are…," she chose her words carefully, "I just…"

Laughter from the village girls interrupted them.

"An'tony!" Rubi held out her hand, "Come, 'ju bring 'jor girl, come."

Before either she or Anthony could refute their relationship, Rubi took Anthony by the arm and grabbed Tess by the hand. She led them down the path where voices and sounds of mingling grew louder. A bonfire burned in the center of the gathering and the bamboo table was full, different dishes overflowing with fruits and other foods the women had prepared. While Rubi and Anthony talked, the men from the village returned. A dozen laborers ambled next to the evening fire; their clothes smudged with the day's work. An older man holding armfuls of large green leaves bound with twine, knelt by the fire. A couple of the women helped him dip the tethered leaves into the water. Another kettle already filled with bundles sat next to him and he placed each one into the outer embers of the fire, covering them up. Rubi's eyes lit up as she squeezed Tess's hands and smiled at both her and Anthony.

"We will celebrate, tonight, 'jes?"

The aroma of spices filled the air. Rubi's contagious smile lifted the mood and Tess once more felt a sense of belonging—far removed from her reality.

Tess laughed and smiled back. "Yes, let's celebrate!"

Rubi led them to the bonfire where two of the younger girls ran up and adorned both her and Anthony with more fragrant flowers. Excitement permeated through the air. Tess sniffed the bright red pedals perfectly arranged on the necklace. A soft hibiscus fragrance floated past her nose and the words of the store clerk rang through her mind. Tess glanced over at Anthony. The children draped more flowered strands around her neck and Rubi donned him with a more masculine, shell-like garland. Anthony's raised brows told her the celebration was not a typical event.

"Why are they doing this?" Tess asked.

He shrugged, "It must be an occasion of some sort, I guess."

"You guess?" she paused. "You mean you don't know? I thought all good pirates were familiar with the local customs."

Tess grinned as Anthony turned towards her. With eyes alert, he arched his brow but before he could reply, the beating of drums sounded. Rubi took him by the arm.

"Come, An'tony! Ju dance Punta 'wid me!"

Anthony took the spry woman by the hand and stepped onto the open dirt floor. Rubi rolled her hips to the rhythm quickening her steps and twisting her arms up into the air. Tess watched the captivating dance and shifted her gaze onto Anthony. Beads of sweat glistened on his chest as his feet moved to the drums. Engulfed by the music, she watched, almost hypnotic-like, the two dancers. Their movement mesmerized her, the same as the night at the Grand Simone. The dance was primitive, yet erotic. Anthony's face brightened and the hard lines from earlier softened across his brow. Joy and laughter erupted as the two Sambaed to the drums.

Tess sipped her drink and ate the prepared foods, gazing over at Anthony as he danced with Rubi. She couldn't deny that she felt something deeper for him than just desire. She shook her head and looked away. They were worlds apart—from occupations to lifestyle. Her mind drifted to the container pulled from the ocean. How could she possibly believe they could be together? She glanced out across the open firepit and watched the dancers through the flames. Anthony looked over at her. The corner of his mouth curled slightly, and his eyes glistened in the firelight. Her heart surged and she found herself smiling back. She gestured with her glass, took a deep breath, and swallowed the rest of her fermented drink.

The sweet taste of her pineapple cooler quenched the dryness in her mouth and relaxed the tenseness in her shoulders, feeling more at ease. Tess was certain that Molly would applaud her spontaneity. Empowered by her freedom, a euphoric sensation swept over her. For now, she resolved, she wouldn't think about rescues, galas, or contraband pulled from the sea. She would answer to no one, except her own desire.

The drums stopped. Rubi touched her palm to Anthony's face, like a mother to her son. In return, he brushed his hand across Rubi's back and guided her to the table. The image warmed Tess's heart and she wondered how it was that they had such endearment for each other. Tess glanced over at Anthony. He took a step in her direction, but the little children rushed to him. They tugged at his leg until he relented and picked up the little round-faced girl. Tess smiled, amazed to see this pirate of a man coveted by the children. She laughed softly and he gave her a pleading, yet playful, look.

"Ju have 'anudder drink, 'jes?"

Rubi's familiar voice interrupted the moment. Tess looked up. The vibrant old woman beamed with hidden youth.

"'Jes…" Tess laughed, "I mean, yes, thank you."

Rubi filled the fruited cup. "He is a 'gude man, An'tony. Ju have a 'gude man, too?"

The question took Tess by surprise. She glanced over at Anthony and considered her options briefly; did she have a good man? Tess could sense Rubi's watchful eyes on her, waiting for a reply.

"No, not exactly," Tess wondered how much to share.

"'Das too bad, 'ju a nice girl. 'Ju should have a nice man too."

Rubi's words lingered on her mind. Tess sipped her drink and peered over the brim of the cup. The children still gathered and knelt at Anthony's feet. His eyes beamed and his hands gestured, completely engrossed in the tales of a story. The children leaned in, eagerly listening. She watched the details of his features, the movement of his jaw, and how the shadows of the flames flickered on his face as he held the children's attention. Then bouts of giggles erupted. Their serious faces burst into laughter as Anthony reached out and startled the unsuspecting listeners. Laughing, his dimples deepened as he turned his attention towards her. Again, desire surged through her veins.

As if reading her mind, Anthony took the young boy that sat on his knee and placed him in his mother's lap. He stood and gazed over at her. With his broad shoulders squared, he strode across the landing. Her heart raced and tingling fluttered through her body. Tess glanced at his sun-kissed skin showing beneath his half-buttoned shirt. Anthony smiled at her; his lips formed into a coy smile. She could see the way he carried himself, the confidence in his stride. Biting her lower lip, Tess anticipated his approach, slamming back the remnants of liquid that remained in her cup. With her legs tucked beneath her, she shifted her skirt and adjusted her top. Her hand lingered just below her neckline. Anthony's eyes dipped, following the curve of her cleavage. Visions of his lips caressing her breasts filled her mind. Her decision had been made, tonight she would be his.

"Anthony!" a woman's voice interrupted.

Anthony turned. The yellow flicker of the fire cast a dim light into the shadows and Tess strained to see the intruder's face. An overwhelming rush of nerves flooded through her mind as the shapely figure stepped into the firelight. Tess gasped and a wave of nausea lumped into her stomach. It was that temptress, the one from the bar! She watched in disgust as Anthony rushed to the newcomer. The woman wrapped her arms around him and buried her lips into his skin. Tess glared at the two, disbelief encompassed her. Horrified, she watched them walk away and disappear into the night— Anthonys hands low around the harlot's waist.

***

THE FAINT rays of dawn broke through the jungle. Tess stirred. Her temples throbbed. With her eyes closed she heard faint footsteps, or perhaps the hut had shaken. Repositioning her woven purse Tess dismissed the noise and sleepily covered her hand over her ear. Still half-awake, she lazily realized it had substituted twice now for a pillow. Her body relaxed and she drifted back into her dreams. An unrelenting hand pushed against her shoulder. She swatted, intending to slap her target but instead her hand waved dozily out into the air.

"Tess!" she heard the familiar voice whisper. "Wake up."

She groaned. "Go away! Leave me alone."

"You need to get up. We need to leave," the voice persisted.

Tess rolled over and saw Anthony crouching next to her. Her head pounded. "Leave? I don't want to leave. Not with you," she grumbled. Tess shoved him away and rolled towards the thatched wall. "Go back to her—why did you come here anyway? Did you think you could spend the night with your barfly and then top it off with me?"

Her face still turned away; she stared wide-eyed at the hut wall waiting for his answer. Her mouth was dry like the desert and her tongue stuck to the inside of her cheek. It had been three days since she had showered or brushed her teeth. She longed for a steaming hot bath. Tess looked down at her once vibrant, hibiscus-print sundress, the legend of love...she sulked, had become her nightgown. Her bikini substituted as undergarments, and she hadn't seen a mirror in days. She could only imagine what her hair must look like.

In any normal situation she would never allow anyone, especially a guy, to see her like this. But this wasn't normal, she mulled. Out here, traipsing through humid jungles and sloshing through thick wiry webs, she shuddered, make-up and combed hair were the least of her worries. It served him right, she mused. He would have to drag her around looking like a monster with her stale breath and web matted hair. She smirked for a moment. Perhaps she would have felt differently though if he had stayed with her last night. She scowled. But instead, he had gone off into the woods with that hip slinging, brunette. Tess turned to face him. Her eyes narrowed and she dared him to comment on her disheveled look.

"Why? Why do we need to leave?" she asked, looking past him. "It's not even daylight!"

"Rolan's men are searching through the villages," he said.

Anthony stood and walked to the door. Tess noticed the gaunt look and the tightness of his jaw. These past three days she had seen a confident man, eyes bright and assured of himself. But this morning, he was different—vulnerable.

"Rolan?" She sat up. "But how does he know where we are?"

"His men must have seen me."

"How? When could they...," she stared down at the floor, her voice softened, "yesterday, when you went to make arrangements for me—this is my fault, isn't it?" She searched his face for the answer.

"This is hardly your fault. But we need to leave now, before they come. If we are gone when they get here the people will be safe. But if we stay, Rolan will hurt them," his voice trailed, "maybe even kill them."

She looked out the open door. In the early morning, a sleepy stillness engulfed the little village. She wondered about the children, about Rubi and her family.

"Can't we go to the police? Won't they protect them?"

"You are naive, Tess," he said, tightening his jaw. "Maybe the police would have helped you, alone. But not now, not with Rolan and his men involved. The police won't help either one of us."

"I don't understand. Don't the police want to arrest men like Rolan?"

"Not unless they're forced to. And an American tourist who got herself mixed up in the wrong place at the wrong time," he raised his brow and threw her a glance, "isn't enough to get the most notorious drug lord arrested."

"Notorious drug what?" she gulped. "What will Rolan and his men do if they catch us?"

Anthony's eyes grew stern, and his dimples set deep into his cheek, "Nothing, they won't catch us. Now, grab your things and let's go."

Chapter Fourteen

Stole Away

ANTHONY'S FOOTSTEPS ECHOED ACROSS THE wooden porch. The people within the small gentle village slumbered under the soft glow of the moon. From the corner of her eye, Tess could see Anthony's towering silhouette filling the doorway.

"We need to move quickly!" he urged.

"I'm coming. I just need to find my other sandal!" she snapped. Both sandals, but not like she needed to be rushed by him, she snorted. She scrambled for her things. Her bag had been easy enough to find. It hadn't been the softest pillow, she thought as she rubbed her cheek, but given the circumstances, it did the job. Her shoes, however, lay hidden somewhere in the shadows.

"Quickly, Tess, we need to..."

"Go! I'll be right there," she cut him off. "Besides," she mumbled, "I certainly don't need you telling me what to do!"

Tess knelt down onto the wooden floor, her fingers flared, sweeping over the planks. Her palms brushed over the smooth bamboo. A bleak hint of moonlight penetrated through the window. But it was of little help and her mind envisioned creepy insects lurking, waiting in the corners ready to pounce. She shuddered. The gooey texture from the jungle web yesterday still lingered fresh in her thoughts. The darkness was eerie and quiet. So much so, that the hair on her neck stood on end. She held her breath and continued to search. Just then, the tip of her finger nudged against the familiar leather of her black shiny sandals. Tess exhaled as she grabbed the pair of shoes. Quickly, she shoved them onto her feet and made her way to the porch where Anthony, to her surprise, still waited.

She could see his silhouette in the moonlight. His shoulders turned away from her as he rapidly descended the rustic stairs. With his long, swift strides, Tess hurried to keep up. Ahead, she could see a thin shadow of a man, standing next to a van. It was Devon. Seeing Devon waiting next to the car brought the gravity of the situation full circle. Traipsing off into the night with a couple of strangers was completely out of her comfort zone. She had taken a one-hundred and eighty-degree turn from her life back home.

Tess glanced over at Anthony, but his back was turned. She had let her emotions get the best of her last night. Her frustration flared that she had even considered giving herself to Anthony. That was, of course, before that woman showed up and Anthony ran out leaving her alone. Tess spent the remainder of the evening realizing how foolish she had been. But still, if he were going to harm her, he surely wouldn't drag her across the ocean and then bring her to this village.

Rubi and the others all trusted him. She had seen it on their faces, the way they interacted with him, and Tess knew she felt it, too. There was something about him, a quality he portrayed. And right now, she needed this stranger. She needed him to get back home to the safety of her life in the city. At least there, drug dealers weren't chasing after her. Tess paused, inhaling the cool air deeply into her lungs. She squared her shoulders then looked ahead to the waiting vehicle but what she saw made her stand fast.

"Are we going in that?" she asked, eyeing the metal heap in front of them.

"I'm sorry, is this not to your liking?" Anthony jeered.

She detected the twinge of annoyance in his voice. A pang of doubt shot across her forehead as she continued to size up the jalopy. The front fenders rounded over the wheels and the nose dropped flat. The year of the car may have even predated Rubi's grandmother, she winced. Welded scraps of misshapen tin pieces patched the rusted holes which were offset by the lined, pitted grill, spanning from one side of the front fender to the other, like bars on a jail cell. Whatever make or model it was, it looked old and vile. Tess cringed.

"Really? This is our only option?" she asked. "Does it run?"

"Yes, it does, and we don't have much choice. Besides, it will be a good cover blending with the locals," Anthony retorted.

She exaggerated a nod and swallowed hard. Her gaze followed its outline. "I'm sure it will. I don't even recognize what it is," she paused, "and the rope?" she pointed to a tattered rope which tied the hood to the bumper. "Camouflage, I suppose?"

"Look, perhaps this is not what you're used to back in New York with your high-rise buildings and fancy porters, but the sooner we get going, the sooner you can get back to your life of luxury!"

His words stung. If there had been any affection for her, he made it clear that those feelings were gone now. She hadn't wanted to be here. She didn't ask for this to happen. Why couldn't something just go right for a change? Was it too much to think that she, Tess Martin, could find happiness? How did I get myself into this? she asked herself. All I wanted was a vacation.

Images of Roger groping over his platinum tease spilled through her mind. Her nostrils flared.

Here she was, traipsing through the dark with criminals and whatever else was lurking ahead of her. Her eyes narrowed as her lips pressed tightly. And Anthony, Tess fired a blaming glance towards him, he's probably no better than Roger the way he ran off with that harlot last night. What was she thinking? Again, she scoffed. She didn't need men like that in her life. It was those types of men that kept causing her heartache. She shook her head. Like a flame doused by a bucket of water—no chance to rekindle, her infatuation with Anthony was over. She was ready to leave, to prove she didn't need these men to survive, or at least not once she was back to her hotel.

Tess tossed her head back, raised her chin, and drew in a deep breath. She would put the last few days out of her mind and move on from those two-timing pigs. What mattered most now, she decided, was to get back to her hotel and finish what she had started—her vacation!

"Fine!" she said.

Anthony yanked at the rear passenger door. It let out an arthritic pop and the door sprung open. Startled, she jumped back, her foot slipped under a vine that wound like a snake around her ankle. It slithered tight and sent her flailing into the metallic heap. Helpless, she gasped and flung her arms out to brace for her inevitable fall. Flashes of Anthony's surprised look and green jungle foliage rushed past her. With a loud thud, her out-of-control fall slammed her onto the side of the car knocking the wind out of her. She gasped. The relic's chalky filth smeared across her chest. Deflated, Tess slumped against the crusty metal. Her lips quivered and tears beaded at the corner of her eyes. She looked down at the green slime embedded into her skirt and fought back the frustration and tears, regaining her breath.

"Why? Why is everything against me?"

"Are you alright?" Anthony asked.

"I'm fine. Let's get out of here!" she demanded.

Anthony stepped beside her. She took another deep breath and recovered her composure, grateful for the blanket of darkened skies obscuring her disheveled appearance. The last thing she wanted was his pity. No, she had to stay strong. She wiped back a tear that slipped down her face. She expected him to scold her for almost waking up the others, but instead, he put his arm around her and held the door open for her.

"Don't worry, I'll keep you safe," he said.

His voice was low and vibrated through her. Undeniable impulses fluttered through her breasts, and she felt the blood rush to her cheeks. Once more, her body betrayed her. No, she wouldn't fall for him—it was all wrong—here, Belize, the jungle, everything. But his tone reassured her. This stranger stirred her emotions, she couldn't deny it. She took a final glance back at the sleeping village and reminisced about Rubi and the villagers. If leaving now could help protect them—she turned to Anthony.

"Let's get going," she said.

***

GAPING HOLES erupted from the hard vinyl as she slid onto the back seat. Course, wiry stuffing protruded from the cushions. She eased herself next to the tattered mess. Immediately, her bottom sank. The crude covering had given way and she found herself slumped into a tattered hole. Tess tried to reposition herself, but the abrasive matter poked at her thighs, snagging the thin material of her flowered skirt. Tess ran her thumb and forefinger over the soiled print. Visions of the old woman and her story of desired love came to mind. She doubted, at least in its present condition, that the gift store ensemble would bring true love. The prickly cushion continued to scratch at her skin. Tess gingerly shifted her weight then tucked her purse under her legs; it did the job, keeping the dry mass at bay.

"How long will it take to get...wait, where are we going?"

"Back to your hotel," Anthony paused, "that is where you want to go, isn't it?"

"Yes, is it nearby?"

"About an hour's drive from here to the buses. Devon will take us."

She could see Devon behind the wheel. His eyes focused straight ahead, uninterested in polite acknowledgment. Figures, he's probably happy to get rid of *'dat gurl*, she sneered. There was no loss of affection leaving him behind either. He had made it clear how he felt about her the day she arrived.

Wrapping the skirt over her knees, a habit from her childhood, Tess settled into the back seat as best she could. With a firm push, Anthony gave her door a good shove, the metal clicked sharply as it latched into place. He then tugged open his own creaking door, hopping into the front passenger seat. Without hesitation, Devon turned the key, cranking over the stiff engine. For a moment, it made a low whirring sound, then whined excitedly before engaging fully. Puffs of exhaust spouted out the back, and a grey, pungent cloud engulfed the entire automobile. Tess covered her mouth and nose trying not to breathe the penetrating fumes.

Devon shifted the lever into gear and the heap lurched down the dirt road. It jarred and rattled as it made its way along the rough path. Tess was sure it would leave them stranded. Every dip they encountered bobbled her up and out of the prickly hole. She braced herself the best she could, but the bumps came without warning, jouncing her into the air only to land abruptly on the unyielding steel frame. She hoped the hour would go by quickly as the vehicle continued down the crude roadway, creaking and groaning through the jungle.

Finally, the car slowed. She rubbed at the muscles aching in her legs and the bruises that had undoubtably formed on her thighs from the bone jarring bounces onto the hard seat. Through the dirt scuffed window she could see a crossroad ahead. Devon slipped the knob into gear, and the engine's high pitch whir resumed, sending vibrations through the cab as the car set into motion. With each rev, the motor roared louder. Gaining speed, he shifted the gears and the rusted cab jumped forward, awkward and ungainly like an overweight toad. A couple of stuttered jerks later, they were steadily on their way. The new route hummed softer under the balding tires.

Tess looked out as the sun peaked over the treetops. In the front seat she could see the two men talking but it was impossible to hear over the loud motor. She stared out the window, leaning her head cautiously into the seat. As the scenery blurred past, her mind wandered back to Anthony at the cantina. She reminisced about the way he smiled at her from across the dance floor. At that moment, she remembered, he had looked straight into her eyes. It had been more like a grin, as if he knew something she didn't.

The brakes screeched and the high-pitched squeal brought her back to the present. In the distance, Tess could see rows of thatched roofs. Devon pulled the heap over, stopping on the side of the road. He turned to Anthony.

"You'd betta' walk from here," he said.

***

THEY STOOD along the edge of the dirt road as Devon turned the vehicle around. More puffs of smoke chugged from the exhaust as she watched the car sputter away. Only the sound of the tired engine could be heard humming in the distance. It, too, quieted as it rounded the corner and disappeared. The smell of dampened earth wafted past her nose. Like the river channel, the area was humid, with the jungle life uncannily still. The idea of trudging through the overgrown foliage made her stomach flop. She was anxious for dry sandy soil, like that near her hotel, and dreaded encountering any more insects or spiderwebs, which were most certainly lurking in the jungle forest.

The trees were thick and dense along the primitive road. Tiny plops of dew formed on the broad leaves and drizzled down their waxy green platters. The droplets steadily trickled onto the ground orchestrating a soft rhythm among the hushed jungle. Tess raised her brow and surveyed the area. The village ahead looked motionless.

"Where are we?" she asked.

Anthony gestured, "This is Jocaab, it's a small village but there's a bus that comes through each morning and if we hurry, we can take it."

"What about Rolan?" she hesitated, "I mean, you said he's looking for us. Do you think he will look for us here?"

"Not likely, but we had better get going."

"And this bus, will it take us to the hotel?"

"As a matter of fact, it will," he said.

"I think we should go to the authorities...," she paused mid-sentence. For a moment she had forgotten. With Anthony being a drug runner, he couldn't take her to the police, he was probably wanted, or at least that's what she assumed. "I mean if we go back to my hotel, won't Rolan find us there, too?"

"Rolan's a businessman who likes to keep his business under the radar. He won't risk the publicity. Besides," he winked, "it's me he's after. You'll be safe at your hotel. Now let's hurry and catch that bus."

Anthony seemed so sure of himself, she thought. Perhaps he was a criminal, but maybe not as bad as some. He did steal the container of drugs from Rolan but then didn't seem to care about it. It was Devon, after all, who went back to the boat for the illegal stash. But that woman, she scowled, who was that woman Anthony had left with?

Swiftly her mind centered on the present as a high-pitched gnat hummed near her face. She swatted at the little beast. Its brazen spirit was bigger than its size and the obnoxious critter flew close to her nose. She snorted. The tiny, winged nymph fluttered, insistent on using her like an airstrip. Tess waived her hands wildly, swatting the hard-shell pest and flinging it into the shrubs.

"Pesky little thing!" she huffed.

Anthony started towards the huts up ahead. Tess put her purse over her shoulder and gave a passing glance in the direction the critter had sailed. The sound of buzzing grew louder and the idea of stinging insects dive-bombing her vividly played over in her mind. She batted her hands through the air swatting at any would-be insects and, in a reserved panic, hurried after Anthony already in full stride.

***

EARLY RISING villagers stood on their porches as she and Anthony passed by. She wondered what they must think of the two out-of-place strangers traipsing down their rural road so early in the morning. Finally, they reached the last storefront on the street. It looked more modern and more established than the primitive bamboo huts they passed earlier. The last building stood noticeably taller than the others and a small crowd had gathered at the corner. Anthony stopped.

"We'll wait here," he said.

"This is where we catch the bus?" she asked.

Tess looked around. Crates were stacked next to the edge of the compact dirt road. Inside, white-feathered chickens with red combs flopping across their beaks clucked nervously. Their plumes protruded through their crudely made cages and clumps of bird dung splotched all around them. She scrunched her nose at the mess and caught a whiff of their pungent odor. Tess shuddered. Her empty stomach made the stench seem worse. On the wooden sidewalk a man squatted next to the creatures. The villager grinned, exposing his toothless smile. Instinctively, she nodded, smiling back then turned to Anthony.

"Are those birds going on the bus too?"

Anthony's eyes brightened, delighted, no doubt, at her unfamiliarity with normal village life.

"Yes," he chuckled, "do you have any objections?"

"No," she lied.

She wondered how the lopsided cages would stack onto the bus without toppling over. But the nagging ache of her feet soon distracted her; she leaned against the building and gazed down at her already aching toes. The thin straps of her sandals had rubbed her skin and made the tops of her feet red and sore. She glanced over at Anthony and hoped he wouldn't notice. She loathed the idea of him making fun of her ill-prepared shoes, or worse, that he would see her as a burden. But it was too late. He looked down at her sandals and shook his head.

"It's not like I knew I'd be traipsing through the jungle," she said.

With arched brow, he tightened his mouth, frowning. Suddenly, the wall next to them rattled. The shutters surrounding the hollow-framed window popped open and a cheerful face peered through the opening. The woman propped the window open with a bamboo stick. Her hair, like Rubi's, had streaks of silver strands pulled neatly back and twisted into a bun. Her eyes twinkled and her brown wrinkled face creased with her smile. A whiff of sweet syrup permeated the morning air.

"Mmm," Tess instinctively mumbled, "what is that delicious smell?"

"Mama Marcos delights," Anthony said.

"And was that, Mama Marcos?" she asked.

"Yes, as a matter of fact, it was. The locals usually come here on their way to work."

With the morning sun rising higher, the crowd at the bus stop grew. Not only did they gather waiting for the bus, but also assembled to order their breakfast from Mama Marcos. The fresh air smelled of warm cinnamon and nutmeg. Thinking of food caused her stomach to grumble. Salivating, Tess would give anything for a sugary maple, pecan pastry, like the bakery back home. Her stomach growled, again. She knew it would be a stretch of the imagination but hoped for a latté to wash it all down with. Anthony stepped through the open door.

"I'll be right back," he said.

Moments later he returned carrying two hollowed out mango halves. Each one was filled with a combination of chopped pulp and seasoned rice. Although it wasn't the fluffed pastry she had anticipated, the sweet, delicious scent of the mango was irresistible, and she eagerly accepted the breakfast offering.

A sharp, almost familiar echo of grinding gears sounded in the distance. The crowd stirred and gathered their belongings. Anthony stepped onto the dirt road. Looking in the direction of the noise, Tess saw an old rickety bus rounding the corner. She swallowed the last of the rice and scraped the remaining mango fruit with her teeth, tossing the roasted shell into the waste basket. Comparatively, Mama Marcos may have outdone the New York deli. With her stomach filled, she stepped next to Anthony as the dust-covered heap screeched to a halt.

The villagers streamed into the tiny coach. They carried their baskets and goods, stacking them high onto the seats. Those waiting for the bus packed next to each other until the oversized van resembled a tin of sardines destined to be sealed. She and Anthony waited to board until the end but there was little room left. Anthony stepped onto the narrow stairs. The driver shook his head.

"No room, you wait here."

"Yes, we go now!" Anthony argued.

"No room!" the driver shouted.

Tess looked at the overloaded bus. Its tires frayed and bulged from the cargo. Fearing their safety, she leaned close to Anthony's ear. "Is there maybe another one we can take?"

"No, it will be too late. We can't risk being seen by Rolan's spies or having the word get out that an American woman and a local are traveling through the village together."

"I thought you said Rolan isn't after me, that it's you he's after," Tess said.

"I said he's a businessman and not to be underestimated. If word gets out that a red-haired young lady tourist showed up this morning, he'll know we're together. We have to be on this one," Anthony said, sternly.

Her nerves tingled and tightness spread quickly throughout her shoulders. Anthony turned to the driver, producing his wallet. He took out a wad of cash and thrust it at the man.

"We go with you!" Anthony insisted.

The man flipped through the money. Satisfied, he stuffed it into his pocket. The brown-skinned driver nodded and stepped back. Anthony motioned to Tess. Any butterflies she had, up to this point, morphed into hornets, buzzing in her gut, and stirring up an almost overwhelming case of anxiety throughout her body. She had more solace a moment ago thinking that Rolan and his sidekicks were more interested in Anthony than her. Somehow, she reasoned, it had seemed safer. But now, hearing Anthony hint that she might be a target, too, Tess shuttered and turned to the open door waiting for them. With a deep breath, she reluctantly stepped onto the aging bus.

The interior looked just as rough as the exterior, she grimaced. Low hanging ropes crisscrossed along the ceiling. The toothless farmer hoisted his chicken crates on top of the vehicle. He wove a heavy cord through their enclosures. Pulling the thin rope tight, the man tightened the cages closer together. The birds squawked and fluttered in their makeshift boxes while feathers randomly floated through the air and inside the bus. Once he was satisfied that they were secure, the old man climbed back down to the ground and scuttled to the back of the coach. As if synchronized in repetitious rehearsal, the bus driver waited as the agile rancher climbed through the emergency door slamming it shut. The driver revved the motor. With the front door still open, Tess braced herself hanging on to the metal post near the driver's seat. Anthony crowded in next to her. Immediately, a sense of desire stirred within her. Tess held the railing tight as the bus lurched down the road.

Chapter Fifteen

Discovered

THE DRIVER FLEW DOWN THE road. Jumbo-sized palm leaves crowded the edges along the rustic dirt path. Anthony shielded her from the obtrusive plants, pushing their waxy stocks back out the open window. The bus swished past, leaving a cloud of dust trailing behind them. As they rounded the last corner, Tess could see another village. This one was busier than the last, more like a small city. Her fingers ached from what seemed like hours of holding on for dear life. There had been moments when she doubted their safe arrival. At one point, she was certain the worn tires had lifted off the surface—only to slam down just in time to lean into the next curve. Tess had been grateful for the embedded grooves formed deep into the road; certain the ruts kept them from sailing over the embankment.

As they approached the small town, she finally released her white-knuckled grip and exhaled—the breath she had held for most of the trip. The brakes screeched and the driver pulled to the side.

"We're here," Anthony said.

Exhausted, she was ready to leave the rickety shuttle. Anthony stepped off the bus first. He turned and offered his hand. She was surprised at his gentleman-like gesture. With her legs fatigued from the constant jostle of the bus ride, she welcomed his help. She took a moment and looked back down the path expecting to see shrouds of belongings scattered amuck, but the road was clear. Tess glanced at the cargo atop the bus. To her amazement, everything still looked intact, not a single crate or chicken had been lost.

No longer cooled by the open shuttle careening down the hillside, the Belizean sun blazed over her, and the humidity stifled her breath. She looked up and down the street. Nothing looked familiar. There were no polished piers leading to the Grand Simone and, for that matter she realized, there were no brick courtyards outlining her inferior last-minute accommodations either. Of course, she rationalized, she hadn't walked around and explored the city very much before running off to the boardwalk and sailing away on the snorkel excursion. She cleared her dust coated throat.

"I don't recognize this area. Are we close to the hotel?" she asked.

"No, this village is just outside of the city. Your hotel is down the road, not far," he gestured and scanned the street. "It's too far to walk though, especially in the heat. But there is another bus coming soon."

"Another bus?" she blurted. "But I thought the last one was taking me to my hotel."

Her nerves sank into her gut. Had she been naïve to trust Anthony? Would he take her to the police or get her back to her hotel? Her mind raced wildly. She glanced down the street looking for someone to help her, to find a way out. But just as swiftly as her nerves heightened, Anthony turned towards her, their gaze met, and she found herself once more drinking in his chocolate brown eyes.

"Trust me, Tess, you'll get there," he smiled, and brushed his hand down her arm. "At the other end of town there are some tour buses that go into the city," he said, gesturing down the road. "It's only another few miles to your hotel, I promise. First though, we'll have to get a couple of tickets."

His soothing tone and the sincere look in his eyes reassured her. He had called her by her name, and she liked how it sounded coming from his lips. Besides, she hadn't a clue where to go. Anthony, she supposed, seemed genuine in helping her. After all, he had brought her this far. As she gazed up at the brilliant blue sky, the Belizean temperatures steadily climbed. The muggy, slightly moist air clung to her clothes—a sensation she was growing accustomed to. Rationalizing that another bus would be better than aimlessly wandering the humid jungle and possibly missing the only opportunity to return to her hotel and real life, she nodded and followed after him.

They made their way down the wooden sidewalks leading to the small shops ahead. The thatched roofs were neat and tidy with trailing plants sprawling up the sides. More of the bright yellow and red flowers bloomed along the thick twisting vines. Sign boards made of bamboo frames sat outside the storefronts. Their advertisements offered jungle adventures or mystic tours, like the Belizean tribal museum which displayed a brilliant-colored headdress attached to a stuffed jaguar. The ferocious animal posed with its sharp pointed teeth showing and lips snarling. The cat's large taxidermy body crouched, ready to pounce. With eyes wide and brows arched, she darted a concerning look around wondering if the animal had once roamed the area, or worse, still roamed the streets. A large-framed man stood at the rustic museum doorway. His arms were folded across his broad chest, giving him a stout and unyielding appearance. Tess continued to size the expressionless man up. She stared at his thick biceps covered in symbolic tattoos. Her overactive imagination flashed an image of the rigid native wearing the feathered headgear, leading his fellow tribe members like a warrior. Still, with no facial emotion, his eyes followed her as she and Anthony passed by. Quickening her steps, Tess nearly ran into Anthony who seemed unnerved by the museum's bouncer.

The narrow streets were crowded, just enough room for oversized carts and vendors selling gifts and trinkets along the edges. Wire trimmed chairs and wooden crate tables sat outside small cafés. The tourists were enjoying their mouthwatering drinks on the crude furniture. Despite the uncomplicated design, there was a certain freestyle charm to the rustic village. While the eating areas were very plain, the drinks, Tess noticed, had brightly decorated fruit wedges and colorful paper umbrellas, a reminder of the tropical and uplifting atmosphere she had felt that day at the Simone hotel.

Squinting up at the sky, Tess figured it must be nearing lunch hour as more tourists filled the tiny marketplace. She envied the carefree persona of the tourists leisurely walking through the streets. A flicker of loneliness swept over her at seeing the myriads of couples roaming about. Tess was eager to get back to the hotel and put the past few days behind her. That is, she frowned, as soon as she could make her police report against Rolan and Sergey.

Anthony led the way through the maze of vendors and cafes. Randomly, she scanned the primitive structures hoping to find some sort of official-like building where she could find a police officer to help her. But there were no police stations or consulate establishments in sight. She was oddly relieved. It would give her more time to think, to keep Anthony from going to jail.

Her mind drifted to that morning aboard the elegant *Charisa* and the captain, Rolan. She chided herself for overlooking all the red flags that should have been so clear. Instead, she was too concerned about getting ahead of Roger. She had ignored the obvious signs, like Rolan's out of place loafers and his expensive watch. Tess remembered how differently he had dressed for a boat captain. Especially his thick layer of gold chains, like a mafia kingpin, or rather the notorious Belizean drug lord that he was. She grinned at the idea of Rolan and Sergey in stripes behind iron bars. Anthony, however, there was something about him that she couldn't completely decipher, but her intuition told her that Anthony was different from the other two. Again, she thought, even Rubi treated him like a son. And because of that, Tess wasn't sure she wanted the police to arrest Anthony.

Tess glanced over at him. Sweat glistened on the edge of his face and beads of perspiration slid down his throat and the opening of his shirt. She felt like a character in a romance novel, a *Harlequin-type* where the hero could seduce the woman with a mischievous glimpse. If she hadn't just spent the last two days traipsing across the jungle with him, she would have assumed Anthony was just one of the locals here in the village. His attire was casual, lightweight denim pants and a linen button shirt. The lines on his forehead relaxed, but with a taught jaw, as if planning his next step. His deep brown eyes sparkled with wit and necessary humor. Her cheeks warmed at the memory from last night, how their eyes had locked and held each other's gaze. It was difficult to think of him as a criminal. Just then they stopped at the corner.

"There's a place over there that sells bus tickets," he gestured. "I'll go see when the next scheduled one is leaving. Stay here, I'll be right back."

Before she could protest, Anthony turned and jaunted across the narrow road. With the afternoon in full swing the walkway crowded with more tourists. A distracted vacationer bumped into her. The man wore a straw hat, like the ones she had seen at the corner shop just moments ago. The round-faced tourist sported a blue seashell print shirt and polyester striped Bermuda-style shorts. A stout woman stood next to him. Tess unintentionally overheard their conversation by the heavyset man as he bellowed to his partner in southern drawl.

"If that's what you want to do, sugar plum, but you know we're meeting Bob and Connie at the caves in twenty minutes," the man said.

"Connie?" Tess whispered, "I wonder if..." she scrunched her nose at the likeliness and peered down looking beyond the man's fashionable golf shorts to his black socks that covered his shins and bulged through his open toed sandals. Tess laughed discreetly and glanced down over her own attire. "Tsk," she groaned and swiped her hand at the dirt splotches.

She looked over to where Anthony had gone. Seeing a line had formed at the small shack, Tess decided she'd have time to buy another skirt at the gift shop. Turning, she glanced down the street. Not far, she could see a hat display, like that of the black-socked tourist, hanging on a spindle with colorful scarves and other items folded on a table.

"It will only take a minute," she muttered, as if speaking out loud would justify disobeying Anthony's instruction to stay put. Besides, she would be back before he would know that she was gone.

The shop was bigger than it appeared from down the street. Working her way through the hats, she browsed quickly through the colorful scarves stacked neatly on the table. The woman behind the counter smiled at her.

"I have a beautiful blue one that would match your sundress," the native woman smiled.

"I'm afraid my dress has been through a lot lately. Do you have any skirts that tie?"

"We carry several beautiful scarves. They unfold and you can wrap them around your waist like a skirt. They're extremely popular to wear at the beach." The woman sifted quickly through the delicate fabrics. "Here, try this one."

The shopkeeper held out a blue and white, midi sarong-type scarf adorned with more hibiscus flowers—the folklore of love. Tess looked down at her garments smudged with dust and dirt. A tiny white feather stuck to the outside hem and the rickety bamboo crate packed with wide-eyed chickens flashed across her mind. She could almost taste the pungent aroma of the smelly bus and the storm of dust stirred up by the tenacious journey. It certainly hadn't done her clothing any favors. It would be nice to have something colorful and new to put on when she returned to the hotel.

"I'll take it," she smiled.

Now, when she gets back to the hotel, the disapproving scowl of the beady-eyed desk clerk flashed through her mind, she could at least cover up her disheveled attire. Tess rummaged through her bag. The once tightly woven stitches had loosened and frayed. She paid the woman with her credit card, thankful to have taken it onto the cruise, and stuffed the wrap into her bag. She stepped back out onto the wooden walkway where the afternoon sun beamed down.

Tess closed her eyes, and for a moment she allowed her mind to wander. The sweet smell of the jungle surrounded her. She breathed deep, inhaling the soft fragrance of the colorful hibiscus blooms that wafted across her nose. For a snip-it of time, she drank in what a vacation should be like. But the moment of joy was short lived. The glimpse of what she had hoped for faded, tainted by Roger's sneering image that worked its way into her mind. Her jaw tensed.

She opened her eyes and leaned onto a wooden railing looking over the street, pondering thoughts of Rolan and the possible danger of him coming after her. After a moment, she pressed her lips tightly and chose not to think about it, at least not right now. Besides, she convinced herself, Anthony was right. If Rolan was after the drugs, he would have no reason to come after her. It was Anthony who took them, not her. She would be back at the resort soon and report the incident, or at least most of it. Then Rolan would stay away, and she could put all of this behind her. A hard lump formed in her throat. What about Anthony? Could she forget him, too? Her heart sank. Yes, she decided, even Anthony. Once she was safe, back at her hotel, she would put him out of her mind, too. Besides, she told herself, criminals were definitely off the boyfriend checklist.

Tess threw back her shoulders, took a deep breath and walked back to where Anthony had left her. There were chalkboard signs everywhere. Some listed menus while others hosted more nearby attractions. She paused next to the fry jacks and banana pancakes menu. There was another poster of activities. She stooped to read the list and skimmed her finger over the options, pausing.

"Ooh, a zipline. Now that would be adventurous," she mused. "Maybe next trip," she continued reading. "Cave tours. Hmm, sounds interesting." The list went on. "Explore drawings and artifacts of the Mayan's. Oh, and the crystalized remains of 'the sacrificial virgin,'" her face cringed. Tess momentarily envisioned herself tied to a slab and shook her head. "Seriously?" she scoffed. "No thanks!"

Glancing around the area, Tess was intrigued with so many things to do. She was looking forward to some real adventure, the tourist kind, and decided she'd look into it when they returned to her hotel. Just then, from the corner of her eye she could see a dark figure briskly walking towards her. Tess froze. How could she have been so foolish to let her guard down? Her stomach tightened and panic spiraled through her. It took all she had to muster her courage and turned to face the looming image approaching. She let out her breath. *Anthony!* His eyes glared and his jaw twitched. She knew in a moment he would scold her. Tess prepared her defense. She hadn't gone far and there hadn't been any harm in her wandering. The closer he got, the more she could see the hard lines softening over his brow. His stride slowed. Did she detect a sense of relief? Had he truly been worried about her?

The sunlight cast across his dark wavy hair. His rough, unshaven stubble edged seductively down his cheek and across his upper lip. She looked up at him; his lips sensual and inviting. Her eyes drifted to his unbuttoned shirt. The folds slipped apart, exposing his sun-bronzed chest. How would she be able to put this man out of her head? Images of their bodies held close together on the dance floor at the Simone played over in her mind. And their kiss on the island, fresh as the moment it happened, lingered in her thoughts. She remembered how sweet he had tasted. His jungle musk cologne had swirled around her with her thigh pressed against him. She remembered his mouth on hers; entwined in his breath as his tongue explored her mouth. Savoring the memory, passion awakened throughout her body; her desire flourished once again.

The crowd dissolved into a blur leaving only Anthony in her view. He exuded confidence in his stride as he closed the distance between them, almost swaggering. Like that night at the Simone, his gaze held hers and his lips alluringly curled. She caught herself smiling. Who are you? Why are you here? A commotion stirred behind him. The sun's bright light obscured her view. The crowded street divided through the middle. People jostled to the side, something, or someone was shoving their way through and heading directly for them. Tess put her hand over her brow and squinted hoping to get a better look. With eyes wide, she looked at Anthony and pointed behind him.

"Sergey!"

Chapter Sixteen

Narrow Escape

SERGEY AND HIS TWO HENCHMEN barreled through the crowd. Adrenaline coursed through her veins as her eyes fixed on the criminals running straight towards her.

"They found us!" she exclaimed.

Anthony glanced over his shoulder, grabbing Tess by the arm. The force spun her around and Anthony gripped her hand as they ran in the opposite direction. Sergey and his henchmen ran after them. They made their way down the small strip of shops and rounded the corner. The sidewalk ended, only a thick wall of palm shrubs and jungle trees lay ahead.

"Where do we go now?" she panicked.

Anthony clutched her hand tighter, and they bolted through the underbrush. Just off to the side there was a wide path with two short wooden posts and a chain wrapped around them blocking the entrance. Dangling from the chain was a sign, *'Next tour 2pm'*. Anthony hopped over the flimsy barrier with Tess following right behind. One hundred yards or so ahead, Tess could see a tall, slender woman raise a bright blue parasol that she waived over her head. The woman bellowed orders to the tourists around her.

"If you'll all just follow me, we'll get right in and begin our tour," the woman said.

A group of thirty or more followers, short and tall, young, and old, complete with camera bags and flower print tourist-like shirts flocked around the dazzling umbrella. The lush foliage along the trail quickly encompassed the group as they wound their way down the path. Tess watched as the guide's umbrella disappeared—tottering down the trail.

"It looks like we're going sightseeing," Anthony said. "Come on, we'll catch up with them."

Tess glanced over at a small sign staked into the dirt marking the path. The placard read, *'Crystal Virgin Cave.'*

"Well, I was hoping to explore some caves, but this isn't how I envisioned it," Tess said.

"Good to see you have a sense of humor, you'll need it," Anthony replied.

They ducked into the green, leafy tunnel-like path lined with thick shrubs and large palm plants, following the direction the crowd had gone. Tess could feel her blood pulsating rapidly. Adrenaline pumped through her. With each step, her legs propelled her faster, while her heartbeat throbbed heavily at the base of her throat. For a moment she wondered if it was actually the footsteps of Sergey and his henchmen rather than her quickened pulse. She didn't dare look back and sprinted straight ahead.

"Everyone keep pace, we wouldn't want to lose you through the caves!" the tour guide's shrill voice shouted.

Relieved that they had finally caught up with the tourists, Tess stopped and breathed deeply, holding her side attempting to alleviate the ache she felt in her gut. She panted, out of breath and couldn't remember the last time she sprinted one-hundred or more yards.

"We need to keep moving," Anthony whispered, taking her by the arm and blending into the group.

She was slightly annoyed that he didn't seem out of breath and that she was still trying to recover from her side ache. One of the tourists caught her attention. It was the man she had seen earlier in the striped shorts. He held a flashlight in his hand and fiddled with it. Simultaneously, other lights illuminated around them. Tess could see the black hole of the cave entrance and the impending blackness ahead of them.

"I suppose we missed the part where they handed out flashlights," she sputtered, still out of breath.

"Don't worry, we won't need one."

The group's leader held the brightest of battery-operated lanterns and rambled off more instructions to the anxiously awaiting group. Like sheep, the tourists followed the waving, illuminated umbrella. Anthony pulled Tess off to one side and the crowd continued on. In the dim light she could see another narrow passage that led off into the darkness. Tess dug the heels of her thin worn sandals into the dirt floor. She braced her hand on the cold jagged wall.

"I'm not going down there! There are spiders and…"

Anthony, again, grabbed her by the hand and pulled her into the dark vein. "Don't worry. We'll be long gone before they realize we detoured." He grabbed her arm. "Quickly, it's the only way. Let's hope Sergey and his men follow the crowd and not us."

"But…," she protested.

Just then, Anthony placed his hand over her mouth and drew her close to him. The warmth of his breath brushed across her cheek, and she could feel his heartbeat heavy against her. With surprised eyes, she looked up at him. Raising his finger to his lips, Anthony nodded behind her. Tess turned cautiously and watched as the all-too-familiar shadowy figure of Sergey pushed his way through the crowd, his knuckle-breaking gorillas were right behind. Tess gasped. Anthony darted a cautious look and motioned towards the eerie passage.

"This is our chance, we'd better go," he whispered next to her ear.

She drew a breath and nodded. Reluctant to leave the group, Tess followed Anthony down the dark narrow path. Adrenaline continued to surge through her veins, sending prickles up her arms and into her shoulders. Her elbows scuffed the cold jagged rocks that protruded from the stone walls as they made their way through the claustrophobic darkness.

The damp sand filled her sandals, sifting between her toes and making it difficult to walk steadily. Barefoot would have been better, but she feared what she might step on. With eyes alert and her nerves heightened, visions of cave creatures hiding in the crevices made her shudder. She gripped Anthony's hand tighter. A shadow of light cascaded down the narrow passage, but the light grew dimmer, near-total darkness, as they continued.

A musty smell, like a cellar of an old brick building, filled her nose. Her handbag snagged and she gasped, certain she had been caught by one of the goons chasing them. Realizing only the woven purse had ensnared on a sharp rock, Tess twisted and jerked the material free. A swatch of fabric hung loose, dangling by a thread.

Anthony placed his hand on her shoulder. "Watch yourself."

She readjusted her purse, slinging it over her head and across her shoulder as she ducked through the rock passage. As they ventured further into the darkness, the walls closed in around them, and her stomach churned. Fearing the overhanging stones, Tess reached out her hand, careful not to hit her head. The jagged rocks scraped her palms. She jerked her hand back and stumbled. More of the cave floor dirt clumped into her sandals, she flicked her ankles, clearing the gritty substance. The idea of wandering aimlessly in a cave made her legs weaken.

"How do you know where we're going? I can't see a thing," she whispered, hoping her voice wouldn't echo too far. She held her breath and her fingers navigated more rocks near her head.

"It's not far, I've been here before," Anthony assured her.

"Let me guess, another drug deal passage?" she said.

Her sarcasm flared, but Tess didn't care. In the last twenty-four hours, she'd been groped, shot at, licked by a monkey, hurled down the side of a mountain with chickens, and now chased through a cavern claiming to sacrifice virgins. She didn't know how much more she could take and certainly never expected to have endured so much already.

Anthony stopped abruptly. She crowded into him. Her free hand slid over his back and down his arm as she braced herself. The cave was colder than the outside temperature, but the rocks and moist sand made the air muggy. She could feel perspiration through his shirt. His muscles were taut, and he made no remark at her stumbling into him. Her shoulders tensed. She wanted to take back her comment. Had she made him angry? Would he decide he'd had enough and leave her? How would she ever find her way out? Her eyes watered and her knees shook.

"Are we lost?" she asked timidly.

"Shh...," he said, his body rigid.

Moments lingered as Tess stood silently next to Anthony, waiting. Just inches from their heads, the crowded cavern with its jagged rocks formed around them. Her body pushed against the dank walls and a soft whirring sound echoed through the tight channel. Tess held her breath, listening into the dark cavern as a cool breeze gently brushed across her legs. The muted plinking of water echoed in the distance. It sounded like a faint cadence— like that of a slow leaking faucet.

"No, we're not lost," Anthony said, finally answering her. "We head towards the dripping water."

Then, just as before, he stepped firmly ahead, her hand still gripped in his as he led her through the dark maze. The path twisted like a switchback as they squeezed past the sharp rocks surrounding them. Once through the narrow passage, a faint glow lit the corridor. Instantly her anxious muscles relaxed, and the aching in her shoulders subsided. Her gaze focused ahead, eager to reach the end.

The closer she stepped to the faint hue of light, the more the claustrophobic walls opened wider. Beyond Anthony's broad frame, she could see up high into the rocks. A sliver of sunlight filtered through the crevice overhead. Finally, they stepped from the jagged entombment and into a small open cavern not much bigger than her shabby hotel room.

Her eyes adjusted to the dimly lit hollow filled with eerie shadows cast about the modest space. A dark shape, like a slab of granite, balanced over the boulder. It was a large stone and filled the middle of the cave. A form shimmered atop the rock. Her attention lingered on the faint, lifeless heap that sparkled on the granite-like stone. Images of zombies clawing their way out of the shadows filled her mind and shivers ran down her spine.

"Where do we go, now?" her voice trembled.

Anthony glanced around the room. His gaze paused towards a darkened arch-like hole on the other side of the shimmering heap. It looked like a doorway of sorts that could lead the way out.

"Is that where we're going?" Tess asked, pointing to the black abyss.

"No, the tour uses that path. They'll be coming through there soon."

"Can't we follow them out?" she asked.

"Well, I suppose if you want to meet up with Sergey and his friends" he said.

"How, then, do we get out of here?" she asked, ignoring his sarcasm.

Anthony turned to the creviced wall furthest from the arched rock doorway. He placed his hand on the jagged surface and muttered under his breath. "It's dry," he said.

"Dry? What's dry?" she asked.

"The wall," he kept his voice low.

A sliver of light illuminated his face, and she followed his gaze as Anthony looked up at the tiny opening. Her eyes widened.

"Uh, no—," Tess stammered, "you aren't suggesting we climb the wall, are you?" she spoke in a loud whisper.

"Look. The rocks form a natural staircase," he pointed up to the stone blockade.

She could see protruding slabs of quartz-like rock that led to the opening overhead.

"A staircase?" Her mouth gaped. "It's got to be four stories high!" she exclaimed, keeping her voice low.

Anthony raised his brow. "More like five," he said and began to climb.

Her legs weakened and she doubted his sanity. "But I ..."

"If we stay here, Sergey will find us. We have no choice," his eyes softened. "You'll be fine, follow me."

Anthony stopped and held out his hand. Tess looked up at the wall then back at the dark mass that lay on the limestone slab—the virgin's mummified body, she supposed. More visions of zombies gnashing about raced through her mind. She sighed heavily, realizing they had no other choice. Reaching down, Tess removed her sandals, shaking out the sand and placing them into her bag.

The cave floor tickled her feet as the cool, thousand-year-old granules sifted over her toes. She situated her purse, slinging it across her chest and resting it onto her hip. Her fingers caught in the loose thread holding the tattered patch of material. Flicking her hand, Tess yanked her fingers free. The torn fabric swatch glided unnoticed to the ground. Mustering her courage, she gulped hard then reached out and grasped Anthony's hand. She had never rock climbed before. Her knees wobbled as her toes curled, gripping the cool stones as the rough surface scraped her feet.

Anthony stepped ahead and turned, standing on a small protruding ledge. He reached his hand out. Tess grabbed ahold and he pulled her up. Her legs trembled. For a moment he held her—his arms wrapped around her waist. She steadied herself and he let her go. Her hands gripped the stone. She took a deep breath, watching him climb up to the next step. Anthony helped guide her as they continued their ascent. They climbed until they reached a slab-like rock that extended from the rockface. Anthony stopped and they both took a moment to rest. Tess looked down where they had started their climb but all she could see was darkness.

"How far up are we?"

"About fifty feet, I suppose. We're almost out," he said.

"Great! Now I can cross rock climbing off my list," she said, panting out of breath. She took a moment and rested against the wall.

"We should keep going," Anthony said, holding out his hand. "Ready?"

"As I'll ever be," she quipped, convincing herself to keep going.

Anthony again led the way. Tess started up the same rock path. Her legs still trembled but this time, she groaned, it was from fatigue, not fear. She pushed on, gripping tight to each crevice offered. Anthony turned to help her, but Tess was right behind him. He nodded approvingly and continued scaling the rock. Swiftly and precisely, Anthony climbed the wall. Tess followed.

Just days ago, he had been a stranger to her. Now, as she scaled the sheer wall, she realized she was again entrusting her life into his hands. Of all the times to wonder, she chastised herself, but perhaps she had misjudged him. The caring side he showed now was endearing, showing a possibility that there was more to this self-assured drug dealer than what she had seen on the Charisa. Pushing her thoughts aside, she refocused on the task at hand and continued to navigate the steep incline.

"It gets a little tricky near the opening," Anthony said, reaching out.

The ledge was higher than the last one and there was little room to maneuver. She stood on her toes to grab his hand. Just then her foot slipped. She gasped. Immediately his grip tightened around her wrist. Drawing in a deep breath, Tess glanced down the steep rockface to the cavern floor below. Tess's head swooned and her legs shook.

"Steady. I've got you," Anthony said.

Hastily, he pulled her onto the ledge beside him. Her heartbeat thumped heavily in her chest and her ears rang deafeningly from the near fall. Anthony looked up at the opening. His brow creased hard. She was sure he contemplated her ability to make it to the top.

"Wait here and I'll help pull you to the next ledge," he said.

He climbed on ahead. Tess could see there were only a few more feet to go and they would be out of the rock tomb hell-hole. She drew in her breath, then gathered her skirt between her legs, tucking it into her bikini bottoms. With renewed courage, she shifted her bag over her shoulder and out of the way. Brushing the loose strands of her hair behind her ear, she then wiped her palms across her hips.

"I came here for an adventure," Tess muttered under her breath, "this is as good as any, I suppose."

Adrenaline surged through her. She stretched her arms gripping the protruding rocks and pulled herself up along the wall, gripping the tiny ledges. Below voices murmured. She turned, looking down. A wand of lights danced across the dark archway. The crowd's awed chatter echoed up the walls. It was the umbrella woman, Tess noticed, leading her troops through the maze.

"Stay close, everyone. This is the exciting part of the tour!" the voice cheered.

"That's an understatement," Tess murmured as she looked up at Anthony who was now climbing out the top of the cave opening.

Without hesitation, Anthony turned back towards her, leaning down with his outstretched arm. The lights flickered more brightly from the group of tourists filing into the cavern. Tess glanced back to the group below.

"Gather around, everyone. Squeeze next to your neighbor," the umbrella leader directed. The crowd shuffled into the entombed cave and Tess could hear the tour guide's voice more clearly. "We're here at the famous virgin sacrifice," she paused for the crowd's gasp. "Here you'll find the crystallized bones," the woman shone her flashlight on the petrified mass. The onlookers, again, gasped in unison. Without hesitation the guide continued her spiel. "It was the Mayan's belief that a pure sacrifice would end their era of drought and famine..."

"Great," Tess groaned, "I'm climbing out the archway of death!"

The mass of tourists filled the cave floor, and the host continued her story. Tess looked up at Anthony. She watched him glance down at the crowd. His face hardened.

"Reach for my hand," his voice rumbled low.

Tess could hear the anxiousness in his voice as he gazed below her. She turned and looked down into the group. Three figures shoved through the tourist mob. A lump the size of a grapefruit formed in her gut as she recognized Sergey emerging from the crowd. His lanky figure twisted in the dim light. Tess gripped Anthony's forearm and with a surge of energy, she pushed off the last step. Her foot slipped, bouncing her hard against the rock wall and brushing her purse against the rocks. The bag caught onto a rock and a patch of loose shale trickled down to the underground chamber. Tess gasped. Anthony held her forearm tight and pulled her the last few feet up and out of the cave.

***

SERGEY PUSHED through the tourists. The faded sound of tumbling rocks caught his attention. He strode quickly over to the cavern wall. Another rock dwindled down. He looked at the cave floor where a rock landed at his feet. Sergey crouched. A fragment of woven material lay on the cool sand next to him. Picking it up, he ran his fingers across the tattered threads. Slowly he looked up. Light filtered up the jagged rocks. Sergey glared at the gaping hole above. Clenching his jaw, he tossed the piece of garment aside. His two cronies stood next to him. Sergey nodded towards the opening then bolted past his henchmen and the oblivious crowd.

"Let's go!" he said.

Chapter Seventeen

The Chase

OUTSIDE THE COOLNESS OF THE cave, the humidity draped over them. Perspiration glistened on her face and the thin ruffles of her sundress clung to her body. Anthony's arm remained securely wrapped around her waist.

"Well, that was close!" she exclaimed.

Had he not grabbed for her in those last moments she would certainly have fallen to her death and most-likely joined the petrified bones of the sacrificial virgin below. She shuddered. Anthony continued to hold her tight. She could feel his breath against the side of her cheek. Tess savored the embrace. Her hand rested on his chest and the thrusting pulse of his heart pounded beneath his linen shirt. Her skirt, still tucked into the waistband of her bikini, exposed her thighs. She lifted her eyes and watched him glance down at her bare skin. His gaze shifted back to her face. Again, she found herself lost in the sweet, luring darkness of his eyes. Her head swooned, aroused by his closeness. She delighted in the moment, wanting it to last.

Her life at home seemed so long ago. The thought of returning to her New York existence, with its endless concrete mountains and suffocating air, filled her with a sense of dread. Rush hour traffic and agendas without meaning were senseless here. She reflected on the day spent with the villagers and Rubi. All this time, she had only focused on getting back—back to the hotel. But as she stood, wrapped in Anthony's embrace, realization awakened and her mind whirled. She didn't want to go back to her old life, her dull old life.

A persistent ringing filled her ears, intensified by his nearness. She could feel him, his desire. Anticipation welled within her, and a surge of passion swept over her. She leaned closer, pressing against his solid frame, her head tilting back. Slowly she closed her eyes and parted her lips. Without warning, he released his grip. She stumbled off-balance, blinking her eyes open and watched the tenderness she had felt just moments ago harden across his face. Anthony turned towards the jungle, turning away from her. He ran his hands through his hair and cleared his throat.

"We had better get going. It won't take long before Sergey figures out where we went."

Oh, why did I let myself do that! Her mind reeled. How could she have been so wrong? Was she so desperate for love that she made up the way he looked at her? Mortified, Tess drew in a deep breath. Resolve replaced desire as she looked past Anthony's shoulders, staring at the thick wall of palmed bushes in front of them. A noise rustled in the leaves followed by a dense sounding thud. Something fell to the ground next to her. Tess jumped back. Startled, she gazed down at the jungle flora. A large, green lizard-like creature glanced up at her. She screeched and the beast scampered off through the palms.

"What was that?" she asked.

"Just an iguana, it won't bother you. Let's get going," he said.

Tess hated the notion of traipsing through more twisted vines, spider webs, and whatever else lay before them. She gathered up her courage, determined to get back to her hotel and stop this fantasy—or rather, nightmare. She scrunched her nose in the prospective direction and hesitantly looked around.

"There? We're going in there? What about the lizard-thing, will there be more?" she said, cringing.

Without remark, Anthony pushed back the overgrowth of palm fronds. She could see the indentation of a worn trail. Thick foliage bowed across its path. Unaffected by her passion or the scaled reptile just moments earlier, Anthony ducked through the leaves and headed down the dense trail.

"Right, don't tell me anything!" she fumed.

Untucking the material from her bikini, she reached into her purse for her sandals. The clasp snagged the woven material, and she yanked it free. A tattered thread draped from the strap. She scoffed at the newly formed hole in her bag. Hurried, Tess tugged her sandals on, wincing as she thrust her aching feet into the thin soles. She wondered which hurt more—her sore toes, or her bruised ego. Clenching her jaw, she slung the bag over her shoulder and rushed after him.

Her thoughts reeled. Could Anthony be playing her? No, she dismissed the idea. He had led her safely through the cave. If they hadn't climbed out, Sergey and his men would certainly have found them. Images of the toothless thug made her shudder. But, she wondered, had he only done that to save himself? Was Anthony really taking her back to the hotel? If not...she bit her lip. Like it or not, she was legs deep into something that was dangerous, and she had yet to know exactly what it was. Her eyes narrowed as she watched Anthony, undeniably involved, steadily trekking ahead. His exact involvement, other than stealing the crate from the ocean, remained unknown. This, Tess decided, would have to change. She stopped on the path and placed her hands on her hips.

"I've had enough!" she said and faced the overgrown trail. "I'm not going any further until you tell me who you really are and why those men are chasing you—I mean chasing us."

Anthony paused. Without turning around, he shook his head and continued down the narrow path.

"I won't follow you!" she called out.

This time he stopped. Anthony clenched his hands and spun around. He walked briskly towards her. "Everything?" he said, scoffing. "What part do you think you need to know? You, my dear, have been a thorn in my side since I met you! I never planned on being your tour guide," Anthony snapped and continued down the trail.

"Oh really!" she huffed. "Well, I was doing just fine without you."

Anthony raised the back of his hand and swished it through the air.

"Oh!" she said, exasperated. "You're impossible!" With that, she started down the sharp hillside.

The path grew steeper, and she found herself taking large jolting strides just to keep up. Anthony's steps were now far enough ahead that the giant green jungle leaves slapped back into her face. A grossly woven web crossed over her lips. Tess sputtered, cringing at the familiar taste lashing itself across her tongue.

Wiping her arm across her mouth, a small piece of foliage, or at least that's what she hoped it was, stuck onto her lips. She spit the sticky clump out and looked ahead to the next over-sized palm leaf blocking the trail. Maneuvering cautiously, she made it past the next thick web, which hosted another craggy legged spider dangling off to one side. Its bulging, bright-yellow, and hairy body twirled over the path. The creature's long legs stretched out helplessly, spinning uncontrollably from the aftermath of Anthony pushing through the fronds. She hurried to keep up. A flutter of birds flew just above her head as she finally caught up to him. He glanced back at her and continued forging ahead.

"It looked like you were enjoying yourself to me, going off with Sergey on some snorkeling excursion," Anthony quipped.

Tess gasped. "And exactly what is that supposed to mean?"

"Just an observation; it seems you don't have any trouble getting men to follow you when you want them to."

"It wasn't my fault I ended up on a drug smuggler's boat."

The argument sounded weak, even to her, but anger had taken the place of common sense, and she was determined to make him obligingly aware.

"And, before the boat?" he baited. "The night I met you at the cantina, you weren't that shy then either. You seemed to rather enjoy hanging on to me in front of your...," he paused as he snapped a branch across the trail, "your precious Roger. How well do you even know him? Doesn't it strike you odd that the snorkeling tour your boyfriend hired turns out to be a rendezvous with a notorious drug lord?"

She reached out her arm and held back a frond ready to slap across her face. Vines tangled across the path.

"That's absurd! Roger didn't have...," she paused as Anthony abruptly stopped.

She looked up. Anthony squatted down on the trail, gesturing for her to stop. Tess froze in place. Another flutter of birds flushed from their perch. The surprised fowl squawked indignantly. Tess squinted. She could see movement and heard swishing noises coming from the brush below. A man swung a machete through the thick leaves and the birds scattered. Loud caws sounded the alarm. More birds flittered from below and landed high in the trees. Anthony motioned for her to get down and pressed his finger to his lips. The argument could wait. She knelt by his side. Her heartbeat drummed into her ears as she gazed upon the unwelcome figures below.

The commotion of the macaws hushed, and the men's voices carried through the eerie stillness of the jungle. She strained to listen, but they were too far away. Tess recognized the man in front. It was, again, Sergey. The other two henchmen crowded behind him. Sergey pointed across the jungle floor with his long knife in hand. Tess could hear his thick Russian accent. Still, she couldn't make out what he said. She leaned in closer. Her weight shifted and a branch cracked under her foot. Tess's eyes widened as Anthony turned and glared at her. Looking down at her sandals and the broken twig, his mouth hardened as he shook his head. Tess shrugged, defenselessly.

The group of men stopped, and the jungle turned silent. A chill crept up her spine and fear pricked at the nape of her neck. Tess feared her heartbeat's deep pounding would permeate beyond her own ears and echo across the brush. The sun filtered slightly through the trees sweeping over her and Anthony. Tess tried her best to be still. One of the men looked in their direction, Tess held her breath. The scoundrel's stone-like face squinted, scanning the forest. She and Anthony hunkered down. The intruder took another step in their direction. Tess froze, fearing their hiding spot had been compromised. Suddenly, a large macaw burst from the thick bush next to the detestable man. The jungle fowl brushed over the low-life and the tip of the bird's tail slapped the startled ravager on top of his balding head. The crook wielded his enormous machete, but the colorful feathered beast squawked and flew higher out of the man's range. The bird's piercing cry disrupted the remainder of the hidden flock and within moments the entire jungle screeched and chattered all around them. The pock-faced thug stood still, glaring back up the hill. She and Anthony crouched lower out of sight. Grumbling, the would-be assailant turned to the other marauders. He raised his machete in the direction of the disappearing birds, swiping haphazardly through the air. Disgruntled, he rejoined the others.

Tess and Anthony waited, gazing intently as the gang reconvened. Looking down the steep incline, she watched as Sergey pointed his heavy steel knife up the hill, grumbling something to his partners. Tingling radiated sharply through her knees. The lack of blood flow was taking its toll. Finally, after what seemed like forever, the criminals turned and went the other direction, thrashing and wielding their machetes through the overgrown jungle, away from where she and Anthony hid. Tess let out a heavy sigh. Her gaze shifted to Anthony who remained crouched and motionless until the men disappeared. Slowly he turned. His lips curled.

"Did you still want to stay out here alone?"

Chapter Eighteen

The Climb

BOTH TESS AND ANTHONY REMAINED hidden. Her legs ached, every muscle burning as she crouched alongside the path. Vigilant, she gazed out across the green jungle foliage. The machete wielding invaders were nowhere in sight, but the oversized fronds below provided the perfect cover should Sergey and his thugs plot an ambush. She strained, listening for the bushwhacking cadence. But the hair-raising sound of sharpened blades slashing through the waxy palms had gone.

The sun shone brighter amidst the lush canopy of trees, and the early afternoon dampness faded as warm, sweltering temperatures rose. Dust particles glimmered in the rays as the tiny spores drifted through the air carried along by the gentle breeze. The sweet scent of palm leaves whirled through the forest. Like fresh cut grass, the jungle oozed with fragrance, no doubt the result of Sergey's chopping through the ferns and other brush along the entangled grounds.

Now, with the marauders gone, the screeching macaws ceased, leaving the jungle peaceful once again. It wasn't long, however, before the buzzing of insects grew louder. She had never been in a forest, at least not one as wild as the Belizean jungle. Giant, black flying beetles meandered in front of her. Fluttering wings, disproportionate to their heavy bodies, gave the insects a rollercoaster-type flight pattern. Agile gnats, disrupted from their deciduous hiding spots, zipped past the circus-like beetles. Simulating five o'clock rush hour on a Friday afternoon, the buzzing mass of insects darted back and forth. Tess found it difficult to avoid the pests flying overhead—dodging near collisions.

The gnats encircled her. Like a pendulum out of control, Tess swished her arm through the air hoping to avoid inhaling them. The beady-eyed combatants taunted her, but their movements were too fast. She feared the pesky creatures landing, biting her soft, and no-doubt succulent tasting skin, at least succulent to bugs, she presumed. Tess swatted more erratically, swinging her arms wildly through the air. Finally, their high-pitched buzzing faded off into the thickets. Darting the irritating imps one last scowl, she turned her attention back to the hillside where Sergey and his thugs had been. Tess caught a sideways glimpse of Anthony. His once angelic brown eyes glared at her, and his lips tightly contorted. With wide eyes, she shrugged then adjusted her skirt and sat quietly.

"Are the men gone?" Tess whispered.

"I think so," he said.

Cautiously, Anthony stood. Tess scanned across the jungle below then back to Anthony. With lines creased across his forehead, Anthony's jaw tightened. Sergey's presence had been unexpected and the worried look on Anthony's face made Tess even more uneasy.

"Now where do we go? We can't go down there," she pointed, "they might be hiding in those bushes."

Anthony stroked his chin then gestured across the hill to another peak. It, too, was covered in dense, overgrown ferns. "We'll have to go around," he said.

As she rose to her feet, sharp tingling sensations surged through her legs. She massaged the back of her knees while eyeing the thick, nearly impenetrable path that Anthony had pointed out. She took a step closer to him, intent on finding another option but the toe of her sandal snagged on a vine. With her legs still numb from the lack of blood flow, she staggered and stumbled backwards. Tess's eyes widened. She reached for a sturdy frond to help steady herself, but the heel of her sandal slipped over the dense trail's edge. Tess gasped. Anthony lunged towards her, wrapping his arms around her waist, and pulling her close to him. She could almost taste the aromatic scent of jungle musk and Anthony's sweet perspiration as her head fell onto his shoulder. Quickly, she regained her composure and pulled away from his embrace. This time, she decided, she would keep her emotions in check. Although their argument prior to Sergey's surprise appearance had ended, there were still questions left unanswered. For now, she rationalized, they could wait.

Anthony glanced down at her tattered sandals. His brow creased and the lines along his jaw deepened. Lifting his gaze, Anthony looked out towards the hilly terrain. She was beginning to understand his sorted look and she, too, glanced down at her feet. The delicate boutique sandals were coming apart. Only a few threads held the strap around her ankle and the stretched-out elastic caused the soles to flap with each step. She had to curl her toes to hold them on. The jagged rocks of the cave had done their worst. Scrunching her nose, she looked up at Anthony.

"These definitely weren't meant for hiking," she said.

"Agreed, but we can't go down the hill and risk running into Sergey or his hoods again. Do you think you can make it across and over to that ridge?"

Again, she looked where he pointed. A blanket of green covered the hillside and, from where they were standing, she couldn't see any clear path. Tess arched her brow.

"I suppose I've made it this far. What's another five hundred feet uphill and practically barefoot?" she said.

"That's the spirit! Now, let's get going."

"Wait!" she said, bending down. Tess grasped the loose strap and twisted it into a knot, then lifted her foot and shook it about. Satisfied, she did the same to the other shoe. "There, good as new."

"I didn't know you were a cobbler," he chuckled.

"Well, stick around," she smiled, "maybe you'll learn more about me."

"Yes, maybe I will," he said.

She noticed his gaze shifted toward her, but this time his expression softened. They proceeded up the path with Tess trailing just behind him. She was glad to be moving on, relieved that the hostility between them had subsided.

***

THE CLIMB had been easier than expected, but the hard twisted knot on her sandals rubbed her ankles. She would welcome any opportunity to rest, and soon. Besides, she reasoned, the air seemed thinner, and each step felt heavier, as if ten-pound aerobic weights were strapped to her ankles.

"Can we stay here a minute?" she asked.

Out of breath, she didn't wait for an answer. Off to the side was a small boulder, like an ottoman, and Tess seized the moment to rest. Sitting down on the smooth rock, Tess rubbed her aching toes. Anthony turned towards her, but she avoided any eye contact.

"We can rest for a moment, I suppose. But we should keep going if we're going to stay ahead of Sergey."

"Stay ahead of him? How could he get ahead of us?" Tess looked back at the hill they had just climbed. She was certain they had tricked Sergey and his cutthroats. Grinning, she reveled in their successful getaway. Suddenly she winced. "Ouch!"

Her hands rubbed over her tired feet and unknowingly across the raw sores from her tattered shoes. The sides of her ankles were an angry color of red, raw from the loosened straps. Two blisters formed on each side of her unprepared foot. She cringed and wished there were some other way down the hill. Anthony glanced at her wounds. His face hardened. Tess tried to make light of the situation.

"Well, maybe we could just fly across the jungle and land at the hotel," she joked.

Anthony's expression remained the same. Distracted, Tess wiped a cobweb from her arm. Removing jungle debris from her clothing and body was becoming all too familiar. She picked at a torn leaf slivered into the threads of her shoulder bag then tugged to release the twig. More of the brilliant-colored material unraveled. Tess sighed. It was silly, she knew, but she just wanted to keep her purse and what was left of her sundress in one piece. They were her souvenirs from before all the craziness, simple tokens to get her through the mayhem. Anthony didn't seem to notice her despair and stood ready to trudge, once more, down the trail.

"We should get going," he said.

She straightened her skirt and grumbled as her hand ran across another tear.

"Really?" she huffed. Exasperated, she turned to Anthony. "Can we just zip out of here?"

She knew it would be an impossible thing to do, but just saying the words made her feel better. At first, he frowned but then his brows arched, and his face brightened.

"You're a genius!" Anthony bolstered.

Bewildered, she noticed the hard lines of his brow soften. Cockiness exuded over him, a flashback to the night at the Grand Simone flickered through her mind. It was the same enchanting look he had when she introduced him to Roger, and Anthony pretended to be her boyfriend. His eyes sparkled then, too. Those deep-brown amazingly magnetic eyes. A warm surge spiraled through her body, leaving a trail of goosebumps down her arms.

"What? What did I say?" she asked.

Anthony reached out and held her by the shoulders. "A zipline!"

He meaninglessly kissed her on the forehead like a pet and rushed past her. Tess scrambled after him.

"Wait! A *what* line?" she asked.

Anthony flashed a mischievous grin. "There's an old abandoned zipline up here."

"But how...where...what?" she sputtered.

Before she could protest any further, Anthony parted the thick underbrush and started up the hill. "It's on the tourist list of things to do," he shouted back.

"Great, I envisioned I would save that for another vacation, you know, one where I wasn't being chased through jungles by machete wielding crazy people!"

Anthony stopped and turned around. "What? Is this the same woman who went scuba diving with drug runners? You're afraid of a little zipline?"

Again, he didn't wait for her reply. Instead, he continued up the hill. She was sure she heard him chuckle. It would be no use arguing, she realized. Taking a deep breath, she followed after him.

"What next?" she mumbled.

Trudging up the hill, her mind wandered. Here she was trekking through the jungle with a man she hardly knew and on her way to a zipline, no less. It was all crazy. Back home her life revolved around appointments and meetings, patterns, and color wheels. She didn't have time for frivolous escapades. Never would she have seen herself on such an adventure, and now she was about to fly through the trees. She couldn't remember what he had said and decided now would be a good time to clarify the details to their destination. Tess hurried to catch up. Her brow furrowed slightly, and she cocked her head.

"Hey! Wait a minute. What did you mean when you said abandoned zipline?"

"Just that, abandoned," he said, matter-of-fact like.

"Uh-huh, that's what I thought you said. And why was it abandoned? It's not like there's a lack of tourists in the area." She recalled the crowd at the cave.

"The locals stopped using it a couple of years back. I don't know all the specifics."

With her hands resting on her hips, Tess paused, panting. Anthony looked back at her. He arched his brow.

"Do you need to rest?" he asked.

"No," she lied.

"Good, we're just about there."

He reached out his hand. With her energy almost spent, she gladly took ahold and let him pull her up. But still, in her mind the question lingered about the zipline and what might be in store for them.

Anthony's swift stride carried him far enough ahead that each palm leaf he held swung prematurely back at her. She pushed through the green fronds trying to keep up. But Anthony was nowhere in sight. Dread spiraled through her, sending shards of tingling sensations carousing up her arm and into her shoulders. Gritting her teeth, she took a deep breath and focused on the path ahead. Rushing forward, Tess pushed through the overgrowth.

Another waxy branch swiped across her face. Tess spewed at the all too familiar taste. Anthony was just ahead, his tall figure weaved through the foliage. Before she could catch up, another palm frond swished across the trail obscuring his sweat-soaked shirt from view and swinging at her like a western saloon door. In the muggy heat, she drew in deep heavy breaths; a sigh of relief escaped her when she caught sight of him again. Anthony stopped in the middle of the overgrown path and looked out across the jungle. Tess was glad to catch up and rest for a moment. She wanted to know more about this mysterious zipline he was taking her to.

"Why was it abandoned?" she panted, waiting for his reply. But, simultaneous to her question, he hurried off.

"Something to do with safety issues," his voice trailed.

This time he remained in sight, and she followed after him. Sweat trickled down her face as loose strands of her auburn hair stuck to her cheek. She wiped her forehead with the back of her hand and tried to moisten her lips with her tongue. But her tongue was too dry, and her throat grated like sandpaper. Wherever they were going, she hoped they would arrive soon. Tess trudged forward, grabbing another group of palm leaves, and pulling herself along the crude path.

"What kind of issues?" she asked, huffing.

Anthony turned and again held out his hand. Perspiration glistened across his brow. She grabbed ahold of his forearm and the sensual aroma of jungle sweat filled her nostrils. The musky scent aroused her, and she suppressed the unexpected urges that spiraled through her.

A frond brushed against her. It tickled her arm, and she shifted her gaze to investigate the sensation. To her horror, a spindle legged spider, the size of a grapefruit, swung dizzily from a thick, silvery web. Its coarse waxy legs stretched out, reaching for her wrist. Tess jumped, letting out a blood curdling scream that filled the jungle. Tears welled at the corner of her eyes. The creature, unfazed, twirled its spindled body as it lowered itself onto the jungle flora. Anthony burst into laughter. He let go of her hand and stepped over the creature then gestured to her to follow. Tess shook her head.

"I don't think so," she cringed.

She looked down at the over-sized alien-like creature. The beast raised itself up on its back legs and fangs pinched back and forth through the air, as if trying to ward off its enemy.

"His appearance is more venomous than he is," Anthony assured her.

"Eww, I don't care what it is. I don't want to be around it!"

Tess shuddered and high-stepped past the monstrous, eight-legged spider. She envisioned the waxy acrophobic leaping onto her head. Convulsing her body, she jumped up and down while swiping her hands over her face making sure the critter couldn't land. Anthony pushed back another large leaf.

"We're here," he said.

Tess looked up. The sun pierced through the brush and the tall trees. The path had led them high up on a hill and over to a landing made of natural stone. Now, instead of looking through the dense green jungle, she could see over the treetops and across the ravine. The forest air smelled fresh in comparison to the dense humid jungle. Again, she tried to wet her lips, but her mouth was still too dry.

"It would be nice to get some water," she said, trying to swallow her saliva but without having any success. "My mouth feels like sandpaper."

Anthony reached into his shirt pocket, pulling out two small star fruit.

"Where did you get those?" Tess asked, salivating.

"They were next to the trail where you did your spider dance," he grinned, handing her the bright yellow fruit. "I was saving them until we reached the top."

Sitting near the edge of the trail, Tess looked across the treetops. Her blistered feet welcomed the rest. Tess bit into the fresh fruit as juice trickled over her fingers. "Mmm," she moaned, "it's delicious!"

Anthony nodded in agreement. The sweet nectar quenched the coarseness of her throat and immediately her body revived.

"This is amazing up here. I've never seen anything like it," she said.

"Yes, a little different scenery than your high-rise in Manhattan, I imagine."

"Well, I don't know about Manhattan but, yes, it's different than the city."

The wind brushed softly across her cheek as she let her mind drift. She tipped her head back, closed her eyes and savored the moment. Life back home seemed so far away. Tess sat up and opened her eyes. She looked over at Anthony; his back faced her as he looked out over the green canopy of trees. She stared, wondering about his life here in Belize, and why he chose a life of crime. The wind rippled across his shirt and lifted the soft curls of his hair. Anthony didn't seem like the criminal type but reading people had proved not to be her strong point. Besides, she had seen him take the drugs from Rolan's yacht. Tess let out a heavy sigh, disappointed by the truth.

Resting on her elbows, Tess looked around the deep green jungle below. She glanced back at the open landing. Just past Anthony's shoulders, near the rock wall, she could see a faint outline, like an old pathway. Her eyes followed the vague, overgrown indentation. The hard-to-see path meandered along the rock wall, intertwining between large, smooth boulders. At first, she didn't think very much about it. But as she looked further down the trail that wound past the boulders, the weathered remains of a small wooden platform came into view. Her interest piqued and she sat up straight. Tess held her hand over her brow blocking the glare from the sun, excitement worked its way up her spine. Tess stood up, pointing towards the disheveled stand.

"Is that the abandoned zipline?" she asked.

Anthony got up, wiping the juice dripping from his hands. He walked up to the weathered boards, half hidden by the overgrown shrubs. Tess gathered her woven bag and followed after him.

At the end of the steep path, the sun-bleached boards lay jumbled along the edge of the hillside. Tess imagined they must have formed a railing at one time, however, now the fasteners had rotted, leaving the boards scattered. She stood next to Anthony, cautious of the drop-off just steps away. Her stomach turned and her heart pounded when she unintentionally glanced down the steep hill. The sheer drop made her legs weak. Her head began to spin as she looked down into the gorge below. Heights were not her forte, she conceded. It had taken her weeks to muster the courage to ride her office elevator to the tenth floor without holding the railing along the elevator box wall. The same had been true for her high-rise apartment. Roger had always made fun of her fear of heights. The unwanted image of Roger spurred her to defy his negative assessment and she stepped closer to the edge. Her legs wobbled. Taking deep breaths, she exhaled slowly, calming her nerves.

The fresh air swirled around her, causing her light cotton skirt with its tattered edges to ripple in the wind. She tucked loose strands of hair behind her ear and looked out across the ravine. In the distance, beyond the trees she could see a sliver of aqua-blue. At first, she thought it was the horizon but quickly realized it was the massive Belizean seawater. She gestured towards the ocean, unable to make out any sign of the city.

"Down there? Is that where we're going?" she asked.

Anthony looked up from his task briefly looking over at the horizon. "Yes, as a matter of fact it is, and this is how we'll get there."

He pointed to a rickety contraption anchored to an enormous rock. Curious of what lay below, she cautiously peered over the edge. The vast drop off was laden with boulders and treetops that stared back at her. Its depth made her stomach flop, sending waves of nausea to the back of her throat. She held back the urge to vomit but the aftereffects of looking down had made her woozy. The ground tilted slightly, and Tess staggered. Anthony put his arm around her waist, pulling her swiftly away from the edge. She leaned into him, grateful for the stability.

"Maybe you should stay back from the edge, at least for now."

"Yes, good idea," she agreed.

He steadied her, then walked over to the boulder. Anthony ran his hand across the metal pegs drilled into the side of the stone wall, anchoring the zipline. The thin cables stretched across the gorge and disappeared into the thickness of the jungle far below. He stepped onto the disheveled platform, but immediately the boards depressed like sea sponges under his weight. Certain that the entire deck shifted, Tess threw a weary glance at Anthony. With eyebrows arched, he met her gaze briefly, shrugging his shoulders. But Tess had other thoughts, and trusting the rusted contraption wasn't one of them.

Anthony pulled on the line. "It seems to be alright," he said.

Tess looked across the gorge and back at Anthony. "How old is this place?" she asked, unimpressed. "It looks like something the *Mayans* left behind, a century ago!"

"Well, I suppose you have a better idea?" he asked.

She pointed at the crusted cables. "Any idea would be better than flinging myself over the edge and imminent death while holding onto those!" she blurted.

Anthony ignored her as he continued tugging at the wire. The line squeaked, protesting like a broken-down shopping cart. Her eyes widened and her shoulders tensed. She would have felt safer in a grocery buggy than riding on the decaying cables. Tess pointed at the rusted bolt twisting and grinding to its precarious tune.

"Like that!" Tess pressed her lips together. "That doesn't look very promising!"

Anthony let go of the first rusted cable and stepped over to the other cable. The second line looked identical to the first. This time, though, the bolt held under his weight without squeaking. He tugged at the line fastener still impaled securely into the giant rock-face wall.

"Perhaps we'll use the other line," he said.

She watched as he stepped from the platform and looked over the coarse rocks below.

"What are you looking for?" Tess asked.

"We need a harness."

"A what?"

"A harness," he repeated, "we need it to go down the line."

"And how does this harness thing work?" she paused. "I mean, have you ever done this before?"

Anthony tapped his hand over one of the roller type contraptions. "Once we find the harness, we can clip on to these pulleys and fly over the jungle," he winked. "After all, isn't that what you wished for?" his smile broadened. "Don't worry; we'll be at the bottom of the canyon in no time at all."

"When you say, 'at the bottom of the canyon' you do mean alive, don't you?"

"Just help me search, will you?" he said.

"Look, I'm all for not walking to the bottom of the canyon, but I'd rather not fall from the sky on some broken down zipline thing-a-ma-jig that hasn't been used in...," she hesitated and looked around the overgrown area, "in quite some time!" she huffed. Squinting from the sun's bright rays, and with her hand cupped over her brow, she stepped closer to a row of shrubs that offered a small amount of shade. "Even if we did find a harness lying around, I'm not sure I'd want to use it," she said, crossing her arms.

Obvious that Anthony ignored her concerns, she stepped forward to confront him. But then a loud buzzing rang close to her head. A giant, lime-green striped bug flew into her face, smacking her in the cheek. She swatted at it, but her torn sandal with its flapping sole caught the protruding board from the dilapidated platform, twisting her foot. Letting out a helpless yelp, Tess toppled backwards landing bottom first into a heap of dead vines.

"Are you alright?" Anthony asked.

His voice sounded sincere but with a twinge of sarcasm. She looked up. The sun beamed down behind him creating his dark silhouette which now hovered over her. He held out his hand. But before taking hold of his gentleman-like gesture, she picked at her lips, removing a decayed piece of frond that had stuck to her tongue. Getting all that she could with her fingers, she leaned to the side and spit out the remaining bits.

"Plah!" The taste of dirt embedded on her tongue. Anthony held out his hand ready to pull her up. Her eyes widened. "Wait!" she exclaimed.

Sitting on the dirt she could see beneath the platform. Obscured by the wooden edge she spotted a lump of twisted thick straps lying underneath the boards. Reaching under the decking, Tess grabbed the knotted mass. The dry braided fibers pricked her skin. Tess winced. The ropes were dirty, stiff, and tattered from the jungle weather.

"Is this what we're looking for?" she asked.

"Perfect!" Anthony smiled. "Tess Martin, you never cease to surprise me."

Anthony took the heap from her. Seconds later he wrapped the bristly tethers around her.

"What about you? Where's your harness?" Tess looked about but didn't see a second belt.

Anthony held up the remnants of another harness. But even Tess could tell the twisted mass was beyond use. The fasteners were all broken and the strap to the clasp looked mangled. She doubted it could hold someone as fit as Anthony.

"It would appear there is only one we can use," he replied.

He tightened the strap around her waist. Tess's eyes widened as she looked over the edge.

"Oh no…I'm not going on that alone!" she said, turning to stare at him.

"Nonsense, you'll be fine. When you reach the first platform, take the belt off and I'll pull it back with this safety line."

Anthony held up a frayed, thin rope which had a carabiner-type clasp dangling at the end. Swiftly, he attached the rope to her harness. He must have done this before, she thought, noticing how expertly he tied the secure-looking knot. Still, fear surged through her arms, creeping to the base of her neck. The idea of making the journey solo and being the first to test the contraption's worthiness was almost paralyzing.

"But that tattered rope looks like it's going to fall apart. Isn't there another way?" she pleaded.

Before Anthony could answer, a loud crashing of limbs sounded from the bushes. Tess glanced towards the jungle. The wall of shrubs parted, and a familiar face emerged. Tess gasped and her body shuddered.

"Look out!" she cried.

A twisted smile lifted from Sergey's lips as he sprang from the overgrown trail, his machete wielding towards her and Anthony. The other two culprits immediately piled through the brush.

"Well, well, well. We finally catch up to you," Sergey sneered.

Sergey's thick accent echoed. His men lined up beside him. Each one folded their arms broadly across their chest. Their eyes narrowed. Anthony stood next to her lifting his arm slowly behind her back. She heard the clank of a clip. A heavy pit formed in her stomach, and she feared how they would escape. Anthony pushed her behind him and faced Sergey.

"We don't want any trouble," Anthony stalled.

"No. Of course not, neither do we," Sergey said, smirking at his men, then back to Anthony. "We just want to talk—don't we boys?"

With that, the lying marauder ran up the path and lunged at them. Anthony spun around. His hand pressed hard into Tess's back.

"Hold tight!" he said.

Before she knew what was happening, her feet slipped out from under her. The solid ground gave way as Anthony pushed her from the ledge. The line dipped and bounced, and she hurled down the gorge. The sound of screams, her own screams, filled her ears. The pulley whirred above her head and fear riddled throughout her body. Tess gripped the harness tight. Her feet dangled as the wind wrapped her skirt around her legs. Afraid to close her eyes, she watched as the ground moved like a blur beneath her. Her stomach leaped to her throat and her head spun. With a daredevil's grip, Tess held on.

Seconds later she felt a tug on her ratted harness. The unexpected jolt slowed her plummeting body, flinging her feet out in front of her. Simultaneously, her dress flew up in front of her face. She continued sliding across the gorge blindfolded by her worn and tattered skirt. She blindly sailed through the air. As the flower printed material flapped at her chin, Tess refused to remove her white knuckled grip from the dirt riddled harness, not even to part her skirt out of the way.

The cable jounced behind her. Tess turned her head, giving herself a partial view through the wind pressed material of her skirt, which still flapped haphazardly over her head. She gasped when she saw Anthony gliding down the steel cable behind her. His arm wrapped through the broken harness which he had clipped onto the second pulley. Tess realized it was his harness she heard clicking onto the cable back at the platform. She looked beyond his shoulders. Her eyes widened in horror as Sergey swung his machete and chopped at the bolt that tethered the cable. She knew the rusty bolts couldn't last long. The whirling noise above her clasp slowed and the cable jerked causing the line to sag even more. Anthony yelled something to her, but she couldn't make out what he said.

"What?" she yelled.

"Your feet…"

Anthony pointed ahead of her. Reluctantly Tess freed one of her hands from its death grip and pulled her skirt away from her face. At that same moment, a shadow fell over her. She gasped and tried to scream but she found herself engulfed in tree leaves that had overgrown along the line. The slick palms brushed over her as she slid by. Instinctively, she released her grip and protected her face, pushing the leaves aside. Ahead, through the jungle's thickness, a huge palm tree, bigger than any she had seen before, was in front of her, approaching fast. The zipline stretched high into its branches and the corner of a platform protruded from the overgrowth. The sag in the line helped to slow her down, but now her momentum was too stagnant. Not wanting to be stranded and dangling high in the air, Tess pulled her knees up close to her chest in an effort to create motion and continue to the tree. But her efforts failed as her body stopped short of the platform. She swung her legs hoping to inch closer. It didn't help. Next, she stretched out her toes as far as she could, but the landing was just out of reach.

"I can't reach it," she yelled.

"Heads-up!" Anthony warned.

Abruptly, his body slid into her, but Anthony absorbed the collision by wrapping his arms around her bringing her close to him. The line bounced and swayed. With his arms still wrapped around her waist she spun and clasped her hands around his shoulders. The force of their collision propelled them together and they glided the rest of the way onto the tree stand. Anthony balanced atop the platform, easing her next to him. Unlike the sun weathered planks above, the stand was more solid under the protection of the tree canopy.

"I guess I can cross zip-lining off my list now," she said.

Anthony chuckled. They looked back across the gorge. The glint of the sun reflected off Sergey's machete as he took another swing at the cable.

Suddenly, the line gave way, and the weight of the cable pulled them both closer to the platform edge. Tess grabbed the railing and held tight. Her feet started sliding off the edge. Tess gritted her teeth and fought to hold on. Anthony scrambled, tugging at her clasp. Seconds later the heavy drag of the cable released.

"That was close!" Tess exclaimed.

"Let's not waste any time," Anthony replied.

He pulled on the cable fastened to the opposite side of the sturdy tree. It held tight. Anthony swiftly clasped Tess's harness, securing it to the second cable. He reached out, placing his hand to her back but this time she stopped him.

"I've got this," she said.

Tess tucked her loose skirt into the waistband of her swimsuit. Anthony arched his brow.

"Very well," he said.

This time, Tess was prepared to glide through the trees. The fragrant scent of the jungle swirled around her face. Her eyes remained open, her adrenaline rushing through her. They were high above the ground, and she could see a small flock of birds soaring beneath her. Their colorful wings gliding back and forth with the breeze. Other jungle macaws sat perched atop their sturdy branches—black glassy eyes following along as Tess sailed past. The zipline jerked and her heart leaped. With nerves heightened, she glanced back, relieved to see Anthony gliding behind her. She turned and faced the trees ahead of her. Within moments they descended onto another platform covered with more overgrown branches. Tess pushed the fronds aside as she landed. She unclipped from the line, leaving her harness on, and hastily scrambled down the wooden ladder, glad to be on solid ground.

"How close are we now?" she asked.

Anthony tossed aside his makeshift harness. He swiftly descended the ladder and stood next to her.

"The trail will take us about a hundred yards through the brush. Then we'll be at the edge of town," he paused, "that's where the bus stop will be."

Anthony's gaze met hers. As if time stopped, she felt herself swept away, engulfed in his deep brown eyes, and lost in the whirlwind of chaos they had just escaped from. Now, his bronzed jawline and broad shoulders radiated a newfound tenderness. Her eyes lingered on his mouth, tracing the rugged stubble that darkened across his upper lip. His cheeks flexed, etching dimples into his skin, and she felt the warmth of his energy enveloping her. If there was ever a perfect time for a kiss, this would be it. She leaned in closer hoping he could read her mind. But, instead of a warm embrace or tantalizing kiss, Anthony hesitated and pulled back, just enough to disrupt the moment.

"We're almost there," he said, shifting his gaze, "you'll be home soon."

The words lingered in her mind. *Almost there.* She wondered what that would mean for her. What about Anthony, would she see him again? Tess realized she was daydreaming and that any opportunity for their lips to touch and ignite a moment of passion had fizzled out. She stood tall and cleared her throat.

"Right, we should get going," she said, fumbling with the harness clasp.

The buckle had become stuck, her fingers were swollen and sore from gripping the zipline. Anthony stepped to her side grasping the harness. His hand unintentionally brushed against her skin. Her desire for him jolted from the tips of her soft breasts to the arches of her slender feet. Anthony yanked the strap to loosen it. The motion, this time, pulled her close to him. She could feel his warm breath next to her face. Her hands rest on his chest, feeling the deep pulsating rhythm of his heart pounding through his shirt.

The buckle released. Slowly, he slid the harness over her hips and dropped it to the ground. They stared at each other. She yearned for his lips, to savor his jungle wildness and to run her hands through his dark curls. His eyes glistened. Anthony lifted her chin up towards him. His mouth parted and her heart throbbed. She didn't care anymore about right or wrong. She only knew that she wanted to be there, at that moment, with him. And this time, she knew he wanted her, too. Anthony leaned in, his lips softly caressing her as he tilted his head. With his hand pressed low around her back, he gripped her tight and held her close. Her head spun wildly, and her knees weakened; her body succumbed to her desire. This was really happening, she moaned as their mouths met. Instantly she knew. She knew she never wanted their adventure to ever be over—to never leave Belize, or Anthony.

"Tony," she whispered, "take me with you."

Anthony's lips slowly left hers. She looked into his eyes, but the brightness faded. His brow furrowed and he released his grip.

"We better get going," was all he said.

Her eyes shifted down. "Yes," she paused, "of course."

Chapter Nineteen

Safe at Last

THEY CONTINUED TO TRUDGE THROUGH the jungle. Anthony's reaction to her plea—rather the lack thereof, played over in her mind. Naturally, he wouldn't rush into her arms begging her to come with him, she sighed. It's not like they were in some fairytale where the girl meets the most incredible man she's ever met, and they ride off into the sunset. And it's not like he's the most exhilarating guy she's ever encountered, she lied to herself. Tess looked up ahead at Anthony as he steadily led the way down the trail. Each step was a step further away from the dangers of Sergey and away from their zipline catastrophe.

Everything around her felt surreal, like a moment in time that she knew wouldn't last. Her heart weighed heavy as they continued down the widened path and on towards the next village where she would inevitably go her own way, without Anthony in her future—a ridiculous idea anyway. It was for the best. What was she thinking? Tess shook her head as if to realign her less than rational romantic standards. She noticed Anthony deliberately keeping his distance as they hiked down the trail. Just as well, she frowned, there wasn't anything more to say. She would go back to her hotel, book the next flight home, and forget Anthony and forget Belize.

She stepped into an opening and the sun's warmth cascaded over her shoulders. Her steps became robotic as she let herself envision how life could have been, traipsing across the jungle or sailing off into the sunset—romance alive and thriving, just the two of them. The more she fantasized, the more deliberate her steps. Tess ran her fingers over the soft fabric of her sundress, a sense of tightness formed in her stomach knowing the store clerk's legend was only empty folklore. There would be no romantic escape with Anthony. With a sigh, she released the material, letting it slip through her fingers along with the fading hope of the enchanting myth.

The foliage, once again, surrounded her as she continued through the overgrown path. Sharp, scratching palm leaves swished at her legs. She barely noticed the rough plants constant scraping anymore. Her mind wandered, silently scolding herself and her inability to perceive the real character of the men she seemed to fall in love with. *In love*, she repeated the words. Anthony blazed eagerly through the jungle. Tess glanced up at him as he pushed past another palm. She pressed her lips tightly. *You picked the wrong guy, again,* her mind scoffed. Anthony cleared away more branches that fell across the trail. *He's a drug dealer, a womanizer and who knows what else,* she nodded, as if convincing herself. Images flashed through her mind, and jealousy swept over her, recalling the full-figured brunette and later the sting of Anthony's rejection.

"Can't wait to get back to your...," she stuttered, *"your brunette?"*

Tess looked down at the path. Matted vines ran beneath the soil, their thin rope-like roots twisted together. She was careful not to trip.

"You mean, Sophia?" he asked.

Of course! Tess fumed, repeating the girl's name silently. What's sexier than a woman named *Sophia*? The olive-skinned woman's image flooded her mind. She huffed, remembering the full-figured woman poured into the slinky minidress, dancing ever so close to Anthony that night—the night they first met.

"Yes!" She tried to conceal her jealousy that quivered in her voice. "Your, Sophia, the brunette."

"Sophia's not my girl," Anthony's words were quick. "But why do you ask?"

Anthony lifted a broken tree limb and Tess ducked under the branch. Perspiration soaked through his shirt and the heavy scent of sweat and jungle musk permeated through the air and across her lips. Her mind raced battling the internal tug of war between her feverish jungle desires and the reality of her safe, almost placid life back home in New York. She had to stop thinking of him in that way, she told herself. He's a scoundrel, a two-timing user who's dragged you through the jungle these past few days, toying with your emotions. What were you thinking? Now he's gotten you mixed up in this whole drug deal thing, or whatever it is! Her emotions flared.

"Well, you two were certainly close that night at the bar, on the dance floor," she blurted. Her cheeks burned at the memory of his hands caressing the brunette's full-figured hips. Tess looked up to watch his reaction. Her sandal caught on a root, and she fell forward. Grabbing a handful of palm leaves, she steadied herself and continued. "Then, when she showed up at the village, you left with her, again!"

Anthony stopped and looked ahead towards the green forest. Fearing another appearance by Sergey, Tess's eyes widened as she stared out ahead of him.

"What?" she whispered. "Is it Sergey?"

Immediately she crouched down and scanned the area. Anthony spun around. With eyes glaring and his jaw tight, he strode over to her. His dimples set deep into his skin; she had not seen him like this before.

"Look, you know nothing about me, yet you assume I am this scoundrel of a person!" he paused. "I have put up with your behavior, gone out of my way to get you back to your hotel, to your precious Roger, or whoever he is."

Tess's mouth dropped open at the unexpected reaction. Her surroundings forgotten by his rant, Tess stood up and composed herself. She defended herself against his words.

"Roger?" she laughed. "He's the last person I care to see!" Tess placed her hands on her hips, exasperated, she looked off into the distance. "He's the reason I'm here in the first place. Him and his...," she snarled at the images of the blonde bimbo wrapped around Roger. Tess turned back to Anthony. "I paid for this trip, not him. I should be the one who gets to go on it," she paused, the realization to the current mess she was in sank deep into her gut, "this lousy trip was his idea!"

"Oh, that's right; none of this is your doing!" Anthony rolled his eyes.

"And what is that supposed to mean?" Tess glared.

Anthony shrugged his shoulders, throwing his hands up into the air. "Why would you get on that boat by yourself?" His arms slapped the sides of his legs as he continued. "Just you," he paused, "alone on a cruise with a couple of well-known drug dealers," Anthony continued. "I don't know, but it seems kind of insane to me."

"How was I supposed to know who they were..."

"Don't you read?" Anthony interrupted. "You know, do a little research as to where you're going?"

Shrugging his shoulders and shaking his head, Anthony turned back down the more open trail and walked away.

"What do you mean, read?" Tess followed him. "Of course I read, and I didn't think..."

Anthony stopped and faced her. "Clearly you didn't. Because if you had read anything about this area you would have known that the Belizean waterways are the most treacherous places for tourists right now, not to mention a single woman traveling by herself!" Anthony's look softened as he walked up to her. "Belize is a major exporter of cocaine and marijuana. They sell to the Mexican cartel, which then takes it to the States." He placed his hands on her shoulders. "Recently, the drug lords have increased their line of business to include kidnapping wealthy tourists."

Her emotional frustrations peaked as tears welled in her eyes.

"Kidnapping! You mean they were really going to kidnap me that day on the boat?"

"I don't know for certain, but Rolan and Sergey's entire family is notorious for drug dealings in Russia and now these two have come to Belize to expand an industry for themselves."

"But you...," she shook her head wiping back a tear that slid down her cheek, "you stole their drugs."

"Yes," he said.

"So, you are a drug dealer too!" she frowned. "Is the village your..." Tess paused and looked away.

Her eyes continued to brim with tears, remembering Rubi and how kind she had been. Tess couldn't believe a woman like that could be a part of an illegal activity. She turned to Anthony, hoping for an answer. But his body was rigid, and his jaw tensed.

"The people do what they must to survive the poverty of their corrupt government. The drug cartel pays the villagers to use their fields," he said.

"Their fields? But aren't they farmers? I mean, the men," Tess remembered the polite village men as they returned from their days work, "they carried hoes and rakes, their clothes were smudged with dirt from farming, working in the fields, right?"

"They were dirty, yes, but they weren't farming. They were rebuilding air strip landings that the foreign government officials decommissioned."

"Foreign government? You mean like the U.S. government?" she asked.

"Yes, the American government and the D.E.A. have been commissioned to destroy all of the known airfields, attempting to stop the use of airplanes transporting drugs in and out of Belize."

"The island," she paused, "you said there was an old airfield when we were on the island. How do you know about that?"

"The cartel has focused on using the tour boats now, instead of the airplanes," he said.

"My snorkel cruise," Tess realized.

"Yes," Anthony turned and started down the path, "and now we need to get you back to your hotel."

"Wait," Tess scrambled after him, "what about the authorities? Shouldn't we make a report, tell them what happened?"

"The authorities are part of this whole circuit. It would be better for you to go to your hotel, pack your bags and get on an airplane back to New York, and let others take care of things here...without your interference," he added.

The hustle and bustle of her office life seemed dramatically unimportant now. How could she return to such an atmosphere when people, like Rubi and the other women in the village, were forced into oppression. And her hotel, she didn't have any bags to pack. The only thing of importance was her passport which she had left in the nightstand drawer.

Anthony sensed her hesitation. "You can't help, Tess. You need to go back where you belong." He placed his hands onto her shoulders and looked into her eyes. "It's me they want; I've interrupted their plans. You'll be safe at the hotel; now let's get going."

***

THE OVERGROWN path led them to a dirt road. They waited in the hot sun. Within minutes, Tess could hear the familiar roar of an engine and the rattle of metal coming from around the bend. Moments later another relic of a bus rounded the corner. Like their previous ride, packages and bamboo cases slung over the edges of the oversized van, strapped tight with twine. It was smaller and newer looking than the first bus. Curious villagers peered from the open windows as the brakes squealed to a stop. The man behind the wheel smiled through the open window, his gold tooth gleamed out at them.

"You need lift?" he asked.

The man's accent was thick. Tess looked at Anthony.

"Yes," he said.

Anthony dug into his pocket and handed the bus fare to the man. The driver turned and yelled something in Spanish to a small boy in the front seat. The young man jumped up and scooted himself between two passengers in the next row. Anthony held open the door and nodded for Tess to get in. The spark in Anthony's eyes faded and the mood slipped into a somber tone.

"Aren't you coming with me?" she asked.

"I think this is as far as I should go," he paused," if Sergey is out there making inquiries, he'll be asking about two people, a man and a woman being picked up along the route. It will be better this way." He looked deep into her eyes. "You'll be fine. The driver will take you into the city. The bus will stop at the hotels along the beaches. Just make sure you get off at your hotel."

"But...," she protested, then shook her head, choking back the true words she wanted to say. Instead, she half grinned, and pretended to be indifferent. "Of course, I can't expect you to do more than what you've already done," she paused, "thank you for helping me."

She searched his face looking for an indication, anything to validate the feelings she had for him—the same ones she imagined he had for her. But instead, he turned away; the muscles in his jaw flinched. As she watched his expressions harden, she wondered if any of the last two days had been real. He held open the door and gestured for her to get in. Tess stepped into the waiting vehicle and Anthony shut the door. He tapped the hood and, once again, the bus resumed its journey down the road.

***

IT WAS early evening when the driver pulled up to the familiar piers of her hotel. She stood at the pathway and watched as the rattletrap bus disappeared down the street. Tess held her tattered purse in her hands and walked through the guest doors.

"Miss Martin!" the attendant blurted. "We were very worried about you."

The beady-eyed man seemed genuinely concerned.

"Yes, I imagine I gave you all a scare," she said, her voice tired.

"Indeed, miss," he paused. "There's a gentleman waiting for you to return." The attendant picked up the desk phone and quickly dialed. "Yes, sir...she's just arrived...very well."

Her heart skipped. She wondered who it was. Anthony? Did he come after her? Did he change his mind and want to be with her, too? But how did he get here before she did? Her emotions whirled. A few moments later she heard the doors open and footsteps quickened behind her. Her head swooned; joy spurred throughout her entire being.

"Tess!" The familiar voice called out.

Tess turned around; her smile faded.

Chapter Twenty

Reunited

"TESS, DARLING!" ROGER'S VOICE ECHOED through the lobby. "I've been so worried about you!"

Tess turned to see Roger, his face looked pale, wrinkles creased deep into his brow. His steps quickened, and his arms reached out.

"Roger?" She barely sputtered his name before he caught up to her. She managed to get her palm braced between the two of them. He was the last person she wanted to see, let alone hug, she cringed. Roger grabbed her hand. He folded it into his own and raised her scraped fingers to his lips. She jerked away. "Why are you here?" she asked, annoyed at his presence.

The corners of Roger's eyes creased. "Don't be silly, Tess." He slipped his hands over her shoulders, "I've been looking everywhere, worried about you for days."

She watched him speak. His words echoed in her ears, like a dream. Days—it had only been days, not weeks or an eternity. Her gaze shifted past Roger to the hotel doors. The evening sunlight shone through the etched glass, and the shadows of palm trees swayed in the sultry wind. It had only been a short ride since she left him, but her heart already ached for Anthony. She wanted him to thrust open the oversized hotel doors and sweep her away—to come for her, to beg her to stay. But the doors stayed motionless. Instead, it was Roger's icy grip that held her hand. The sound of Roger's voice broke her trance.

"I feared the worst," he said, glancing around the room. The desk clerk and other workers gathered nearby. He then looked back towards Tess with her jungle smudged face and tattered clothing. Roger shook his head and gasped glancing at the audience around them. His eyes dipped, looking down at her blistered feet and ragged shoes. "Sweet, Tess. I can't imagine what you've gone through," Roger continued.

She must have been a dreadful sight to the onlookers, she imagined. Her eyes watered slightly. Roger pulled her close to him. In her weakened state she let him, she let herself be held.

"I missed you, Tess," he whispered.

His lips brushed across her cheek. Roger held her theatrically tight. The awkward embrace sent pain pinching into her neck. Like waking from an all too familiar nightmare, she pushed his arms off her. Tess looked around the lobby. The small-framed clerk cast his eyes down and shuffled through papers on his desk, now seemingly uninterested in her return.

"Roger, what are you doing," she cringed, "why are you here?"

"I've been crazy worried about you, Tess," he glanced around the uninterested room, "don't be silly. That night, at the cantina, and you were with that local," his eyes shifted. "Tess, you were so beautiful. When you didn't show up the next day, I went crazy looking for you. I told the clerk to call me the moment you returned."

"Really? Where's your girlfriend, Roger?" Her face tightened and she realized she didn't even know the blonde tarts name.

"Kat didn't mean anything to me, she was just...," Roger lowered his eyes, "I was such a fool. I don't know what got into me," he arched his brow over puppy dog eyes. "It was pride, the pride of wanting to give you more. I'm a washed-up actor, Tess. What could I have given you that you couldn't already provide yourself?"

Unmoved, Tess glanced just beyond Roger's shoulders and looked around. "So where is...Kat? Waiting for you at *our* hotel?"

"She's gone, Tess. I sent her away. I realized what a fool I've been. It's you, Tess. It's you I want," he reached for her hand. "Oh, Sweetness, can you ever forgive me?"

Tess pressed her lips tightly. She doubted his sincerity, but she had also never seen him this adamant before. Was he truly sorry for all of this...his affair, his rejection? Tess pondered the idea. The girl's name played over in her mind. *Kat.* How fitting, she huffed. Like a platinum sorority daddy's girl, Kat had dug her claws into Roger's thin skin. Tess glanced around the lobby then back to Roger. She could see tears welling in the corner of his eyes. She wondered if he was really sincere. She couldn't remember seeing him like this before, this vulnerable side of himself.

Her mind drifted. She had once idolized him—or was it just the idea of him? Her head ached, confused. He had dumped her and now stood before her pledging his love once more. A few days ago, his pleas may have won her back, but not now. She pressed her lips tight. After everything she had been through, never again would she be the gullible woman settling for the lies of a philanderer, no matter how good looking he was.

A warm breeze blew through the open foyer and the soft scent of the jungle filtered into the lobby. Tess inhaled the fragrance. The sweet scent of palms and hibiscus blooms filled her lungs. Like wind to a sail, she knew her direction. She had seen a glimpse of what she wanted and recognized what she no longer would fall for. Roger is over and Anthony, she reflected on his chocolate dark eyes that sent goosebumps spilling down her arm, he was what she wanted.

"Tess, we must go to the authorities. We have to tell them that you're all right." Roger said.

"No!" she blurted, remembering Anthony's warning.

The police would only make matters worse, Anthony had said. Besides, they might arrest him. She couldn't let that happen. He had helped her, protected her from Sergey and his bandits. She wouldn't risk it. If Anthony was a criminal, there must be a reason. She glanced over at Roger who wrinkled his brow.

"Tess?" Roger said.

She quickly recovered. "I mean, I don't want to stir up more trouble. If Rolan..."

"Rolan?" Roger stiffened.

"Yes, he's the one who kidnapped me on the boat, you know, the snorkel cruise," she said, frowning.

Roger looked her square in the eyes, his voice hollowed. "Rolan kidnapped you?"

"Yes, he and his cousin, Sergey, they were waiting for a drug drop and then," she paused, "and then another boat came by and interrupted them. He's the man who's been chasing us—me," she corrected her words.

Tess was relieved that Roger hadn't pressed her for details. The less Roger knew, the safer Anthony would be. But Roger's tone and detached reaction after mentioning Rolan's name caught her off guard. She watched his brow furrow deeply as he looked beyond her. A second later, he glanced back towards her. For a moment, their eyes met. She studied his face, puzzled by his cold, blank stare and the tightness in his jaw.

"Do you know him?" she asked.

"Who?" Roger said, innocent-like.

"Rolan," she said, watching him carefully.

"Know him? No...no, of course not." He gave a quick smile. The lines on his face softened. "We'll talk about this later. You must be exhausted. C'mon," he said, gesturing. "Let's get you out of those rags. I'm sure you'll want to get yourself cleaned up after everything you've been through."

She was relieved to end their conversation. Her ordeal surreal, Tess looked over her once brilliant-colored sundress now pale and faded. Its threads embedded with jungle flora and dirt from the craggy zipline. The lore the store clerk had shared, *'when you wear the hibiscus, you will meet your true love,'* panned through her mind. She exhaled a weary sigh, dismissing the foolish notion. Sensing the eyes of onlookers staring at her disheveled state, her cheeks flushed. She gripped her purse tight, her souvenir for what should have been her romantic getaway. The journey had taken its toll. Not just on her clothes, but her emotions, too. Anthony was gone. He'd left her to find her own way back to the hotel, alone. He hadn't cared for her. He merely wanted to be rid of her. And Roger...*was* he sorry? Could she trust him?

Roger put his arm around her shoulder. Too exhausted to protest, she let him escort her upstairs. She was glad he didn't ask any more questions about Anthony, the boat, or Rolan. She needed time to think, to figure out what she would say. Keeping Anthony's name out of it, though, seemed like the best thing to do, at least for now. They walked down the hallway and stood outside her room. When she told him she wanted to be alone, he didn't argue.

"Take your time. I'll make the arrangements for our flight home, and we can meet up later this evening." Roger said, turning to leave.

Home, the idea sounded sweet. Yes, she wanted to go back home, to her life, to her *real* life. "Thank you," she half smiled at him, surprised by his doting attention.

Maybe she had been wrong, that he was genuinely sorry. Only days ago, she had envisioned his proposal. Certainly, she must have some sort of feelings for him. Her mind raced. Events of the past two days, blazing through the jungle with Anthony by her side, played over in her mind. Had it all just been a fantasy? Was she that blinded by her own expectations that she made herself believe it was romance? Tess shook her head, too exhausted to think about it now.

With Roger gone, she stood outside her room. The key the desk clerk had given her slid effortlessly into the lock. The echo of the latch clicked as she opened the door. The whir of the ceiling fan sounded in her ear while the familiar smell of dust and bamboo rushed to greet her. She set her bag down onto the bed and pulled open the nightstand drawer. The small, blue covered passport lay just as she had left it, untouched. A wave of loneliness blanketed over her. Like the emptiness back home in her apartment, here too, everything was untouched and unchanged.

She walked over to the sliding glass door, pushed back the plain linen curtains, and stepped out onto the balcony. Vibrant red-orange and yellow with streaks of pink swept across the sky as the sun began to set. She rested her forearms across the balcony railing and with her eyes closed she took a deep breath, inhaling the lush fragrance of the tropical oasis. The flavor of ocean salts and persuasive jungle musk comforted her. Her heart ached.

"Tony," she whispered.

Chapter Twenty-One

Betrayed

TESS STOOD IN FRONT OF THE mirror. The hot shower had given her time to reflect. If she was going to meet up with Roger, it wasn't going to be here, not in her dumpy hotel room. She buttoned her blouse and smoothed the tight fitted office skirt over her hips. Two days crumpled up in her purse had left her clothes musty and riddled with wrinkles, making her uncertain if she could salvage them. Discovering an iron hidden in the closet was a welcome surprise, given the otherwise sparse offerings of her humble hotel room. She pressed the fabric the best she could. The camisole looked decent enough, she thought, holding it up and glancing at her reflection in the mirror. But the blouse still curled around the buttons and collar. *Probably should have packed a suitcase,* she muttered silently. *Not like I knew I'd be trudging through the jungle.* The flowered two-piece tropical garments lay heaped on the bathroom floor. Glumly, she stared at the clump of tattered clothing. *Maybe I'll stop in and buy another one before I leave.*

Tonight, her office attire would suffice—not too seductive, yet it flattered her figure. She didn't want Roger getting any wrong ideas about their meeting this evening. Fumbling through her tattered woven bag, Tess found the sunscreen lotion she'd bought for the snorkel cruise. Her scraped-up hands and elbows drank in the moisturizer as she obligingly lathered more onto her dry skin. Its coconut fragrance soon filled the room, camouflaging the stale scent of her clothes. She sniffed her wrists and shrugged content the lotion would work. Reaching for her purse she noticed the corner of her midi sarong, her memento just prior to running through the caves. The petite scarf protruded from the woven bag. Tess pulled it out and held it to her nose. It smelled faintly of the jungle mixed with the scent of burlap. As she ran her hand over the printed flowers, images of Anthony flooded her mind. She stuffed the delicate scarf back into her bag, then looked back to the mirror and stared at her reflection.

"Chin up, Tess, you can do this," she half-heartedly rallied.

Walking out the door, she headed to the lobby. Her heels echoed down the stairway. She was glad to have her patent leather slings on rather than the tattered sandals with their makeshift repair that rubbed her feet sore. The office shoes, however, were more rigid, causing her feet to ache where scratches and blisters had formed while hiking the miles of jungle trails. At least the straps were tight, and the shoes stayed put, she winced. She would take them off once she reached the nearby cantina. Tess left a message with the desk clerk to tell Roger she would wait for him at the bar.

The small-framed man nodded politely. "Yes, miss. I will tell him when he arrives."

Tess walked out the side door of the hotel and onto the familiar path that she had taken that first day. She drew in a deep breath. The air was fragrant, filled with the sweet scent of the Plumeria blooms. The blisters were too much, and she slipped off her shoes letting the sand sift through her toes. The cantina was just ahead down the path. Soon, she could see the familiar bamboo half-wall that boarded around its perimeter. As before, the tiki torches flickered from each corner. A slight breeze caressed across her face and the flames danced to its cadence. She had worn her hair up, gathered in the back then twisted and pinned loosely. After days trudging through the humid jungle, Tess had been glad to use shampoo and remove the dust and cobwebs that had embedded themselves in her auburn curls. She tucked a couple of windswept strands behind her ear and took a seat at the bar. This time, the mellow, almost empty establishment was inviting, and she looked forward to a low-profile evening.

Tess set her tattered purse next to her. She skewed her lips, thinking she should have left it in her room. Habit, she guessed. It was empty except for her credit card and the scarf she had bought before running into the caves. She would have to wait until morning to get a new phone, to replace the one Anthony had kept. Oddly, she realized, the anxiety she previously felt, not having her phone by her side, had ebbed away. She liked the freedom without it.

The sun lay low just above the water's horizon. The blue, pink and orange hues deepened across the sky. The muffled lap of the ocean waves provided a surreal backdrop to her exhausting ordeal. Further down the beach lights twinkled.

"The Grand Simone," she muttered.

Tess gazed towards the resort. The bar would be packed full of tourists—unsuspecting and naïve tourists. Tess turned and faced the counter. Tonight, she didn't want to celebrate or pretend that romance existed. Instead, she would change the course of her life.

"What'll you have?" the server asked.

It was the same cheerful bartender from the first night she had arrived. Before she could answer, the young man's smile widened.

"Ah, I remember you, miss!" he wiped the bar towel across the counter. "You don't want to party at the Simone tonight?" his brow arched.

"No. Not tonight," she glanced the direction of the big hotel then back to the young man, "I don't really feel like dancing."

"A beautiful woman like you shouldn't be so sad. Let Ramone fix you up. What can I get you to drink?"

She sighed softly, acknowledging her mood. "Oh, I don't know," she paused, "how about one of those blue peachy drinks?" Tess had forgotten its name, but the thought of the fruity taste made her mouth water. "At least my taste buds can enjoy the night." she said, attempting to smile.

Ramone chuckled and turned to make the drink. After a couple splashes of peach liqueur, a dose of unidentified blue liquid, and a tumbler of ice with some coconut crème, Ramone presented his masterpiece setting it in front of her as he bowed his head, jesting.

"Viva!" he shouted. "Enjoy!"

This time, Tess earnestly smiled at his attempt to cheer her up. "I'm sure this will make the evening more bearable. Thank you."

She sipped through the tiny straw the bartender had poked into the glass alongside the blue paper umbrella that speared morsels of fruit. The bitter sweetness of the drink made her cheeks pucker, and the aftertaste of the alcohol warmed her throat. With another sip, the tenseness in her shoulders subsided. Visions of Anthony danced through her mind. She remembered his sturdy embrace, his arms wrapped tightly around her as the zipline dipped and disappeared into the trees. She recalled how safe it had seemed with him. Tess closed her eyes and her mind drifted further. Flashbacks of his touch tantalized her. She could still feel the warmth of his breath brushing against her cheek and down along her neck. She swooned thinking about the warm sensual sensations. Desire swept throughout her body. But her thoughts came full circle causing her to abruptly open her eyes.

"And then he pushes me away," she whispered.

Tess looked into the tall wispy shaped glass in front of her. She swirled the bits of ice and gulped the remaining blue beverage. She clenched her teeth. The last bit of the drink made her eyes water, and she wiped the corner of her lip with the back of her hand.

"I'll have another one, Ramone."

"Now you will feel better, miss," he smiled.

Ramone set another Belizean Special on the counter then waited on another customer. Again, thoughts of Anthony played over in her mind. She could almost see his brown eyes gazing down at her. Ramone passed behind the bar.

"You know, Ramone," she paused and bit the slice of mango speared by the tiny umbrella, "you're a nice guy. Why can't I find a nice guy like you?"

"But miss, surely there is someone special that you know, right?"

"No," she said. "No, Ramone, there's not. I mean, there was, and then," her voice pitched higher, "he turned out to be an unfaithful jerk. In fact, Ramone," she leaned in closer and held two fingers up to her face, "he's a beady-eyed snake!"

Ramone studied her then nodded his head, amused by her tipsiness.

Tess continued. "He's the reason I ended up being here in the first place!"

"Ah, I see." Ramone placed a plate of papaya next to her glass. "Have some fruit, miss. It'll make you feel better."

"You see, Ramone," she paused and took a bite, "you are a nice guy."

"I'm sure you'll find the right one soon."

"Oh, I did, Ramone. I did!"

Tess ate more of the fruit stuffing her cheeks full.

"You see!" Ramone tried to make light of her situation, "I told you— you'd find one!"

Tess looked into her near empty glass. She chewed the last of the fruit the bartender had given her. Her attention drifted to the melting ice.

Twirling the straw, she watched the small pieces swirl. With her purse lying next to her, she sized-up the tattered woven bag. The end of the scarf still protruded from the pouch. Tess ran her fingers over the silk flower print and continued her conversation.

"But," she paused, "he's a drug dealer."

"Oh? "No, miss, that's not good," Ramone's brow wrinkled, "you don't want that. You are much too good to be with someone like that."

Tess lifted her head and stared across the room. "I know, Ramone. I know," she said.

She looked back at the bartender. His eyes softened and suddenly she saw him look beyond her, His demeanor stiffened and Ramone leaned back, throwing the bar rag over his shoulder.

"There you are!" a familiar voice sounded.

A wave of repulsion slithered up Tess's spine. She turned to see Roger. He walked briskly over and sat on the stool next to her. Ramone looked at Tess and raised an eyebrow. Tess motioned to the bartender, pointed her two fingers to her eyes, and mouthed the word *'snake.'* Ramone nodded.

"Roger, where were you?" She studied his face.

Roger smiled at her. "Don't worry, everything's been arranged."

***

MOLLY SAT in her boss's office. Her six-inch stilettos rested on the mahogany desk; ankles crossed. The overstuffed leather chair tilted back. Molly liked looking out across the tops of the buildings, watching the cars and people below. The images brought back memories of her brother's ant farm, a Christmas gift from years ago. She recalled how he had set it on his dresser and watched the ants work relentlessly through their sandy tunnels. The neighbor had come over later that day, showing off his new football. Her brother was more into bugs than sports at that time, she remembered. Her brother's friend threw a long one. The ball bounced off the closet door, banged it shut and headed straight for the ant colony in perfect spiraled form. It had been an awful scene. The neighbor jumped up on the bed squealing in terror. Looking through the tinted glass, Molly shook her head. Yep, all those people running around on that concrete down there, each one headed somewhere different, just like all those ants scattered across her brother's room.

The sun beamed through the high-rise windows, its rays glistening across Molly's sequined shoes. She admired how her high heels accentuated her appearance. Raising one leg off the desk, she pointed her toe, flexing it in the light. The shiny black heels elongated her legs. Despite her petite height of just five foot two, Molly commanded attention. She was Tess's right-hand girl and knew how to get things done. An attractive quality, so she'd been told, and all too often for her liking. She'd been pursued by some of the wealthiest and most high-ranking gentlemen within the company and their clients. Molly just did what she always did and let them down easy. Most of the time, the men didn't even know they were being rejected. She had quite the charisma when it came to getting what she wanted, or what Tess needed. There was one good looking gent, however, that Molly fancied. Once her mind was made up, she didn't take no for an answer.

They met at a client opening Tess hosted. Molly helped with planning and facilitating the event. She'd been a sucker for a man in uniform and Tess's uncle was no exception. Tall, dark, and scrumptious, a little on the older side, but sexy as all could be. She and Tess's Uncle Ray had kept their relationship on the hush side. Molly figured it would be best if Tess could focus on her work rather than on the low-cut dress that Molly wore for her date. Ray picked her up every Friday, just like clockwork, he was always on time. He'd tell her it was because of his years in the Coast Guard commanding his crew. He didn't go out on boats anymore, instead he was some secret mission director, or something like that. Molly didn't pay that much attention to the details of his job. She was more interested in having a good time draped across his arm and directing the wait-staff at some of the most elite restaurants around town.

The sun on her face was warm as she closed her eyes in Tess's chair. But the muffled ringing of the office phone made Molly sigh. She looked at the caller I.D. and scrunched her nose at the name. It was Mr. Becker, one of the wealthier clients of the company. He may have money, Molly huffed, but he sure didn't have any friends. At least not that she thought were worth knowing. Some people had money and didn't have to tell you, but not Mr. Becker. No, he made a point of always letting you know he was some high and mighty because his grandfather invented some gadget that made him millions. As far as Molly was concerned, this generation Mr. Becker was just a fat-scaled, bottom fish sucking up on someone else's riches. She picked up Tess's pen that lay on the desk and pressed the blinking light.

"Good afternoon, Marcus and White, Miss Martin's office," she attempted a smile as she spoke.

"Yes, this is Mr. Becker, Mr. Tom Becker," he blustered. "I want to speak to your boss."

Molly rolled her eyes and twisted the pen through her fingers, "I'm sorry Mr., ah...," she paused.

"Becker! Mr. Tom Becker and I don't appreciate your attitude young lady!" he bellowed.

Molly stifled a chuckle, certain the man's big, puffy cheeks were turning red. It gave her a slight sense of satisfaction to hold the end of the receiver while Mr. Becker lashed out. He couldn't do anything, and she knew it.

"Of course, Mr. Becker, Miss Martin is out of town. Is there a message I can give her when she returns?" Molly's tone rose with just a hint of patronization.

"Yes!" Mr. Becker stormed. "You tell your boss that I don't much like the guests your company associates with at those client openings you host!"

Molly tilted her head, twisting her spiked heel in the sunshine. "Oh, is there an issue with one of our guests, Mr. Becker?" she inquired, but Molly paid little attention to his words, glancing at her recently manicured nails.

"As a matter of fact, young lady, there is! Some scoundrel calls himself Roger Van de Camp. If you ask me, anyone whose name sounds like a can of beans shouldn't make the guest list."

Molly dropped her pen. "You said, a Mr. Van de Camp?" she asked.

"That's right! He's a no good, money grabbing sleaze ball preying on our well to do society, if you ask me!"

"Please, Mr. Becker. What details should I tell Ms. Martin when she returns?" Molly focused.

"You tell your boss that the Becker family is considering taking our account somewhere else. Someplace that provides a more reputable guest association."

"I'm sure Miss Martin would be interested to know the details of what has happened, Mr. Becker," Molly said, her interest piqued.

"Some fancy-pants, smooth talker seduced my baby girl into running off to Belize with him. Then, once he got her out there, he started spending all her money! My money! So, I had him checked out."

"Oh, checked out, you say?" Molly asked.

"Yes! Maybe your firm should do their own background checks before they start inviting just any 'ol swindler off the streets! Then maybe your clientele wouldn't have to clean up this mess," Becker scolded.

"What did you find, Mr. Becker. I mean, on this Roger person?"

"Well, his name isn't even Roger Van de Camp. No telling what kind of beggar scum he comes from. I had to pay for a first-class ticket to fly my little girl home, away from that low-down scoundrel. You just tell your boss she's on notice. If we decide to keep our account with your company, we'll let you know!" he said, near hollering.

"Of course, Mr. Becker," Molly said, pausing. "Thank you for calling." She slid the receiver down the side of her face. Her eyes squinted and she pressed her lips tightly. "Hmm," she tapped the pen then dialed a frequent number. The line picked up on the other end. A familiar voice answered.

"Hello?" the voice said.

"Hey, Baby, it's me. I need a favor."

Chapter Twenty-Two

Farewell Dinner

TESS SET DOWN HER EMPTY glass. Roger's re-appearance changed everything. Her reasons for coming to Belize were to spite him, to make him jealous. But now, none of that seemed important. There had been a glimpse of life beyond Roger. She had experienced excitement and the possibility to be with Anthony—although impossible given his career choice, she frowned. She had seen a new outlook, new parameters that she wanted for her future. Somehow, through her fateful clumsiness and poor choices, she'd gone on the adventure of her life. Leaving behind the sheltered walls of her apartment and the fast-paced boredom of the city, she stepped outside her comfort zone for the first time.

It was a stark reckoning—reality had awakened within her. In the past two days, she had embraced a more fulfilling life than during the last two years of grueling, long work hours and relentless appointments. It wasn't until this very moment, that she realized how capable she was of taking risks, ascending rock-faced caverns, and careening down death-defying ziplines. The last forty-eight hours had shown her that it was possible to take charge. Not only could she oversee her own destiny, but also change its course when *she* wanted to. She glanced over at Roger sitting next to her at the bar. Tess fumbled with the coaster under her drink.

"Look, Roger, about us...,"

"Tess," Roger interrupted, "you've been through so much. I don't expect you to run back to me," he shifted his gaze and softened his tone, "not after what I did. Just that you're here—now, that's more than I could ever have hoped for. A chance, a chance that you'll forgive me, that's all."

He took her hand into his. Tess could see tears brimming in the corner of his eyes. Unmoved, she tried not to scoff at his words...a chance to forgive him? What an understatement, she tightened her lips and turned her attention to the melting ice at the bottom of her glass. Roger placed his hand on her arm. His cold fingers made her skin flinch. She could honestly say she held no more affection for Roger Van de Camp. A week ago, she'd hoped he would propose to her. But now, she saw a stranger before her.

In these past few days, clarity dawned on the relationship she thought they had shared. With a sobering realization, she understood that all this time, she truly knew nothing about Roger. They had always lacked a deep connection; she could see that now. She had been desperate to fill a void. Maybe it was loneliness, or a lack of confidence that drove her to him, she wasn't certain.

They moved in together sooner than she wanted, with him pressuring her for a place to stay. Roger had told her he had to leave his home suddenly, saying he didn't have any place to go. She didn't know his family; he never talked about them other than one time, but only casually. He mentioned a distant cousin or maybe it was an uncle, she couldn't remember. Either way, he hadn't been on speaking terms with any of his relatives for quite a while.

If she asked about his family later in their relationship, he always said that he didn't want to talk about it, that it was too painful to bring up.

Tess focused on the melted ice. The tiny cubes clanked against the glass. It became clearer to her, sitting under the dim light of the little cantina, that the reality of their relationship had only been a fabrication in her mind, a fairytale gone wrong. Tess realized that her weakness—to be true to herself—had blinded her to the red flags blatantly waving right in front of her. She hadn't wanted to see them; she knew that now. As the realization of her one-sided relationship flooded into full view, Tess took a deep breath and exhaled.

They had met at one of her company's galas. She had just landed her first big account and her nerves were in full swing. The guest list and decorations had to be perfect; it was her opportunity to impress the firm's important clientele as well as her bosses. If it hadn't been for Molly's connections the guest list might have been slim. Molly's undeniable ability to woo even the most difficult of clients brought a grin to Tess's face. Her thoughts continued to drift, and she remembered the first time she had seen Roger. Like the fairytale she had always envisioned, it was as if everything and everyone had faded into the background except for him as he walked into the room that night.

There was an aura about him. Time stood motionless the moment she laid eyes on him. He hesitated at the door for just a moment as he scanned the room, then smoothly he took a glass of champagne from a waiter's tray. She remembered how he sipped the sparkling wine, stepping out onto the gala floor, mixing with the guests—as if he belonged. He had worn a white semi-formal tux, red handkerchief folded into the breast pocket, like a movie star. Elongated European-style shoes made his lanky figure look even taller. His skin glowed—not from the faux tanning beds that flooded the city, but real sun bronzed rays. Even his hair shimmered—sun-kissed, as if he'd just stepped off the sands of the Caribbean. Then, he turned his head from across the room and their eyes met. His broad shoulders, defined chin, and enchanting swagger were like that of a spicy fiction novel, and she had been anxious for a hot, steamy romance. It had all blinded her, she realized now.

Her memories of the past faded and the present sat before her. Tess glanced over at Roger who momentarily turned away. His shining armor–his demeanor and suaveness that she once foolishly admired–felt tarnished and dull. He was just another slimy frog to throw back into the swamp. She wasn't going to fall for him again and this time, she decided, she would let him know it was over, and over for good. Tess straightened her posture. She pressed her lips tight then turned to face him.

"No, Roger, I don't think another chance would do either of us any good," she said.

Roger slammed his fist on the bar. Ramone looked up warily, his conversation with the blonde at the other end of the counter interrupted. Tess noticed Ramone's heightened stance as he glanced over towards her, his brow arched. Tess held her hand up assuring the bartender that all was well.

"Calm down, Roger," Tess fumed quietly.

"It's him, isn't it, the guy from that night," Roger said, harshly.

"No, it's not him or, at least not now," she fumbled with the strap of her purse. "Look, I just need time on my own to think all of this through."

Roger took another drink. He looked back at her. The hard lines of his brow softened. "I'm sorry, Tess. You've had a lot to deal with. Let's not quarrel. Let's just enjoy the freshness of the night," he lifted his glass. "A toast," he paused and moved nearer, "to good friends." Roger downed his shot of vodka. "Come with me and have dinner," he pleaded, casually.

"That wouldn't be a good idea. I just don't think we should…"

"Oh, come on Tess," Roger interrupted, "let's be adults about this. It's just a meal. When was the last time you ate?"

He did have a point, she thought. Her stomach grumbled.

"I promise you I'll be on my best behavior. Besides," he ordered another shot, "we won't be alone, there will be others onboard as well. And then, after tonight if you still think its best, you can go your own way."

She hesitated, ignoring the pangs in her belly. "No, I don't think it would be a good idea, Roger."

"Tess let's put this ugliness behind us. Besides," he persuaded, "it's the evening dinner cruise you booked, remember?"

Did she remember? She scoffed at his implication. Of course, she remembered! If he had asked, she could have recited the entire brochure—*a two-hour evening tour along the enchanting coastline. A full menu dinner cruise featuring lobster, Caribbean crab cakes and chocolate banana chimichanga for dessert, drinks included.* Tess looked out over the water. A few yachts sailed near the shore. Their bright party lights strung across the deck with guests mingling near the railing, enjoying their cruise. The sun setting in the background painted the perfect picture.

She wanted to be one of those guests, to have that ideal, picture-perfect life. She scoffed. Life hadn't been perfect, just fake. If only Anthony..., she stopped herself and closed her eyes. His image filled her mind as she took a deep breath. The scent of ocean air hinted on the evening breeze but the smell of sweat and jungle musk, the familiar cologne she'd grown fond of, no longer drifted past her nose. Belize could never be the same for her. Anthony was gone and she would be going home tomorrow. Tess methodically looked out towards the horizon. It had been a long day, she rationalized. Roger had been right, the meals she had eaten over the past two days were meek, at best. Her stomach rumbled again. Just one more excursion, she told herself, and besides, there would be others on the cruise, too.

"Why not, what harm could there be?" she agreed. "Yes, I'll go to dinner with you. But that's all it is, Roger, just dinner."

"Thank you, Tess, of course, yes, just two friends having a farewell dinner." He lifted his glass to Ramone. "Bartender, another round, please."

***

THE WEATHERED boards sounded hollow under their feet as Roger led Tess down to the dock. The remote marina was the furthest away from the hotel and only a few boats were moored along the edge. Such a contrast from the bustling pier the other day, she noticed.

"This marina doesn't look like it's used much. Are you sure this is the right place?" Tess asked, glancing down the boardwalk.

"Not to worry, the yachts are all chartered out. It's a popular excursion for tourists," Roger assured.

For a moment, she wondered how he would know, but the warped decking, cracked from seawater and intense heat, caught her heel. Her foot sank between the rough boards; Tess focused on freeing herself rather than making small talk. She would rather nibble on caviar and look out over the setting sun than have idle conversation with Roger anyway.

"Damn!" Tess exclaimed.

"Are you alright?" Roger asked, shifting his gaze.

"Yes, fine. Is the boat close?"

She tugged her foot free leaving her shoe behind. When she bent down to retrieve her uncooperative heel, her purse snagged on a nail sticking out from the weathered railing. Annoyed and without looking, she yanked her bag free, intently focused on liberating her low-heeled sling from the plank crevasse. Tess groaned, noticing fresh gouges on the smooth patent leather shoes. Her favorite heels ruined, she sighed, irritated. She slipped the shoe back on and this time she watched where she stepped more closely. Roger continued walking ahead of her. The oddity briefly crossed her mind that he would leave her to trail behind. But Tess shrugged indifferently, realizing she liked the distance between them. He seemed intently focused, she noticed, as he hurried down the dock. Tess glanced up the wooden pier to the end where she could see a yacht; thirty feet in length, she guessed, recalling the brochure's description. The craft was just as elegant, if not more, as the *Charisa*. It didn't surprise her. Most of the charters looked like newer yachts.

Ahead, as with the boats she had seen earlier, lights were strung across the back deck area, where an attendant stood waiting next to the boarding steps. The idea of getting on another charter made her stomach queasy and her shoulders tight. Her pulse quickened sending heavy cadences drumming into her ears. The effects from her earlier cocktails were wearing off and dread consumed her mind rather than pampered visions of a relaxing farewell evening dinner. She chided herself for letting her guard down and agreeing to a last meal with Roger. Taking a deep breath, the tension in her arms relaxed. That was the solution, she thought. She'd just have another Belizean cocktail. Surely, downing another drink or two would make her ordeal more bearable. After all, this dinner would provide Roger with the closure he needed.

His persistence at the bar made her realize how pathetic his life really was. She gave Kat points for figuring it out sooner, rather than later. He probably spent all of her money, or rather her daddy's millions. In some strange way, she glanced over at Roger, she felt sorry for him. Not a penny to his name and a life of mooching off of others seemed to be his only future. The sooner he truly realized there would never be anything between them, the better off she would be. Two hours, she quickened her strides, she could manage another two hours.

They reached the end of the pier and walked over to the yacht. Roger bowed at the waist and extended his arm. Like a knightly gesture he rolled his hand for her to take. The gold band of his wristwatch slipped from under his cuff. She hadn't remembered him owning a watch, especially one with diamonds studded around the face. It looked familiar and she wondered for a moment where she had seen it, but then decided not to dwell over it. Roger was always one to dress extravagantly, it was probably just the spoils of a shopping excursion with his blonde sorority pig. She furrowed her brow and looked up at him. He got the message and put his arm down. Grabbing the metal railing, Tess stepped on board. The attendant she'd seen from the dock moved to the lighted area at the back of the cruiser. She walked the narrow pathway to the rear deck. Roger quickly followed behind her. He slipped his arm around her waist.

"Roger! I told you this is just a farewell dinner, nothing more."

"Yes, you said that. But I can still be a gentleman, can't I?"

Hostility resonated in his voice. Tess glanced up, noticing the hard lines creasing along his forehead as his jaw muscles twitched. Good—he was getting the hint. She stepped onto the open back of the boat, just catching a glimpse of the attendant's white coat as the man ducked back under the overhead salon. She stopped cold. There was only one table. A bottle of champagne chilled atop the glass dinette.

"Roger, what is this? You told me there would be others, but there's only one table. And where did that man go, the one who was here just a minute ago?"

Roger stepped past her. He took his hand from his pocket and reached to open the bottle.

"Yes, I wanted to surprise you. If I had mentioned it would only be the two of us, you wouldn't have agreed, would you?" he said.

"Come on, Roger, you broke up with me and brought your bimbo to Belize instead. Why would you even think I would want to get back with you? I said I would go to dinner only because I wanted to eat, nothing more!"

He took the bottle out of the ice and swiftly popped the cork. With her nerves already heightened, she jumped at the loud noise. Champagne bubbled down the side of the bottle. Roger, with his back facing her, filled the two glasses then turned and held one out to her. She scoffed.

"Okay, I apologize," Roger said, mendaciously.

Tess crossed her arms as Roger stepped closer. She avoided eye contact.

"Look, Tess, I am sorry. For all of it, I...I just needed to know for sure," he said.

"I knew coming here would be a bad idea," Tess huffed.

"No, you were right. I should have told you. We'll just eat dinner and enjoy the view along the coast. Please stay. You might as well, at least take in the sunset. Here, a peace offering," he said.

Roger again extended his arm and offered the glass of champagne. With her lips still pressed tight, she looked out over the water. The gentle waves glistened, and the sky burned bright with a deep orange-red color. She had to admit, the sunset was beautiful this evening. The warm breeze wisped over her, and the sweet ocean fragrance surrounded them. Her mind drifted to Anthony, and she wondered where he was, now—at this moment. For one more night she could pretend that this was her life, a tropical getaway. She would stay and have dinner but then she would never see Roger again. Tess turned to face him ignoring his pouting face. Taking the glass from his hand, she gulped the bubbly wine.

"So, what's on the menu?" she asked, stepping over to the table.

Roger smiled and filled her empty glass. She raised it to her lips and took another sip. Avoiding eye contact, Tess let her gaze cast just over his shoulder towards the dock.

Her eyes followed the boards leading to the beach. Off in the distance she saw a woman standing near a small sailboat tied to the pier. The woman, it seemed, looked right at her. Tess shifted her gaze, noticing a taller, broader figure standing alongside the shadowed woman; a man, she assumed. Tess watched the mystery couple, intrigued. She sipped her drink, continuing to focus on the two beach goers. Methodically, Tess strolled to the railing. She brushed past Roger, ignoring his presence and leaned against the cool metal barrier. A soft breeze passed over her as she held back loose strands of hair wisping across her face. She strained to see the two figures. Their silhouettes moved aside then slipped out of sight. Disappointed, she churned her lips. It had been an exhausting day, perhaps her tired mind was playing tricks in the dim evening light.

Tess continued to look out along the beach. In the outspread of the shore, the twinkling lights of the Grand Simone shone bright. The lighted hotel stood majestic and beautiful, glistening—just as it had been at the beginning of her journey. The yellow-flamed tiki lights flickered from the bar, waving in the evening wind. Tess's smile faded as she took in the surreal and fitting moment, the last evening setting to her vacation. She closed her eyes. Anthony's crooked smile and his seductive sweet-chocolate eyes filled her mind. Despite her present company, she was glad she had stayed.

***

THE DINNER yacht cruised along the shore just beyond the secluded marina. Her anger waned as she settled for moderately annoyed, avoiding the chit-chat Roger persistently offered. She barely noticed his presence as she continued to let her mind fill with images of Anthony and their whirlwind trek through the jungle. The caviar spread did little to impress her compared to the sweet star fruit Anthony picked from the trail. Tess took a bite of the blackened roe, chasing it down with more champagne. Her mind and body relaxed as the drinks took effect. The boat rocked—or so she thought. She took a step and steadied herself. Her eyes grew heavier as she strained to keep them open. The yellow flickers in the distance blurred. Roger's image appeared out of focus as he stepped past her towards the helm. Nausea lay at the base of her throat and her head spun. A loud rumbling sounded from the back of the yacht. Tess could see the water churning—blurred.

"What's happening? Roger, what are you doing?" she slurred.

Like an empty corridor, her words echoed inside her head. Dreamlike, as if watching everything from a distance, she could see Roger standing next to the captain who then pushed the throttle forward. The sudden lurch caught her off balance. Her glass slipped from her hand and shattered. The sound echoed in her head as she groped for the railing.

"Roger, answer me! Where are you taking me?"

Roger looked over his shoulder. His lips curled. Tess could see the blurred shape of a man approach her. The hair on her neck pricked as her body swayed and her legs buckled. Anthony's words, warnings of the Belizean waters, flickered through her mind. She looked out at the shore as a wave of darkness engulfed her.

***

THE DINNER cruise captain took the envelope filled with cash, stuffing it into his belt. Roger signaled the awaiting boat. The familiar yacht approached, and the merciless crew transferred Roger and his unconscious guest.

***

HER HEAD pounded. She opened her eyes, squinting in the dull light. Tess stretched her hands out across the smooth bedding. With her mind foggy, she tried to remember where she had been. Voices murmured—men's voices. There was something familiar about their tone. She sat up, slowly regaining her senses. Waves cadenced against the boat and the moonlight filtered through a tiny window. Her eyes adjusted, straining to see her surroundings. In front of her was a narrow louvered door. To the right she noticed another smaller door. The room seemed familiar. Like *déjà vu*, she knew she had been there before. Her legs, still weak, shook under her weight, stepping from the bed. Tess looked out from the small porthole. A life preserver lashed to the railing faced her. Her body trembled as she whispered the name.

"*Charisa!*"

Chapter Twenty-Three

Rescued at Sea

GREY CLOUDS SCUTTLED ALONG THE skyline, illuminated by the moonlight. At the dock, the slender brunette placed her hand on the man's shoulder next to her. The woman turned and faced him. She looked deep into his brown eyes.

"You would risk your life to rescue her?" the woman asked. "Tony, she went with him, you saw it. She must be involved."

Anthony reached down, picking up a silk flowered scarf that still stuck to the weathered post. He slipped it off the rusted nail that had snagged it from its owner. Rubbing his fingers over the silk material, his jaw clenched. Anthony stared towards the yacht then back to the dainty fabric. He tucked the wrap into his pocket and turned towards Sophia.

"No. Tess may have gone with them, but she's not a part of this."

The woman shook her head. "How do you know? You've only known her for a few days."

Anthony ignored Sophia's question. He reached for the rope, untying the skiff.

"Tony, you're not thinking right. Tess Martin is working with Rolan and his nephew."

Anthony jumped on board the craft. "Call Devon, tell him where I've gone. Tell him to bring all of it."

He turned the key and the engine roared. Moments later the boat sped out to sea.

***

TESS EASED over to the closed cabin door. Dizzy, the room tilted like a bad carnival ride and her head pounded. She pushed past the grogginess, reaching for the cabin handle. It was locked. With her ear pressed against the wooden slats she could hear voices, men talking overhead. Rolan's thick accent bellowed.

"She'll make up for the last one," he said.

"I still don't feel right about this," Roger chided.

"Shut up, you idiot! It was simple. All you had to do was bring Becker's girl. We could have gotten millions. But instead, you had to *play house* back in the States! You just had to move in with her. If you weren't my brother's kid, I'd...," Rolan's voice trailed.

"Tess wasn't supposed to be here! I broke it off," Roger whined. "I did what you said."

"Then why is she locked in the cabin below and the heiress," Rolan paused, "on a plane headed back home to daddy?"

"How was I supposed to know she'd follow me to Belize?" Roger said, sulking.

Tess clutched her fists. "That lousy maggot!" she fumed.

She drew a deep breath and pressed her ear tighter to the louvers. The slats on the frame gave way, creaking with the force of her hands. She gasped, covering her mouth. The voices hushed. Adrenaline surged through her body. She glanced around the tiny room, straining to see the layout. The moonlight filtered through the small porthole, faintly illuminating the stateroom. It shone well enough to see there was no other way out except through the louvered doorway. Suddenly, the cabin door flung open. Tess stumbled back. Her knees hit the edge of the bed, almost knocking her down. Regaining her balance, she squared her shoulders. It was Roger's hardened face she recognized. Rage welled within her as she glared at him.

"You bastard!" she sneered.

Tess flung herself at him, landing a blow to his cheek. Her nails clawed at his skin and blood oozed from his face. Roger grabbed her arms, pushing her back. Her legs buckled as she fell onto the bed. Tess scrambled to her feet and lunged at him again. Rolan stepped through the door.

"Stop!" Rolan shouted.

He raised his hand, landing a hard slap to her face. Tess fell to the floor. She held her cheek, rubbing at the stinging sensations burning into her skin. Rolan turned on a lamp that dimly lit the small room. She glared up at him. The up-close sight of him made her nostrils flare as her stomach tightened, snarling into a knot.

"That'll be enough out of you!" Rolan said. He turned and glared at Roger. "Get back on deck, keep a look out for the arrival."

Tess scowled at Roger as he swiftly obeyed. Rolan turned back around.

"You've given me a lot of grief, young lady."

"What do you want?" she said, clenching her jaw.

"It seems we have quite the situation," he taunted.

Walking callously to the louvered door, Rolan closed it—slowly and methodically. Tess could hear the latch clasped shut. Rolan turned around.

His gaze dipped, roving over her body. With his arm still behind him she could hear the key twist locking the door. Her eyes hardened. He let go of the knob and stepped towards her.

"What do you mean, situation?" she backed away slowly. "Why did Roger bring me here, what do you want?"

"Ah, yes, Roger. That is what you call him, isn't it?"

Rolan curled his lip. Once more, his gaze roved over her body, lingering at her breasts before his haunting cold eyes met her glaring stare. Her adrenaline heightened and her nerves prickled, rushing down through her arms and out to the tips of her fingers. The nape of her neck tingled with fear. Tess glanced around the confined space and scanned over the small table under the porthole. She thought about grabbing the marbled lamp and hitting Rolan with it, but she saw the small brass bolts that fastened it to the tabletop. There was only one door out and Rolan stood in the way. Her mind raced. She needed to distract him, to keep him talking.

"Yes, that is his name," she said, defiantly.

Rolan's lips sneered as he taunted her. "No, my pet, Roger is not his name."

"What are you talking about? Of course it is. We lived together; he was going to...,"she paused, "what are you telling me?"

Rolan grinned. "His name is Ricondo Petrov, my nephew."

"Your nephew?" Tess blurted.

"Yes," Rolan chuckled, "my dead brother's son. So, you see I must look after him as my own."

"Why did he call himself Roger? Why did he lie? None of this makes any sense!" she said, shaking her head.

Rolan sighed, arching his brow. "You see, about a year ago the D.E.A...," he paused, grinning as he continued and took another step closer, "I'm sorry, my dear, that's Drug Enforcement Agency. Well, you see, they had gotten a little too close to Ricondo. They were going to arrest him, sending him to prison for a very long time. Now, I couldn't let that happen, could I? So, I sent him to the States. I gave him money to take care of his needs but, well, let's just say Ricondo has never been good with finances."

"I'll say he isn't," she muttered. Tess stared at him. Her mind reeled. Roger, or Ricondo, whatever his name is, she clenched her jaw, had been lying to her all along. "Is that why he had to leave his home in such a hurry, to get away from the authorities?"

Rolan's eyes lit up, delightedly. "Precisely! You see, it was better if he went on holiday, more like a vacation for a few months."

It was all coming together. She pressed her lips tightly. Roger was a slime bucket. He had used her all along. Tess drew in a deep breath, her nostrils flared. Nothing had been real, not the romance, not the love she *thought* she had with him, nothing. It was all just an act. Tess looked Rolan square in the eyes. The hate she had for both Roger and Rolan boiled under her skin.

"No, I don't see! What I do see, though, are kidnappers and drug gangsters! That's what you are, isn't it?" she said, pressing her lips tighter.

Her face flushed with anger as the stale humid air surrounded her. The muggy temperatures caused her blouse to cling to her clammy skin. Beads of perspiration ran down her face. She held her head high, defying him and his scoundrel family. Tess held no regard for Rolan or Roger-what's-his-face. Rolan's gaze roved over her. Suddenly, he strode across the room. With his jaw tightened, Tess could see the anger raging in his eyes. Rolan grabbed her by the arms. His towering body loomed next to her slender frame, and the pungent odor of his unkempt clothes and sweat wafted past her nose. His closeness repulsed her.

Tess struggled in his grip. "Let go! You're hurting me!" she squirmed.

His breath lay heavy across her face. She turned her head and twisted to free herself, but Rolan's grip was too strong.

"I can see now why my nephew grew fond of you. You are very...feisty and it brings me pleasure to see you like this."

"No! Stop! What do you want with me?" Tess stuttered.

She turned her head away from his mouth, struggling in his arms. His hands groped at her breasts. She fought, hitting him with her free hand. Rolan pulled her arm down, bending it behind her and pressing his body hard against her.

"You will make up for the loss we suffered the day we first met," his eyes glistened. "You've cost me over a million dollars. Let's just say you owe me a debt and I am here to claim it."

Rolan leaned his head into her neck. His mouth ravaged her throat, and the unshaven stubble of his face brushed harshly along her pale skin, scratching into her cheek. Tess writhed at his touch.

"Stop! Let me go!" She tried to pry her hands free. "You can't do this."

Rolan twisted her arm harder. He leaned in closer, and the stench of his breath roved over her.

"On the contrary, my dear, I can do what I please," he whispered into her ear.

As his grip tightened, her back arched in pain. Rolan brushed his coarse lips down her chest. His hand followed the outline of her hips then over her thighs. Tess squirmed to free herself. Rolan laid his mouth over hers, thrusting his tongue between her lips. Fury rushed through her.

"No!" she could hear her muffled words.

Tess's anger surged, spiraling adrenaline throughout her body. With conviction, she bit down as hard as she could. Rolan yelled in pain. He pulled back and let go, wiping his hand across his mouth. Staring at his blood-stained fingers, he glared at her. Tess could see the anger raging in his eyes. Rolan lifted his hand high, but before he could strike her, Tess straightened her arm and dealt a blow to his nose. She shoved her hand against him as hard as she could. And, just as the self-defense instructor had taught her, she further jabbed her fist into Rolan's throat. With one swift motion she brought her leg up and landed her foot hard into his groin. Rolan doubled over.

Tess bolted past him. She turned the key in the lock, flinging open the cabin door and racing up the stairs. Just then, the boat thrust forward, turning hard to starboard. She lost her footing on the slick steps and fell onto her knees. Rolan made his way up the steps grabbing at her. His hands caught her ankle, pulling at her leg. Once more, the boat turned sharply. Tess could hear the other two men yelling on deck. Rolan stumbled but still gripped her ankle dragging her down the steps. Tess reached up and grasped the railing. She held tight and turned to face him. Adrenaline raged through her. She gritted her teeth, pulling her free leg up close to her chest. She drew a deep breath and, as before, thrust her foot as hard as she could into Rolan's reptilian, ugly face. The heel of her patent shoe landed squarely on its mark. Rolan's eyes rolled back, and the cold-blooded ingrate fell in a heap onto the floor.

Again, Tess made her way up the staircase. She looked out to the sea. Darkness surrounded her, but her eyes quickly adjusted to the dim, reflective moonlight. She could see a commotion on deck near the helm. It was that snake—Roger and his hoodlum cousin Sergey, she fumed. Roger turned the wheel sharp while Sergey stood at the edge. Tess grabbed the banister, steadying herself. The two men bellowed orders at one another. Tess looked past the railing. Another speedboat approached, fast. The water churned fearlessly in its wake. Sergey fired his gun in the direction of the vessel. Simultaneously, the speedboat rammed the side of the yacht and sent Sergey flailing overboard.

Moments later Tess's heart skipped. She stood motionless and watched as Anthony leaped over the railing and onto the deck.

"Anthony!" she gasped.

"Are you alright?" he asked—lines creasing along his forehead.

She ran to him, and he held her. Tess felt the warm strength of his arms wrapped around her. For a moment, she laid her head on his chest. Anthony caressed her hair. He placed his hands on her shoulders and looked into her face.

"Seriously, you really need to stop going on boat tours," he smiled.

Tess gave a slight laugh, but the reunion was short lived. Anthony glanced past her. His jaw tightened as he pushed Tess aside. Tess turned just in time to see Roger charging towards them. Roger grabbed a fishing gaff stowed along the railing. Raising it high over his head, Roger held the spear poised to strike. Anthony ran full force and barreled into Roger, tackling him to the floor. The two men brawled. Tess watched in horror. Her eyes darted back and forth between the two fighting men while keeping a watchful eye on the cabin steps. She feared Rolan might appear at any moment.

Roger held Anthony from behind, his arm crossed over his throat. Anthony pulled at Roger's grip. A loud, deafening rhythm rang in Tess's ears. Her hair whipped in the sudden breeze. She reached across her cheek, holding back the loose strands forcibly whipping in front of her face. Spattered seawater misted through the air as a bright light beamed across the deck roving back and forth over the pirate yacht. The night shadows turned to daylight from the hovering aircraft's intense lights. Tess looked up, holding her hand out and blocking the bright beam. She squinted and watched as dark uniformed shadows slid down ropes, dangling from the helicopter. The thumping continued to cadence through the air and the ominous machine hovered. A voice rasped out through a speaker.

"Attention on deck. This is the US Coast Guard, Marine Corps Forces. Put your weapons down and prepare to be boarded."

The deck quickly filled with the armed men in black uniforms. Tess watched as the soldiers slid down their ropes, unclipping in rhythmic unison. The military men stepped quickly towards Anthony and Roger with their weapons drawn, ready for action. Roger released Anthony and both men raised their arms high into the air. From the corner of her eye, she could see another man being pulled from the stairs. Two Marines gripped Rolan tightly while a third soldier cuffed him. Tess noticed another shadowed figure approaching. Through the turbulence and vortex of the blades the slender man leaned close and shouted to her.

"Are you alright, miss?" the soldier asked.

Tess nodded to the uniformed man. Her hair still whipped across her face and her shear blouse rippled against her body. The mechanical rhythm of the blades beat fiercely in her ears and the cadence thumped deep within her chest. The man looked up and motioned overhead. A cable lowered near them. The soldier strapped the dangling harness around her. Once secured, he stepped back, giving a thumbs-up signal. Her body spun as the cable hoisted her from the *Charisa*.

There had been no conversation, just swift maneuvers by the military men. Once at the hovering craft's opening, another uniformed soldier pulled Tess inside. He swiftly removed the harness. She held his arm and steadied herself into the empty jump-seat. The attendant buckled her in as she looked at the officer sitting next to her. Tess gasped.

"Uncle Ray!"

Chapter Twenty-Four

Leaving Belize

THE NIGHT AIR SWIRLED THROUGH the helicopter. A uniformed man of medium build heaved at the sliding door. Tess felt the centrifugal force of the chopper lifting as the door latched. Despite the warm temperature, her body shivered. Her uncle put his coat over her, wrapping his arm around her shoulders. She squeezed him tight as he sat in the seat next to her.

"You gave us quite the scare, young lady," her uncle's deep voice bellowed over the whirring of the motor.

The chopper veered sharply. Tess grabbed the edges of her seat as her uncle patted her knee, slipping a com headset over her ears. The loud throbbing noise quieted.

"Don't worry we're getting you back to the ship," her uncle said.

Tess nodded, hearing him clearly through the headphones. She leaned her head against him. She didn't know where he had come from or how he knew where to find her, but sitting next to him made her feel like a little girl again, safe.

"How did you know where to find me?" she asked.

"Let's just say I have a secret weapon."

Tess arched her eyebrow, curiosity piqued as to what he meant. But right now, in her exhaustion, she didn't have the energy to delve further with more questions. With her adrenaline fading, she closed her eyes.

***

EVERYTHING HAPPENED so fast, her mind spun recounting the events. The idea of Roger and Rolan working together shook her reality. She re-lived the moment Anthony jumped on board the yacht. It was then she knew she couldn't leave Belize without him. She thought about the fierce brawl between Anthony and Roger. If the soldiers hadn't come when they did, she pressed her eyelids tighter, horrified at what could have happened.

Tess opened her eyes, glancing up at her Uncle Ray. She knew he was important in the military, just how big of a deal he was, she hadn't a clue until now. Her head spun with thoughts about the swarm of military soldiers that dropped out of the sky and onto the yacht. She grinned remembering the look on Rolan's face as the men dragged him from below in handcuffs. Then there were Roger and *Anthony*—she bit her lip. Tess looked out towards the window and wondered what would happen to Anthony.

Finally, after what seemed like hours, but knowing it was only moments later, the helicopter hovered as it descended aboard the waiting US Naval ship. The high-pitched whine of the engine quieted and the rhythmic thump of the blades diminished. Ray Martin took Tess's headset off and helped her unbuckle. The uniformed man seated across from them unlatched the door, heaving it open. To her surprise, a familiar face waited on the deck.

"Molly!" Tess's eyes widened. Tess looked back at her uncle; her mouth gaped. "How do you..."

"Meet my secret weapon," he grinned.

Her uncle helped her down from the sleek whirlybird. Molly quickly stepped over, planting her lips hard onto Ray's mouth.

"Good job, Baby, I knew you could do it!"

"Baby?" Tess said. She looked at her friend, then quickly realized the connection between her uncle and her resourceful assistant. "Oh, Molly," Tess laughed, "only you could tame my uncle!"

Molly let Ray go and walked up to Tess. "I'm glad to see you too, kiddo!" Molly smiled, hugging Tess as she gave her a peck on the cheek.

"Am I ever glad to see you! But how..." Tess looked around.

"Yep!" Molly laughed. "We sent the whole naval fleet out after you!"

"How did you know where to find me? And what's with you and Uncle Ray?" Tess laughed. "In fact," she looked at her uncle, "how did you get the Navy to come rescue me?"

"Let's just say, your 'ol uncle has connections," he said, grinning. Chuckling, he put his arm around Molly's waist pulling her to his side.

"I'll say!" Tess laughed. "But seriously, how did you..."

"That 'ol snake in the grass, ex-boyfriend of yours, that's how." Molly scoffed. "He messed with the wrong kind of people. Turns out he tried to bilk money from one of your clients using their daughter." Molly pressed her lips tight as she nodded her head. "That fool went too far and riled the wrong blowhard. You know 'ol Mr. Becker, he wants everyone to know how important he is. So, when your dear 'ol reptilian boyfriend..."

"Ex-boyfriend!" Tess interjected.

"Ex-reptilian boyfriend," Molly obliged, "tried to put one over on the tightest tight wad in town, well let's just say Roger sunk his own battleship."

"I don't know how you did it, but I love you!" Tess hugged her friend.

Her mind drifted to Anthony. Quickly, she stepped back.

Molly rested her hand on Tess's shoulder. "What is it, honey? Are you okay?"

The blood drained from Tess's cheeks. She'd gotten distracted, the helicopter, her uncle, then seeing Molly, Tess choked on her words. "U...Uncle, what about the men on the boat, the one you rescued me from."

Her uncle's eyes hardened. "Don't you worry about those criminals; my boys have them in custody. I just got word the boat crew has them and they're bringing them on board now. We'll hold them in the cells below. Those low-down scum will be spending a long time behind bars. That, you can count on!"

"All of them?" Tess asked, softly.

Tess's heart sank thinking of Anthony in jail. She knew he was mixed up in Rolan's drug deal somehow, but she also knew that he was a good person. After all, he had risked his own life taking her through the jungle and back to the hotel. And again, to come alone and risk his life to save her tonight. She didn't know if there would be anything her uncle could do to help, but she had to try. Anthony had fought for her; she couldn't let him go without a fight, too.

"Uncle, the one man, his name is Anthony. Will he go to prison? He didn't kidnap me, he tried to help me. Could you help him, too?"

Her uncle glanced at Molly then back to Tess.

"You don't know...," his brow arched, "about Tony?"

Oh, God! Her heart sank. They killed him. He must have tried to escape, and those military men must have shot him. Tears welled at the corner of her eyes. She walked over to her uncle and placed her hands on his shoulders. Almost sobbing she looked up into his face.

"Please...," her voice trembled, "tell me, what happened to Anthony?"

"Don't ask me, little girl," he smiled and nodded behind her. "Why don't you ask him yourself?"

Tess tilted her head and looked up into her uncle's face. Her brow furrowed. "I...I don't understand."

"Did someone mention my name?" the familiar voice said.

Tess turned. "Anthony!" she exclaimed, running across the deck, wrapping her arms around him. She kissed his mouth, his cheek, and then back to his lips.

"Ahem," Ray Martin interrupted.

Anthony looked up. He immediately released his hold on Tess and stood at attention. Tess looked at Anthony then to her uncle, her expression puzzled. Anthony saluted. His shoulders squared and his face went rigid.

"At ease," Ray Martin said.

Tess watched her uncle pace a couple of steps methodically. Each stride stepped heavily onto the ship platform as he held one hand regimented behind his back. Tess had seen her uncle do this with officers under his command before, but why now and why on Anthony? Confused, she watched her uncle's eyes grow narrow and his mouth stern as he approached the couple. Tess realized her uncle wouldn't understand. He might harm Anthony. She stepped between the men.

"Uncle, I can explain. If it hadn't been for Anthony rescuing me, I...I don't know what would have happened. Rolan and his men, they kidnapped me and Anthony...," she paused. Tess didn't know how to tell her uncle that Anthony was also a drug dealer, but she couldn't stand by and let him go to prison without pleading for him first.

"Stand aside young lady," her uncle demanded.

"But, Uncle, please, if you only knew..."

"I'll take it from here my dear." The Commander nudged her out of the way. "Am I to understand, Lieutenant that this young lady has no idea who you are?"

Anthony's eyes focused straight ahead. Tess noticed his jaw was taut. A twinge of pride came over her. Looking at him now, Anthony actually looked as if he *could* be in the military. She snapped back to reality, fearing her uncle would soon learn the truth, that Anthony was a drug dealer who she just happened to fall madly in love with. She bit her lip. Suddenly, her uncle's words carried across the deck. Did he just address her drug dealer lover with a military rank? Tess gawked.

Anthony replied to his commander's question. "That is correct, sir."

"Sir? Lieutenant? Uncle, you know Tony?" Tess asked.

"As a matter of fact," his face softened, "I do." Tess's uncle reached out and took Tony by the elbow. He shook his hand firmly. "I'd like to thank you for the chance you took with the possibility of exposing yourself in attempts to rescue my niece, Lieutenant. I know that you took a significant risk in revealing your identity to the cartel."

"Yes sir. Thank you, sir." Anthony replied.

Tess arched her brow, bewildered, and looked over at Anthony.

Her uncle glanced at her. "And I further commend your care in not revealing yourself any sooner and risk exposing years of hard work and dedication on this project. To my knowledge, our intel has confirmed our targets are unaware of your involvement in their capture."

Tess looked at Molly who gave a wide-eyed nod, shrugging her shoulders.

"Project?" Tess looked at Anthony. "You mean you're not a drug dealer and you aren't going to jail?"

"Hell no, this man has been under my command for over two years. He's our top undercover agent," her uncle paused, winking at Tess. "Looks like he's been professional through and through, keeping his identity secret, even from you."

"You mean all this time you really were a good guy?" Tess smiled.

"Tony, here, has been working for our government orchestrating a sting operation on the Belizean drug cartel. Through his efforts, we've been able to apprehend Rolan Petrov and his unsavory family ties, of which lately has included trafficking and kidnapping rich heiresses," Ray Martin nodded. "Seems your ex-boyfriend had ideas he'd cash in on Mr. Becker's wealth by holding his daughter, Katrina Becker, for ransom. After Becker gave Molly, here, an earful, she figured out your boy Roger was using you to get to your clients. Only wish I had found out before you had to go through this ordeal. We could have picked him up sooner."

Tess's mouth gaped. "Wow, I really know how to pick 'em, don't I," she shook her head.

"Don't blame yourself," Anthony stood next to her "it's a sophisticated group and Roger, or actually..."

"Ricondo," Tess uttered.

"Yes, Ricondo Petrov. We had been watching him for several months. Almost had him, but then he disappeared. We lost all eyes on him until you showed up at the bar the other night."

Tess looked up at the stars, she laughed. "The night we met and I...introduced you as my date." Tess held her head between her hands. "Oh, God, how could I have been so stupid?" She looked up at Anthony. "And you, you played along. You knew! The whole time..." she pulled back from him, "you let me think you were..."

Anthony stepped close to her. He put his hands around her waist. The warmth of his touch made her heart leap. Her arms tingled as he leaned in close to her, lifting her chin to meet his eyes. "I couldn't tell you, Tess. It would have put you in more danger. Roger..."

"You mean Ricondo," she pouted.

"Yes, he wasn't the main player we were after. His connection to Rolan is what we were using. Rolan had cut a deal with the Belizean police who were letting top known cartel bring heavy loads of cocaine from Russia to Belize.

We've been watching them...," he looked into her eyes, "intercepting their cargo. Our intel told us they were setting up for a large drop, one of the biggest this far. They smuggled their shipments using tour boats..."

"Like the snorkeling boat," she said.

"Yes. While the guests are off snorkeling, Rolan's man stays on board and waits for the drop."

"I don't get it, why don't they just fly it where they want?" Tess asked.

"Oh, they have," her uncle added, "they've been busted when they cross the border, that's why Rolan and his crew started using the locals and their fields."

Tess began to see the whole picture. "Like the airfields where Rubi and the villagers live?"

"Yes," Anthony clenched his fists, "the villagers have no choice but to let the cartel use their fields to land on. If they don't comply the police destroy the villages. They've even been known to take some of the older children and force them into labor camps."

Tess recalled their early departure and how they had snuck out of the village before anyone was awake. "That's why we had to leave, that morning at the village, isn't it?"

"Yes, I'd gotten information that Rolan had sent his men to the area, searching for the cocaine I had taken from him. If he'd found you or me there, I don't know what he might have done to Rubi or her family."

"You had information?" Tess asked.

"Yes, you met my contact at the bonfire," Anthony said.

Tess thought about that night, how she had watched him from across the flames. Her heart had ached for him, for his touch. She had wanted him more than any other man she'd known. She would have given herself to him that night but, instead, the woman from the dance floor, the brunette, took him away. Tess bit her lip.

"Oh, Anthony!" Tess searched his face. "Was she an agent too?"

Her cheeks flushed. All that time Anthony had been looking out for her, keeping her safe.

Anthony smiled and brushed back her hair. "No," his eyes sparkled as he spoke. "Sophia lives in the village with her Aunt Rubi. She and her brother, Devon, provided information that only the locals can get. She came to the village to warn us."

"What about the night at the hotel, on the dance floor. You were with her then, too? Weren't you?" Tess said.

He smiled as he caressed her arm. "We had to keep her cover, she was getting information from Rolan's man—where and when the drops at sea were taking place." He brushed his lips across her forehead and looked into her eyes. "She gave me the coordinates when we were dancing. It was less suspicious that way."

"Oh, Anthony," Tess tensed, "can you forgive me for being so crazy?" She looked up at him, searching his face for the answer. "All those things I said, on the trail, the bus. I was so...," she cast her eyes down, "I was jealous." She had almost lost him once, she wasn't going to let him go, not without telling him her true feelings. Afraid of how he would react, she couldn't look at him and instead turned her head aside. "I love you, Anthony! I'm crazy in love with you!"

Anthony caressed the side of her face with his hand and turned her towards him. He reached into his pocket, pulling out the silk hibiscus print scarf. "I think this belongs to you," he said.

"My scarf! Where did you find it?" Tess asked.

"Tonight, on the pier."

"But how...," her voice trailed.

Then, she remembered her heel sinking into the plank and her purse catching on the post along the dock. She had tugged at it not realizing the material snagged, pulling the scarf from her bag. Anthony put the scarf around Tess's waist. He drew her close and his eyes brightened.

"There is a myth among the elders," he paused and looked deeply into her eyes, "they say that when you find the woman of your heart, wrap her in the flower of love and she will be yours forever." Anthony pulled Tess close to him. Her heartbeat quickened and her body swooned against him. Tilting his head and brushing his lips gently over hers, his voice vibrated softly next to her cheek. "And I am crazy in love with you, Tess Martin."

About the Author

Debbie Zessin has a heart for adventure and loves to bring thrills, laughter, and entertainment to others through charming and memorable characters. Her life-journey has been filled with interesting situations and many wonderful people that encourage her to create thought-provoking and vivid worlds for her readers. When she's not writing, she enjoys traveling, jet skiing, exploring the Northwest, gardening, and hanging out with her animals. Debbie resides in Graham, Washington, a small town nestled in the viewshed of Mt. Rainier, where she and her husband raised their two children. She is currently working on her next novel featuring enticing characters, more witty bantering, and further exotic travel adventures. *Captured In Belize* is her first published novel. You can find more about the author and her books at her website www.DebbieZessin.com as well as her author's page on Amazon.com.